Going Back

Eugene O'Brien has written for the stage, screen and radio. His work includes the critically acclaimed TV drama *Pure Mule*, winner of five IFTA Awards, and which, according to the *Irish Times*, 'spectacularly raised the bar for Irish TV drama'. The show was inspired by his play *Eden*, which debuted at the Abbey and has since played the West End and Off Broadway; it won the Rooney Prize for Irish Literature in 2003. The film adaptation won Best Actress for Eileen Walsh at the Tribeca Film Festival. A new play, *Heaven*, set in the same fictional midland town debuts at the 2022 Dublin Theatre Festival. Eugene is a regular columnist for the *Sunday Independent*. This is his first novel.

Going Back

Eugene O'Brien

Gill Books

Gill Books
Hume Avenue
Park West
Dublin 12
www.gillbooks.ie

Gill Books is an imprint of M.H. Gill and Co.

978 07171 9427 8

Designed by Bartek Janczak
Edited by Alison Walsh
Copyedited by Neil Burkey
Proofread by Emma Dunne
Printed by Clays Ltd, Suffolk
This book is typeset in 12 on 18pt Minion Pro.

The paper used in this book comes from the wood pulp of
sustainably managed forests.

*This book is a work of fiction. Any references to historical events,
real people or real places are used fictitiously. Other names,
characters, places and incidents are products of the author's
imagination, and any resemblance to actual incidents or persons,
living or dead, is entirely coincidental.*

A CIP catalogue record for this book is available from the
British Library.

5 4 3 2 1

Printed and bound in Great Britain by Clays, Elcograf S.p.A.

MIX
Paper from
responsible sources
FSC® C018072

To my parents, Eugene and Ingrid

prologue

Scobie Donoghue is thinking about that scorching-hot Australian dog day afternoon when he told her that he loved her. He had opened his eyes to stare at her. Ella, perfectly relaxed. In a half-doze. Ella, strawberry blonde hair and a smile that would light up all of Melbourne. She was the *numero uno*, the most unbelievable member of the female race that he ever had the good fortune to be with.

That afternoon, they had just come out of the sea, lying on the white fine sands of Anglesea Beach, along the Great Ocean Road, all traces of hangover washed from their bodies by the gorgeous salty water. It was a far cry from the canal water at home, Scobie's first ever dip, jumping in off the bridge with his older brother,

Shamie, when they were only little lads. Ella opened her eyes then and looked at him. His heart leapt. Her beautiful brown eyes melted him. Made him come out of himself with his hands up – *I surrender!* Nowhere to hide. Scobie had leaned across and kissed her then, and said:

'I love you.'

The three magic words, and for the first time in his life he actually meant them.

She hadn't reacted immediately. Her face was very still. He hoped she wouldn't laugh at him. She was a great woman to peg abuse and take the piss and kid around, but she had no laugh this time. She had just smiled, and eventually replied, 'And I love you too.'

That night they had stayed at an old-style frontier hotel in Torquay. Scobie kept thinking of Basil Fawlty, and tried to explain it to Ella.

'Like, there's this mad English lad, and he runs this hotel and his wife is bossy and there's a useless Spanish waiter and a sexy maid type of one, and Basil is always chasin' his tail to try and rescue something that he's made a bollocks of … like there's an episode with a rat—'

Ella had interrupted him. 'It sounds shit.'

'No,' Scobie insisted, 'it's really funny.'

Ella had never seen *Fawlty Towers*, or indeed any TV, growing up in Tasmania, as her 'artist' parents hadn't allowed one in the house. Her parents were a million miles from anything Scobie would have known. That evening they had sat out on the hotel veranda drinking beer.

'It's like the Wild West,' Scobie had remarked before springing to his feet and getting ready to draw his pistols. 'Dyin' ain't much of a living, boy. Fill your hands, you son of a bitch!'

Ella had drawn first and shot him. Scobie fell to the floor. Later that night they had sex on the old-style squeaky-spring bed, and they were loud and did it every which way and he couldn't help thinking that the people in the next room could hear them and this gave him an extra thrill. Scobie Donoghue, loud and dangerous! The lad was like mahogany, boys! It could bate cattle up Mount Everest!

Later, as they had settled into a kind of lovely half-asleep, half-awake state of heads together on the pillow, Scobie said, 'I had sex with a married woman one time. Like about ten or twelve years ago.'

'Any good?' Ella asked.

'Pretty good. Yeah. I'd have to say it wasn't bad. It was the first time I ever did it in a bed, actually.'

'And where had you done it up until then?'

Scobie immediately replied, 'Graveyards.'

Ella had laughed. 'Kinky. Stiff among the stiffs!'

On the way back to Melbourne, they had stopped off at Hanging Rock. Ella told Scobie that there had been a book and then a film based on a supposedly true story of how three schoolgirls from a nearby college disappeared on the rock on Saint Valentine's Day 1900. But it had been a hoax. It had all been invention. Ella didn't care. She had always found it beguiling and haunting.

'There is an ancient belief,' she told him, 'that when we sleep, people come and steal our bodies.'

They walked on up under the famous hanging rock itself, a boulder suspended between other boulders, under which is the main entrance path. They walked on up into the rest of the volcanic structure.

'I don't think much of it,' Scobie remarked.

Ella was entranced. 'It's amazing. Mystical. I can feel vibrations. From the past.'

Scobie felt no vibrations. 'It's just a Jaysus collection of rocks, like. So what?'

Ella shut him up with a big wet kiss, then put her hand down on his erection and whispered in his ear, 'Scobie-Wan Kenobi.'

Scobie sighed. 'Jesus, Ella, I used dream about a woman like you.'

That was nearly three years ago, but this is now. All Scobie can think of today is those romantic, in-love, can't-live-without-you days. Not long after that first day that he'd told Ella he loved her, they'd moved in together, into the flat in Gisborne, a real nice town near enough to the mountains and about 60 kilometres outside Melbourne. But today he is taking a last walk through Gisborne. Away from Ella and the flat. With the last of his clothes in a holdall on his back. Himself and Ella are now officially over. Split. He is single again. Scobie Donoghue is on his own.

The V/Line train approaches. Scobie lifts the bag to get on. The train stops. He can't get on board. Not just yet, because he can't stop the tears rolling down his face. He feels horribly self-conscious so he stalls the ball to wipe his face and just about makes it on before the doors slide shut. He takes his seat. He was going into the city and then on out to the suburb of Melton, where Shamie and his wife Therese were set up, with a seven-year-old son and a pool and a barbecue and the whole nine yards. Shamie, who had never slept with anyone else in his life other than Therese, and the Scobe, who'd ridden the range, but it's Shamie who has ended up the happy one. The contented one.

Scobie could do with a drink, even though he still feels pretty rough. His head is heavy. He leans it against the window. He closes his eyes and seems to slip into a dream. He is walking into the bush. Like the Aborigines used to do. Disappearing into the land and being free of it all. Being free to walk until you dropped off the world. He dreams that the world is flat after all. He would simply walk until he dropped off the edge. Falling forever but landing eventually. He can see that clearly now. Where he must land. Back to the county of Uíbh Fhailí. Where he was born and reared. To the county of bogs and Biffos. He had run out of road. He had nothing left.

His eyes open. He looks around the train. The first step back starts from here. Home, James, and don't spare the horses.

one

The wind whistled and howled against the window as Scobie lay in bed and scrolled through his phone. He stopped at a sexy photo of some former TV star and an invitation to see what they looked like now. But first, an ad, and then a hundred other loads of shite that you didn't want to see. So he gave up and put the phone aside. He looked across at the empty single bed opposite him. Above it, there was a poster of a blonde model in her underwear called, JEANETTE, THE PERFECT GIRL. Beside it, a poster of a large red Corvette car. A neon sign that said BAR propped up on a bedside lamp and an Offaly GAA wristband draped around it. Nothing had been touched in the ten years since Shamie had last slept in the bed.

Scobie imagined that he could see his older brother's head sticking out the top of the duvet. Like he was around 14 or 15.

'Are ye awake, Shamie?'

'No, I'm not. Some of us need eight hours' kip.'

Scobie would throw something at him then. A shoe or a Dinky car or something, and Shamie would sit up and be genuinely upset at being disturbed. 'I'm gonna ask to be allowed sleep downstairs in the sitting room. Honest to Jaysus, I'd rather the sofa than having to share a room with you.'

But Scobie could distract him with talk of the girls in school. 'I tell ye that Fiona Kelly has a great little bod on her.'

'She's a nice-looking girl all right.' Shamie would be awake now, seeing Fiona Kelly in her uniform draped across a desk in the classroom.

'Or the new one in my year, Karen. She's got some pair on her. Bord Bainne!'

Shamie would imagine Karen and her breasts and what they might look like.

Scobie knew he had his attention now. 'I'm going to get my hands on them this year. Oh yeah, boy!'

Shamie would realise that he had been hooked in and diverted from sleep, while Scobie would doze off then and leave poor Shamie wide awake. Lost in hopeless fantasies about these girls and how and where he'd seduce them.

But now, it was Scobie who was wide awake without a hope of sleep, whereas his brother Shamie slept soundly every night with his wife and son in Melton. He and Therese had moved there in January of '09, ten months before Scobie landed, and he had kipped on their couch for a few weeks before moving into a mad-house full of Irish builders.

Shamie had worked hard and made it to foreman, and he loved his wife as much as he had that first time he'd seen her, when Therese came into the town to the secondary. They had kissed after a youth-club disco, but they were only 15, and Shamie was slagged over it by the others in school because Therese was a real farmer's girl, and they said things like did she smell of cow shite, and her father was strict and wouldn't let her into town that much, so nothing came of the kiss. Then Shamie was gripped by a disabling awkwardness around girls. He just got shy and tongue-tied, and it was worse for him because his younger brother Scobie could talk any amount of shite to them.

This all came to a head one sunny May Monday, when Scobie snogged the face off Julie Ryan, after the sports day in school, at the back of a field next to a tree known as Dinny's Hole for no good reason other than there was a large hollow in the middle of it. Shamie had asked Julie out to the pictures earlier that day and she'd said yes, but now his 15-year-old younger brother had ruined it. It went around the school like wildfire. Scobie had wiped his eye. Shamie lost it, and there was a huge fight that their father had to break up. Determined that his two sons would never fall out like that again, their father declared a rule that they would never compete for the same girl from that day forth.

Things only got worse for poor Shamie after that, as Therese started to go out with the Bomber Brennan, a local desperado trying to go straight. Scobie witnessed his brother's quiet pain as Therese and Bomber got engaged, and no one was as glad as

Scobie when the relationship broke up and Shamie managed to somehow make his intentions clear to Therese. The two of them had been truly happy together ever since.

Back in his bedroom, Scobie thought about going out for his walk but the weather was so shit he might have to give it a miss tonight. It was a thing he had taken to ever since he landed back in the town nearly a month ago. He was finding it very hard to sleep, so he would put the coat on and head out around the empty streets of the town. Sometimes he'd end up on the back roads. Out as far as the GAA pitch and the new estate and back into the main street, where three of the four pubs he used to frequent lay empty. Killed off by the last crash. He still felt like he knew every brick and bit of pavement of the place, and the air smelt the same and was a lot cooler than Oz, but on the other hand he felt he didn't know the place at all. Like the town was a ghost of its former self. Or was he a ghost of his former self? It was as if nobody really saw or knew him anymore.

Scobie had got into the habit of borrowing his mam's car and spent a lot of time driving around during the day. He drove into the bog and stopped and stared at the browns and blacks and listened to the birds and the breeze and he felt a sort of calm. He walked on the peaty land and met very few people. He avoided people as a rule. Not that he knew many people now anyway. His only venture down the town was to go to the new Lidl on the outskirts to get shopping for the ma.

He did run into Niallers, his old workmate, in Lidl one afternoon. He was pushing a trolley with two wild-looking young lads, and they exchanged chat and Scobie spotted the white hairs on

Niallers' temple and the lines in his face. Good old Niallers, laughing with his big toothy mouth and shaking his head, 'Ah, sure, ye'd be strangled – Bobby put that down, ye little fecker!' as his eldest picked up a giant bottle of red lemonade.

Scobie laughed and could see Niallers' eyes shining with happiness as he dealt with his kids.

'Last I heard from your ma you were goin' great guns down below. A steady woman an' all. I said to her, "Wonders will never cease, Scobie-Wan Kenobi with a steady woman."'

Scobie laughed. 'Ah well, you know me, Niallers. It lasted a good while, and she was cool and everything but ... things happen.'

Niallers winked at him. 'Ye fucker, ye. I'd say they did.'

Scobie remembered to ask him 'How's Aine?' like he pitied Niallers in some way for being stuck with the same woman for 15 years while he, Scobie, roamed the earth seducing and discarding women at every turn.

Niallers smiled and shook the head. 'Ah, grand. Grand. Not a bother, like.'

There was a pause then. Like a 'we should have loads to catch up on but we don't really' kind of awkward, making noises that don't mean anything like 'Jeany' and 'Jeez' and 'Good to see ye' and 'we had some great auld nights'. 'We did' ... 'We did.' But neither was really motivated enough to recall any incident from these great nights.

Eventually, Niallers indicated the two boys, who were wreaking havoc in the crisp aisle. 'I better go. Sure, I might see ye around the town. I don't get out that much for pints or nothin' anymore, but like we should ...'

Niallers didn't finish the sentence.

Scobie smiled. 'Does the Pope shit in the woods?'

Niallers had walked on and laughed, and Scobie had laughed. Neither had been really sure what they were laughing at.

When Scobie did manage to shut his eyes and sleep, he would have nightmares. In one very vivid recurring dream, himself and Shamie and their da found a kangaroo's head in the bog. Decayed and flies eating out its eyes. Their da picked up the kangaroo's head and put it on his back, then walked on with Shamie and disappeared into some sort of cloud of red bog dust. Scobie called out for his da and then for Shamie, but he got no answer. When the dust cleared Scobie was on his own and felt a huge wave of anxiety. He would wake up with that feeling lodged in his stomach. Not able to sleep for love nor money. Just like tonight.

He looked at the time. Twenty to three. He thought of a drink on these nights. He had sworn himself off it since he'd got back from Oz. Nevertheless, he couldn't help picturing the bottle of 12-year-old Scotch downstairs that Cliff kept for special occasions. He thought of creeping down the stairs and reaching for the bottle. Taking off the cap and smelling it and looking at it. And the delicious threat of destruction that he knew it would wreak on his life if he succumbed. He imagined the feeling of the first sip. The burn in the throat. The gradual loosening and tightening of everything as a glass was poured, and another, and one particular part of the brain got switched off and another part of the brain got switched on and was let loose and ran amok, turning everything to shite and you landed home to your mammy Angela and stepdaddy Cliff just in time to turn 40.

In fairness, Cliff made her happy: she giggled a lot with him and her eyes shone, and she deserved all the joy in the world because Scobie remembered that same face being far from happy on so many occasions across the kitchen table. A woman widowed in her late forties. The light gone out in her eyes. It was so strange, but since Scobie had arrived home, he had begun to see her as a woman. Was this because another man regarded her as a sexual being? It was mad when he thought about it. They did it. He'd heard them at it one night. He'd put his earphones on. He'd listened to AC/DC for old times' sake, and thought of him and Shamie headbanging in the front room. ANGUS. ANGUS. Oh, please, Angus, rock god, block out any sounds coming from the couple next door. Scobie's mind had wandered to terrible places. He did his best to try and control his thoughts, but they crossed boundaries of decency and led to his mother's vagina. The place he came out of and into the world is now being occupied by the Viagra-fuelled lad of a … aaaahhhhhhhhhh! Scobie closed his eyes and tried to think of anything else – but he couldn't deny the fact that his ma was a woman. A person in her own right. A person who was due happiness even if it had come in the shape of a slightly anal English man who supported Sheffield Wednesday.

Scobie looked out at the empty, windswept street. The rain had eased slightly. He would chance it. He had to get out. He put on his clothes, crept downstairs, grabbed the coat and slipped out the front door. Outside, he relished the wind on his face. He had driven around the town at this time of the night on so many occasions, bringing young ones home after the shift or charging around for the craic. Now he walked alone through a town that needed a lick of paint or some sort of make-over. Kelly's newsagent was gone, where Therese used to work. There was a vape shop there now, next to a tattoo parlour and two charity shops, and that was your lot, really, bar Morgan's medical hall and a BoyleSports bookies. Dessie the barber had closed down too, where him and Shamie used to get their hair cut every Saturday. The market in the square still happened, but with fewer stalls. Scobie passed Reds night club, which was now called Club 52. The scene of some of his finest hours.

The rain had completely subsided now, so Scobie headed off in the direction of the back road that did a loop around the town. He strolled on out towards the national school and saw himself and Shamie traipsing along the path with heavy school bags and arguing over Euro 88 football stickers. Shamie walking slow because he liked to arrive just before the class started. He hated the playground, because it was all rough and tumble, and lads sitting on you and teasing and being useless at football and hating the outcast group that he was a member of and desperately wanting to be part of the herd. Scobie ran with the herd. He made sure he was a card-carrying member of the mainstream. He was a handy enough GAA player without having to try too hard.

A new teacher, Mr Moore, asked him one day, in fourth class, 'So, Sean, how did you get the name of Scobie?'

The class laughed. Scobie looked around, loving the attention, sensing, even at nine, that this was gold. The usual way a lad had a nickname was because he got it from his da. Like the Rat Finnegan. Or Mouse Maher, or Fluggy Flynn, but Scobie's da never had any name other than his own. He was known as Eddie.

He drove a truck for a local timber merchant, the words *Tyrell's Timbers* emblazoned on the front of the truck.

So, Scobie explained to Mr Moore, 'Ye see, sir, when I was smaller, like, I'd say that I was only four or four-and-a-half, I started to watch *Scooby Doo*, and it was my favourite programme. I loved the bit at the end when they took the mask off the monster and it was only some lad pretending. So, sir, I just was mad into *Scooby Doo*, and Shamie, that's my older brother, he started calling me Scooby, but my father couldn't get it right and called me Scobie, and then it just … ye know … I'm Scobie now, like.'

Mr Moore had smiled. He liked Scobie, the way most teachers did when he was that age. Scobie wasn't up to much with his schoolwork, but he could always manage to charm them.

Scobie looked in through the fencing and laurel bushes at the darkness of the playground beyond. He could still see the birds swooping down on the playground to pick up the crusts of bread left over from a hundred lunch boxes. Even though he was younger than his brother by a year and nine months, he would often have to step in and protect Shamie from people trying to steal his Penguin bar.

The great thrill was when their father dropped them to school some mornings. They'd sit with him up in the cab, and it was especially brilliant if he was delivering a full load of timber. Sometimes they'd sing the song out of *Convoy* and shout, 'Hey, Rubber Ducky', at the tops of their lungs. The truck would roar to a halt outside the gates of the school, scaring the shite out of the other parents and kids. Sometimes Eddie would even honk the horn for the craic, as the two lads hopped down from the cab. Scobie loved it. Shamie was not so at ease with the attention, but deep down he got a kick out of the grand entrance. Eddie would wave to them then and rev up and drive off.

Scobie could see Eddie very clearly now in his mind's eye. Sometimes he couldn't picture his face properly, as if it had faded from his memory, but now he was getting a very clear signal. A full, unpixelated image of the man who left this world on 7 August 2004. Aged 50. He had been complaining of headaches, and like any self-respecting Irish man he avoided the doctor and took Panadol until the headaches got so bad that he could barely drive the truck. Angela insisted that he make an appointment with the local GP, Doc Byrne, and he referred Eddie to hospital in Dublin to get X-rays.

Scobie remembered the day being just a normal Thursday. Coming home from work at the site with Shamie. Parking up their pride and joy, the red BMW 3 Series, in the front yard of the house, like they always did. Bounding in the back door, ready to eat a farmer's arse through a hedge and expecting the smell of the dinner. But today there was no smell in the kitchen. The oven was off, and there was no sign of Ma hard at it. They found her and Da in the sitting room. In a weird silence. They were sitting together on the sofa, which was very unusual. Their faces were pinched and worried and drained of colour, and Da smiled at them and told his two sons to sit down.

Angela found it hard to look either of them in the eye as Eddie Donoghue cleared his throat to speak: 'They found somethin'. A brain tumour. Maybe a second one. They're too far gone so, like ... *sin é.*'

Scobie remembered staring at the photo of them on their wedding day, which had pride of place on the mantelpiece over the fire, Angela looking like a million dollars and the da coming over all Steve McQueen. Eddie loved Steve McQueen and Clint, and all the strong, silent ones. He had made his two sons sit with him and watch all the classic westerns in this very room, and later, when they got older, he insisted that they watch Steve McQueen in *Bullitt*, and the boys were suitably impressed with the famous car chase up and down the mad streets of San Francisco.

Scobie looked back at Eddie. He had either finished speaking or was taking a very long pause. Shamie couldn't wait for that to be decided. 'What do ye mean, Da?'

Eddie slowly rubbed his hand over his arm as if he was unconsciously soothing himself. Angela held his other hand. The lads noticed this, as their parents, as a rule, were not overly tactile with each other.

Eddie's eyes narrowed, and his voice sounded tight. 'It's terminal, boys. I'm not coming out of this. They give me six months. Maybe more. Maybe less.'

Shamie instinctively went over to them on the sofa and put his arms around them both. That broke everything. No words. Just the sound of quiet sobbing. Eddie looked to Scobie but he did not move. His eyes were clear. He had no tears. Angela gestured at him to come over and join the family. Scobie shook his head. To do that would be to accept the unacceptable. Eddie Donoghue did not get sick. Eddie Donoghue drove trucks, hauled timber and had hurled for the town, and he was fit and strong. He was not sick. Scobie backed away out of the sitting room. He backed away from his own flesh and blood as they tried to find some ounce of comfort and solace. All Scobie felt was a coldness in his veins. A hardening of his heart.

He hopped back in the car and backed out of the yard and screeched on away out the road and picked up Fidelma, a girl from Castle Hill Park, who he'd been kinda seeing on and off, and he whisked her out the bog road and parked up in a spot covered by trees and he leaned over and kissed her passionately on the mouth. Fidelma was taken aback, but kind of thrilled that she could drive him so wild. Scobie mauled her breasts and sucked and kissed her mouth and tongue and grabbed her hand and put it over his crotch.

'I need you,' he kept saying. 'I need you now.'

Fidelma was excited by this show of desire. She opened up her legs. She was willing to be needed like this.

Scobie wasn't hanging around. He took her into the back seat. It didn't take long. Fidelma had never known him to be that rough, or to finish that quickly. He pulled out of her and sighed, and then he cried. Fidelma tried to take his hand. He pushed it away. He put the keys in the ignition and started up the car. Fidelma was left at her doorstep at the back end of Castle Hill Park. Her mother, with a fag in her gob, parted the curtain to look out at her and the departing car. Fidelma stood there, and all her daydreams of a house and garden and little Scobies running around disappeared in a puff of smoke.

Scobie turned away from the school and headed for home. It was near enough to five o'clock, and he was beginning to feel the bite of the bitterly cold December morning. He began to think about the week ahead, and his fortieth birthday, and how he'd avoid any sort of fuss, but his ma was determined to mark it. Scobie headed on past the church and thought of his father in the graveyard across the road. He thought about going in to see the headstone. He heard his father's voice in his head.

'Well, Scobe, what's the story?'

Lying in the hospital. Not much time left. On the way out. Himself and Shamie and Ma holding a constant bedside vigil. The night before Eddie went, Scobie was left alone for an hour with him. Eddie Donoghue was only semi-conscious, but he leant into Scobie and murmured, 'You and Shamie are to look after her. We all owe her so much ... you know that. She always put the three of us first. Especially me. No care for herself.'

His eyes dropped shut again, and it was the last thing Scobie ever heard his father utter on the planet Earth. Fourteen words forever etched somewhere in his brain, but that he hadn't thought about in a long time.

Out of nowhere, Scobie heard footsteps hurrying down the road behind him. He swung around. A girl was walking towards him. She had a red party dress on. Make-up smudged. She'd been crying. She was young, pretty, maybe around 20 or 21. The closer she got to Scobie, the more lost and alone she looked. She reminded him so strongly of someone, but he just couldn't put his finger on who it was. She was shivering with the cold. Scobie had an urge to throw his coat around her. The girl glanced in Scobie's direction, surprised that anyone else would be mad enough to be walking around at this hour of the morning in the shit weather. Scobie nodded at her and was about to ask if she was okay when a car sped into view and pulled up sharply.

A man in his thirties got out quickly. He had a jacket, which he immediately draped over the girl. He had an air of unruffled authority about him. He threw a very direct glance in Scobie's direction and smiled. 'Okay?'

Scobie nodded back at him. The girl shook her head and went to walk away. The man grabbed hold of her arm.

Scobie instinctively stepped forward. 'Hey, boss, what's the story, like?'

The man smiled again. He seemed very composed. 'No story. It's a private matter. A disagreement at home. I'm a family friend. Just helping out.'

While keeping a firm grip on the girl, the man pulled out a wallet of some sort from his inside pocket. He held it out so Scobie could see who he was. A photo ID. Garda Padraig Delaney.

'I work with her father. Sergeant Eamon Freeman.'

Scobie now knew who the girl was. He knew why she looked so familiar to him. He couldn't help but have a pornographic flashback to the time himself and this girl's mother, Deirdre Freeman, went at it hammer and tongs. He'd got the mother of three high as a kite on an ecstasy tablet, and then had the most 'horn on a brass monkey' kinda ridin' that had stayed with him forever.

This was ages ago. Sometime in 2005. It was when she was going through some deep, restless shit with her marriage, and Scobie's flute was being played for comfort. He hadn't minded of course. He'd loved it. But then he started to think about her and want her, and for two weeks he thought that he was in love, which of course he wasn't. It had just been an infatuation fuelled by the exciting, snatched sexual encounters and thrill of going offside with the sergeant's wife.

Garda Delaney guided the girl back into his car. 'That's it, Keelan. Your dad will be worried about ye.'

Keelan seemed to decide to give in and do as she was told, and she got in and shut the car door behind her. Garda Delaney nodded to Scobie again, and he said, 'I don't know you. Are you from the town?'

'Oh, I am. Scobie Donoghue. I was away in Oz for the guts of ten years.'

'Ah, right. Good man. We might keep this to ourselves. Save the poor girl the embarrassment.'

Scobie nodded. 'Sure, yeah, whatever.'

'Good to meet you, Scobie.' Delaney tipped his finger to his head in a friendly gesture of 'See ye around', and got into the car. Scobie stood and watched as they drove away. The last time he'd seen Keelan she was only 10 or 11. A quiet young one by all accounts, but puberty can do terrible things to ye. Scobie couldn't help feeling that there was an odd tension about the girl. Like all was not as it seemed. But what the fuck did he know. Maybe it was just him. He felt as odd as fuck these days, and not even a drink to steady himself up. Scobie grabbed hold of his coat collars and pulled them up. The rain was beginning to spill again. He hunkered down and headed for home.

two

Angela

Angela was all ready for a big blowout for her son's birthday. He hadn't been around for the last ten of them, so now she was determined to make a proper occasion of this one. 'I thought we'd get the back room in McKeon's and invite a few people. We have to celebrate the big four-oh!'

Scobie was clearly aghast at the idea. 'No way, Ma. Like, I'm off the drink for the moment, okay, so I'd just like to keep it low-key.'

'But it's your fortieth,' Angela persisted.

'Will ye let it go now? Bake a cake or, actually, don't bother. We'll just ignore it. I'd be grand with that. We'll just pretend it didn't happen. Who the fuck cares!'

Angela was upset and worried. Her son was not the same man as the one who'd gone away in 2009. He was much older looking, but it was more than that. His face had dropped. He was a bit jowly, even. His eyes were heavier, and he carried a general weight on his shoulders, as if he was weary of the world. Her heart felt heavy for him, but anything she said seemed to just aggravate the situation.

'I was so sorry to hear about Ella. There's no way ye might get back together?' she'd asked him one night around the dinner table as they'd dug into a chicken broccoli bake.

'Not going to happen,' he'd mumbled through a mouthful of food.

'Was it a mutual decision?'

'Yeah, no. I dunno. I can't remember, it's over anyway.'

He continued eating, and she hadn't been able to prise anything out of him. She had even sent Cliff to Lidl with him one day, on a fact-finding mission. Maybe a man-to-man chat might help her to ascertain some of the goings-on in Oz and what his future plans might be. But Cliff returned with no new information in his report to her.

'I offered him work, like, told him there was loads of building starting up again. But he just said no thanks.'

Angela absolutely insisted on a fortieth, no matter what. Her son needed cheering up. Even if it was just Scobie, herself and Cliff around the table at home. She had been busy all day making the things that he and Shamie had loved as kids. Rice Krispie buns and Belford biscuits with jam in the middle and a chocolate or icing top.

Angela laughed. 'Remember I used to do the jellies and write all the first letters of each child's name with cream? Used to take ages with me having to remember all their names.'

Angela produced a present for Scobie, one that she was sure he'd need. She watched him open it, and he found a collection of socks and boxer shorts and two heavy jumpers. 'For the winter, like. You won't be used to the cold after Oz, unless you're thinking of going back there.'

She was hoping Scobie might reveal something of his plans, but he said nothing, leaned over and kissed Angela and went to shake hands with Cliff but found that he was suddenly being enveloped into a tight bear hug. 'Happy birthday, Scobe. Good to have you back.'

Angela could see that Scobie got out of the hug as soon as he could. She made him put the jumpers up to his chest to see if they would fit. 'They look a bit on the small side,' she said. Angela couldn't help but catch sight of Scobie's newly acquired gut, which he had to hold in or otherwise it would spill out over his belt and jeans.

'Too much of the Aussie beer and shrimp on the barbie,' quipped Cliff in the worst attempt at an Australian accent in history.

Scobie laughed and patted the belly. 'I'll get rid of this in no time.'

Angela pointed to her own tummy. 'I'll have to do something as well.'

Cliff, rosy-cheeked from the wine, leaned over and kissed Angela. 'Not at all. I'll take as much of you as I can get.'

She could sense Scobie's discomfort as he looked away to the television and sipped his cup of tea. She didn't care. She was a bit tipsy on the mid-priced supermarket red wine, so she whipped up a Rice Krispie bun and proceeded to let Cliff eat out of her hand. She was a bit pissed off with Scobie anyway, so feck him. Cliff had been making a big effort all night, but Scobie had barely exchanged two words with him.

Cliff was undeterred. Bolstered by the few jars, he turned to Scobie and launched into a story. 'There was this young lad I worked with on a site in London who was called Blacksod, after the bay in Mayo where he was born. I mean, this lad didn't know what his real name was, as he had always been called Blacksod. Anyway, he was wired to the moon this lad, mad as a brush but kinda soft underneath it all.'

Angela prayed that there would be some point to the story and he wasn't just rambling.

Cliff went on, in full flow: 'He was mad for trying to get me to go to Kilburn with him at the weekends to go on the piss and pull women. So one weekend I agreed. The other lads said I was mad, as Blacksod liked fighting more than anything else. That I'd better be prepared for a scrap if I was going into the Kilburn clubs and pubs with him. I liked the young lad though, so one Saturday I joined him in the Galtymore ballroom, and soon enough Blacksod turned and started getting all mouthy to people. I went to the lav and had a think about doing a runner, but when I came back, Blacksod had pints and whiskeys lined up for me and I got rightly tanked up, and sure enough, before I knew it, Blacksod was causing bloody mayhem and I was right bang in the centre of it and ...'

Cliff paused to take a drink. He looked to Angela. 'I ended up with two black eyes and a swollen face. Two teeth knocked out and a ruptured rib.'

Angela laid her hand in Cliff's and squeezed it. 'God love ye.' Then Angela shook her head and slapped his hand. 'Ye fuckin' eejit.' She said this lightly with a laugh; it was a way they had with each other. The tongue-in-cheek quip or slag, which held no edge – just an ease that she appreciated more than she could express to him.

Cliff grinned, but turned his gaze towards Scobie. 'I didn't drink for three months after that. So I get it, you know. Giving up the drink like. No harm. Just for a while.'

Scobie nodded. 'No harm.'

'Did anything happen you, like?' Angela asked. 'Did ye have a run-in or anything?'

Scobie shook his head. Cliff eyed Angela to let it go. She smiled and took his hand and squeezed it again. He was right. Now was not the time.

Angela had first met Cliff when he'd been foreman on the building site that Shamie and Scobie worked on in the mid-noughties. He was clumsy and overeager at first, trying too hard and full of an insecurity that had both annoyed and endeared him to Angela. He'd been lonely in the town, going out to Reds nightclub, trying to chat up girls half his age, and the lads used to slag and laugh at him. Too much aftershave, bad polo necks and cheesy chat-up lines. He even bought an iguana from Fox Foley's pet store, but he got locked one night and the iguana escaped from the flat and ended up by the canal and scared the shite out of a child and had to be put down. Angela roared laughing when he told her this, and she could see that he no longer felt embarrassed about it. She was so pleased that he was able to tell her things that he said he'd never dreamed he would ever tell any woman. About how his heart felt free to burst with love and affection for her, and his need to spend the rest of his days with her. Angela had never experienced such undying declarations. Eddie had uttered the odd word of affection and love, but if she was honest with herself, there had been too many times when she had felt a kind of loneliness with him.

'My first marriage wasn't perfect, Cliff,' she'd said one evening as they lay in the bed. 'But we did what had to be done. I was mad for him, ye know, physically, but he could be an odd fish. He could be there, with us, in the house, and then he could make strange, disappear or something, into himself.'

She said no more than that. She didn't need to. She had been so young the first time around, and had felt so lucky to be marrying Eddie Donoghue, the best-looking lad in the town, the envy of all her friends at the shoe factory, where she'd gone straight after school. Nine to five, six days a week, sticking the heels on high-end fashion ladies' shoes. Eddie was quiet on the big day, as was his usual demeanour, and she had an ache in her belly at the reception afterwards, because he didn't seem to be as happy as she felt he should be, or at least he didn't express it. She was very aware of the two empty spaces at the top table where his parents would have been sitting if they had been invited. But he had insisted that they were not welcome.

'They didn't give me nor me brother any kind of proper rearing. Just the opposite, in fact. I won't be talkin' to them for as long as I live.'

It saddened Angela to her core to hear that you could hold that much resentment towards the people who had brought you into the world. Her own ma and da had shyly smiled and nodded all the way through the day, as their only child, born to them when they were both in their forties, took to the floor for the first dance. 'Wonderful Tonight' by Eric Clapton, which was Angela's favourite slow song. Eddie had danced out of duty and then sat out the rest of the night. But she knew that he loved her in his own way.

She could see Cliff grow in stature as their relationship got more serious, as if he trusted himself and who he was for the first time. After a few years together, he asked her to marry him.

When Angela met his mother, Ethel, for the first time, at the wedding, she could see immediately how her son might have struggled with basic self-esteem.

Cliff explained to Angela that Ethel had been in what she called the entertainment business in her younger days. She had danced and sung in revues, pantos and musicals, mostly in rep, travelling around the country, staying in dodgy boarding houses and existing on pork pies and gin. Ethel had nearly been in the very first of the *Carry On* movies with Kenneth Williams, and when she missed out, she took to the bed for a week and decided to give in and accept a proposal of marriage from Ian Jones, a steady if rather dull post office clerk who had adored her for years. Ethel knuckled down to domesticity, had her only son two months prematurely, in a hospital in Leeds, naming him after her favourite singer, Cliff Richard, whom she had met once after a show in the Liverpool Playhouse. Cliff said that he hadn't taken after his mother in terms of ever wanting to tread the boards, but he did retain some of her wandering spirit. He certainly didn't want to end up like his buttoned-up father, who had pandered to Ethel's every wish until his death in the early noughties.

Angela dealt with her new mother-in-law in a very friendly but very firm 'I am not one to be pushed around, so don't fucking try it' manner, which, Cliff told her, made him love his new wife all the more.

It had been a perfect day, even though neither of her sons were able to make it back from Oz for the occasion.

'Sure, they weren't there for me first wedding either,' joked Angela, determined not to let it spoil the day.

Cliff told Angela how much he loved her at hourly intervals, and she never grew tired of it. He would cherish her and never let her go. He was warm and childlike and opened his mouth sometimes without thinking, and she wasn't sure whether the two lads respected him fully but she didn't care. She felt a great ease with him. Her tummy relaxed and softened around him.

Angela curled up with Cliff on the sofa now, as a film was starting on the television. It was an English romcom with people falling in and out of love, the kind of thing that Angela pretended to think was 'shite' but secretly enjoyed.

'It's what do ye call it. *Love Actually.*'

'Shite actually,' said Scobie.

Angela was beginning to feel tipsy after just the two glasses of wine. As Shamie used to say, 'Ma, ye wouldn't drink spring water.'

She looked across at Scobie, who had a face like a smacked arse, grimacing as Hugh Grant did the dance around Number 10.

Then Cliff rubbed his hands together, easing up out of the chair. 'So, anyone for a nice little whiskey?'

Angela shook her head. 'Ah, no, I'm grand, Cliff.' She knew she'd reached her limit. A drop more and she'd be neither use nor ornament.

Cliff fetched the bottle from the cupboard. 'Scobie, I have a bottle of Baileys in here, surely you could have a small glass, lots of ice.'

Scobie shook his head. Cliff poured himself a measure of his 12-year-old malt and Angela put her head on his shoulder, thinking that it was a good thing that her son was taking a break from the jar. She got the feeling there'd been a fair bit of drinking in Oz, so it was no harm in him giving the system a chance to recuperate.

Cliff looked every inch the contented man. He was ready to hold forth now on the state of the nation. Angela would have preferred a bit of *ciúnas*, as she loved the bit where your man who does Mr Bean makes a big song and dance about wrapping the present for the cheating husband. But she left Cliff off to have his say, and with any luck he'd settle then and sip his whiskey, as happy as a pig in shite.

'Housing,' announced Cliff. 'That's the big issue. Even in this town there's nothing to rent, let alone buy. People are getting antsy, Scobie. Ye hear people around the town talking about too many immigrants. I mean, there is a fierce amount of foreign people knocking around now. A load of Poles and Eastern Europeans still here, and there's Chinese and even a few Mongolians. And like, that's fine, but they kinda keep themselves to themselves.'

Angela interjected, as she had no problem with people arriving in, as long as they were genuine folk just wanting the best for their families, 'Well sure, their English wouldn't be great, so it's hard to fully, ye know, join in.'

Cliff pressed on. 'I'm just tellin' ye what I hear – that these people stay at home to drink. Never go to a pub. They don't spend in the town. They shell out the few euro in Lidl, but that's it. The money is being sent home. Which is fine, and they're totally entitled to do it, but it's fuck-all use to here. To this place.'

Angela lifted her head off his shoulder and gave Cliff a sharp look. 'I know exactly the type of people sayin' that kind of thing.'

Cliff went on. 'They'll start looking for certain types of people to vote for. Like they do in England.'

Angela shook her head. 'I know, all right. And as I say to them, who are we to be anti-immigrant and we in every country in the world? Irish people are like rats, you're never more than ten feet from one!' She settled back into Cliff's shoulder. 'We're not gone as bad as your shower of Brexit eejits.' She glanced up at Cliff to see if she'd got the rise out of him.

'That shower are nothing to do with me,' protested Cliff.

Angela laughed and kissed his cheek. 'I know, I know. I'm only trying to annoy ye.'

Angela's phone sounded and she pulled it out and let out a squeal of excitement as Shamie Jr's face appeared on her screen. He was standing in his swimming trunks beside the pool. Angela lifted the phone so Scobie could see him.

'How are ye, Shamie, how are ye, love? Look at ye. I swear you're growing every time I see ye.' Angela felt a leap in her heart. He really was the sweetest boy on God's earth.

Shamie Jr nodded politely but looked off camera as if he was being given a signal. 'I want to talk to Uncle Scobie.'

Scobie moved in beside Angela and gave his best dinosaur growl into the camera.

Shamie Jr laughed, but was concentrated on the task in hand. 'Dear Uncle Scobie. We miss you very much every day and hope to see you soon. But until then …' He took a big breath and started to sing 'Happy Birthday' to Scobie. Shamie and Therese joined in off camera. Scobie watched with a huge smile on his face. Angela was close to tears and Cliff sipped his whiskey and squeezed her hand. They applauded loudly when the child finished the song.

Scobie gave him a big thumbs up. 'Shamie Jr, you're some man for one man.' Scobie let out a growl, getting louder and twisting his face into contortions.

'I'm calling back to the spaceship to send down my special laser gun to kill the monster,' said Shamie Jr, thrilled that a 'monster' game had started.

Therese intervened. 'Okay, this is earth calling. Your lunch hour is nearly over. He has to be back in school in five minutes!'

There was a chorus of, 'Ah, Mam, can I not skip this afternoon?!'

Therese insisted. 'Listen, Space Ranger, that's it now.'

Scobie stepped in. 'Ah sure, I'll call ye real soon and read you the rest of that story. What was it? We never got to finish it.'

'*The Land That Time Forgot*,' said Shamie Jr immediately. 'Like it's set on a prehistoric island with a giant volcano which is about to erupt and these lads off a World War II submarine get caught in the place and have to fight pterodactyls and triceratops and of course T-Rexes.'

Shamie moved into the screen and took his son's hand. 'We better move, Scobe. I hope you're doing good. I'll give ye a call soon. Have a proper chat.'

'Bye, Uncle Scobie.'

'Thanks so much. See ye soon, bud.'

Therese stuck her head in and smiled and waved. The image disappeared.

The joy and love of the young lad thousands of miles away had lit up the room, and for a moment, Angela felt that things would be all A-okay with her son. He was just taking time out from a break-up. He'd soon get back to the land of the living. Angela felt a pull inside of her, between hoping he'd stay around and knowing deep down that he was better off in Oz, or somewhere else.

Still, Angela had really liked Ella. She'd been to Melbourne three years previously with Cliff and had really taken to Scobie's girlfriend. She saw the good effect Ella was having on her son. She was bright, full of attitude and affectionate, but took no shite from him either. She had a bit of a wild side, was a bit of craic, but was knuckling down to something, having just recently gone back to college to study teaching.

She spoke freely to Angela about herself: 'When I was 16, I wanted to go to a nursing college in Hobart, but my mother wanted me to travel and have experiences. I told her to get fucked, and that I didn't want to turn into a big hippie like she was! We fought about everything from clothes to how I cut my hair to me liking sports, which she hated. But what do you know, I ended up following my mother's advice and spent my twenties and early thirties travelling the globe and, ye know, having adventures.'

Angela was impressed. 'Well, Ella, I never went anywhere nor took nothing, bar a glass of cider and a packet of fags.'

'Maybe you were better off. I ended up having a fucked-up toxic relationship with a very controlling man 15 years my senior. Lenny, gifted musician. Absolute a-hole. But I fell hard for him. He abused that devotion, Angela.'

'So my lad's not so bad, so,' Angela laughed.

'No. He's kind of an innocent, really,' said Ella, 'all dressed up with bluster and cocky charm, but he's got a good awareness of the world around him. The main thing is that I'm able to be totally relaxed in his company. He makes me like myself a bit more.'

Angela was thrilled to hear all this, and was sure that wedding bells might be a distinct possibility, especially when they announced a year later that they were pregnant.

Angela had been absolutely thrilled when Scobie told her the news. She had cried and made a holy show of herself. She had counted down the days and months, and was all set to book flights and be there when her second grandchild came into the world. But then, one night, as she was walking home from the bridge club, she got another call from Scobie. She knew something was up, as he never rang her usually. It was always a Zoom call. She dreaded the worst as soon as she heard his voice. Ella had lost the baby.

Angela tried to offer her condolences as best she could, sensing that he was trying hard not to cry on the other end of the phone. Angela's heart broke in two, and by the time she reached her house she stopped outside and looked up at the stars and cursed God, and she hoped against hope that Scobie and Ella would survive the disappointment and try again. But obviously they hadn't been able to.

Now her son had landed back, very much on his own, hiding above in his room or driving around with not a squeak out of him about what had happened with Ella, or what he might be planning to do with himself. She started to say little prayers for him last thing at night. Just to herself. She had never been overly religious, had liked the traditions and rituals of the Mass, although she had stopped going when the abuse cases came out in the late nineties and beyond. Angela knew she wasn't getting the full Johnny Magory about what had happened down below.

Angela could feel the old instincts coming back to her. The compulsion to put Scobie first, before anyone else. She had almost forgotten how it felt to be a ma. She had been Angela, a wife, a woman, for the past few years. But now she felt that old familiar need, to provide comfort and to scold and cajole him into action and to provide food and to look at him with eyes of pure love – no matter what he'd ever done.

Angela looked across at her son and was glad to see him holding his phone with a smile on his face. He got up then and hugged her tight, and he'd even hugged Cliff. 'I'm off to the *leaba*, thanks for everything today. Sleep well,' he had said, and he seemed, on the surface at least, to be all cheered up as he left the room.

Herself and Cliff continued to watch the couples in *Love Actually* bumble their very British way through things, and Angela teared up at the bit she always teared up at, when the stoic wife gets the Joni Mitchell CD instead of the jewellery from her husband, so she knows he's cheating on her. Cliff stroked her arm, but a fear had come over her. A vision of what might happen if Scobie settled back here and one day went into the next and he slipped back into his old habits. The drink but probably not chasing girls anymore, because they wouldn't be interested. He would no longer be the one and only Scobie Donoghue, famous for craic and drink. No longer Scobie Donoghue, king of the holy trinity of Friday, Saturday and Sunday night. The fact was, he was now Scobie Donoghue, aged 40, looking burnt out and depressed, back home with her and Cliff and not able to do much of anything about it. Or so it seemed to her anyway. And a mammy knew these things.

He had always been such a little live wire as a kid. So watchful and alert to a room. She had had such high hopes for him. But now she frets and worries about him, and she allows herself to wonder how well she really knows him. Something had altered in him while he'd been away. He had experienced loss, of course, and that is bound to affect a person. But there was a distance in him now. He was becoming more like his father. And that, more than anything, was keeping her awake at night.

three

Scobie hurried upstairs, along the landing and into his bedroom. He lay down and looked at the phone again to make sure he hadn't imagined it. A text from Ella, 'HAPPY BIRTHDAY. HOPE YOU DOING WELL. X.' Scobie smiled. He had wondered if she would contact him. He felt lighter. He saw her walking towards him. Three years before. She'd organised a surprise party in his favourite pub and his head had swum with Coopers Pale Ale and shots, and they clung to each other and kissed and he took her hand and they found a secluded spot out the back of the place and they managed to have a quick rough ride up against the wall. Scobie had never been as turned on in his whole life. Then back inside to the booze and band and they took some pills and danced the night away on a blissful high.

All he could think about now was calling Ella and hearing her voice. What time was it there? Two or so. She'd have just finished the lunch, would be rushing back to the class. She was never a great woman for timekeeping. He pictured her in the mornings: hair frizzed from the shower, like a mad thing, always late, running out the door. He settled his head back into the pillow and shut his eyes, and couldn't help himself going right back to the days in Oz before he met her. All-nighters followed by all-day seshes and the terrible lows of the Persian rugs, which he'd been using more than he ever did.

One weekend he started going to Crazy Girls, a strip club, and some of his workmates paid for a lap dance for him. The girl's name was Cindy, and Scobie was transfixed by her. He kept coming back for more. He offered to take her out one night. She refused, but hinted that if he was willing to pay, she could hang with him exclusively. So that became an arrangement. Scobie was spending most of his money on Cindy in the club. She would sit with him and drink and then gradually he found out that if he put down a bit more money, she would let him masturbate while she stripped for him. Then for a little bit more money she would give him hand relief with a guaranteed happy ending. Scobie was both excited by the sheer, basic no-strings-attached nature of the deal and repulsed that he should be such a sad sack, handing out a fortune for nothing really, bar being wanked off.

So Scobie fell into this pattern of drinking with the lads from the site and then installing himself in Crazy Girls and paying Cindy. He felt a desperate loneliness, but would never admit it. He nearly said something to Shamie one Sunday on the phone. He'd been too wrecked to go over to them for the dinner.

'In a bit of a rut, Shamie, ye know. Same ol' shite, different day. Ever feel like that?'

'I do of course, Scobe. But is it not time ye found a good woman, settled down? No?'

Scobie replied, 'Would ye go way from me. Scobie Donoghue has plenty of ridin' to do before he settles down, thank you very much!' But he knew deep down that this was the very thing he was ready for. That he longed for. He even began to imagine who she was. What she was doing at any given moment. When would he meet her?

One spring day, he was walking from work, tired and filthy but with no desire to go back to the madhouse of Irish builders and all the craic. There had to be craic at all times. He was kind of almost sick of the craic. Sometimes he just wanted peace. Olé, olé, olé, fuck off for two seconds. Maybe he was getting old, or just maybe he was lonely, but anyhow, he kept on walking past the house of builders and the takeaway food and beer and sweat and slagging. Past all the craic. He kept going on down the street and on out of the district. He just kept walking. He had no idea where he was going. He ended up somewhere in Brunswick. He had been walking for hours. He slipped into a bar for a drink and a burger. He ate while watching a rock band on the small stage at the back of the place. The girl playing bass was gorgeous-looking. She had a long, angular face, short blonde hair and great eyes, and he ordered another pint and endured the hackneyed grunge music, just to watch her. When the gig was over, the bassist girl approached the counter to order, and their eyes met.

'I liked the band,' Scobie said. 'Let me buy you a drink.'

'The band are shit and I've just left them. We had a big bust-up in the dressing room!'

'A bit like the fuckin' Commitments,' Scobie quipped.

'What?'

'The Commitments!' Scobie repeated.

She wasn't getting the reference.

'I'm Scobie. From Ireland.'

'Hi, I'm Ella, from Tasmania!'

They headed off out of the bar and the rest, as they say, was history.

He opened his eyes, sat up in the bed and grabbed the phone. He was determined to do it now, this minute, before he talked himself out of it. Make the Jaysus call! He held his breath. He heard the ring tone, and was preparing what to say if it went to message, when Ella answered.

'Hi, Scobie. That you?'

'It is indeed.'

'There was no need to call, but seeing as you did ... happy birthday.'

'Thanks. I'm sober. Would you believe that?'

'Yes. Well, why's that?'

Scobie hesitated for a moment, and then said, 'Because I haven't drank since I left Australia. Just decided it was good to give the aul' bod a rest.'

There was a pause on the other end of the line, before Ella said, 'Anyway, good to hear you but, like, I have a classroom of eight-year-olds waiting for me.'

'How's work going?' Scobie asked.

'Really well, thanks. There's a really pretty principal who has just started, and he's really on my wavelength in terms of new ways we can introduce difficult issues to the kids. The last guy paid lip service but did fuck-all. This new guy is great.'

Scobie tried to sound like he was slagging her. 'Oh, I see. Taken a shine to him, have you?'

A longer pause. Ella's voice was filled with a slight irritation. 'Yes. To his views on children's developmental progress.'

'Nothing else.'

'No. I really have to go,' said Ella curtly.

Scobie was about to say sorry and wish her well and hang up the call, but instead he heard words coming out of his mouth, which he had no control over. 'Well, no problem if you did want to have a thing with him, like. You're single and I'm single and I hope you do manage to land him if that's what you're after. Like me, now, I have kind of started up a thing with a girl since I got home. She's a bit younger than me … but super bright, has her own nail business here in the town. She's a fine thing now, I have to say.'

Ella gave a little laugh down the phone. 'You still got it, Scobie.'

Scobie laughed. 'It seems that I do.'

'Good. I'm glad. See ye around. Thanks for the call.' Ella hung up.

Scobie held the phone in his hand. As if he was frozen in time. Why the absolute fuck had he said that? He felt a terrible bile of heartburn and sickness rising up in his system. His ma's fucking cakes and too much tea, and he rushed out to the bathroom and vomited into the sink. He looked up at his face in the mirror, and he never felt such a wave of self-disgust almost strangle the breath out of him. He wanted to hurt this stupid man in front of him. This thick fucking body that he had the misfortune to have to occupy. He slapped his head repeatedly with his fist. His head became really sore, but he wouldn't stop.

'FUCKING IDIOT. YOU ARE A FUCKING IDIOT!' Scobie beat his head until it pounded, but he could still feel an emptiness inside him, a sinking feeling full of what am I at? What's next, like? Is this it? A voice inside that wouldn't shut up.

four

James Bond was tied to a chair and some lad was batin' him in the bollocks with a thick rope. Cliff loved the Bond movies more than anything. He had an A-to-Z nerdy knowledge of all things double oh seven.

'Did you know that more actors have played the arch-villain Blofeld than have actually played Bond?'

'No, I didn't know that, Cliff,' said Scobie.

'Not a lot of people know that,' Cliff said, this time making a pathetic attempt at a Michael Caine accent.

Angela was dozing after her two glasses of wine. Cliff was in the mood for chat after his four glasses and one whiskey.

'But of course, the favourite Bond movie of the Official James

Bond Fan Club is not *Goldfinger*, as many people think.'

'Can we just watch the Jaysus film?' pleaded Scobie.

'No, it's *On Her Majesty's Secret Service*.'

Scobie didn't respond. Daniel Craig took another blow to his bollocks but Scobie reckoned that it wasn't as painful as having to sit in on St Stephen's night and listen to Cliff.

Scobie was struck by the absolute weirdness of not going down the town of a Stephen's afternoon with that super-excited feeling of being let off the leash after the one day of having to stay in your own house. And then to stride on into McKeon's and everyone would be home and everyone would be out and Reds would be stuffed to bursting and you'd feel a lovely E under your tongue and laugh at Shamie's look of disapproval, and every sinew would strain to absorb the beautiful light that rushed around your body and made you feel like you had just fallen in love ten times all at once, and that your heart was bursting with a need to feel communion with every soul on the packed dance floor. But this year the height of Christmas had been sitting in, chocolates and turkey sandwiches, and his mother with her red pen marking what she wanted to watch in the *RTÉ Guide*, pulling crackers with Cliff and drinking Jaysus Shloer.

Scobie saw Angela wake to see Daniel take another blow to his goolies, and she winced and looked away. Scobie eyed the whiskey in Cliff's hand. He had refused wine at the Christmas dinner, and a Baileys and ice before *Casino Royale* started. But something struck him then. A way out. A get-out clause from sobriety. He would never see Ella again, so what was the point of keeping himself sober and straight? He was stuck here now. At home. He had to make the best of it. He needed to get back to work. He had been in limbo land for the past month or so. He needed to get back into the swing of things. Scobie would have to reintegrate properly back into Irish life, and the only Jaysus way to do that was to take a drink and go out on the town, into the pubs, back to the nice safe familiarity of his old territory.

He wanted a drink, but he didn't want to ask for one or just take one. He hoped against hope that Cliff would offer again. He waited. The clock ticked. Daniel Craig continued to show audacious courage and humour in the face of adversity. But no move from Cliff. Come on, Cliff! Even a Baileys and ice would be a lifesaver. Get him started. Scobie focused all his attention on Cliff, trying to play a Jedi mind trick on him: 'Offer me a drink Cliff … please … like you did earlier … please … come on.'

Cliff noticed Scobie looking at him and, as if he had felt some special vibration from him, as if he was truly in Scobie's power, Cliff said, 'Hey, Scobe, are you sure you won't have something?'

Scobie-Wan Kenobi's Jedi mind trick had worked.

He shook his head immediately. 'Ah no … well look it – maybe, seein' as it's Christmas. Not to be rude, like. I'll chance a Baileys with the bit of ice.'

Cliff sprang up and slapped Scobie on the knee. 'Good man,' he said, and he scuttled off to get ice in the kitchen.

'Are ye sure?' said Angela.

'Ah yeah,' smiled Scobie as he poured the Baileys into a glass. Cliff landed back with the ice and dispensed a generous amount.

Scobie took the glass up in his hand. The last drink he had had was approximately six weeks before, in Australia. He leaned in and took a sip. He felt like he was home again. Like even the merest tincture of booze, in whatever form, filled something up deep down inside him. He took a breath. 'Thanks Cliff. This is grand.'

They all settled back into the film, and by the time Bond had sat down at the big card game with the baddie with the bleeding eye, Scobie had his glass drained.

'Cliff, any chance of a nice whiskey there?'

Angela had dozed off again. Cliff picked up the bottle and poured. Scobie tapped the glass. Cliff increased the measure.

'Sláinte, Cliff.' They clinked glasses and drank. 'Thanks for being so good to my ma. For looking after her when I was gone.'

'Of course. I'm her husband, like. We've been together over 14 years.'

'Is it that long?'

'Yes. So, I don't need thanks. You know.'

'What do you mean?'

'We look after each other and we always will, till death do us part.'

'Fuck's sake, okay. Whatever.'

'No, Scobie, it's just time you took me seriously. I'm your step-father, so, you know, try and see me as a proper member of the family.'

'Jaysus. Okay, Daddy.' Scobie smiled.

Cliff was still in serious mode. 'Okay. Just know that I have your back and I hope that you have mine.'

Scobie couldn't help laughing. 'Fuck me. Grand.'

Cliff settled back on the sofa. He had said his piece. He put his arm around Angela. Her eyes moved and she stirred. 'Is Bond still on?'

'He's still on,' said Cliff.

'Are his bollocks still intact?'

'They are.'

Angela whispered in Cliff's ear, 'Are *your* bollocks intact?' but Scobie heard it. He saw the self-satisfied, smug look creep across Cliff's ugly excuse for a face. Scobie drained his whiskey. 'Hey, Cliff, do ye know who I met in Melbourne. Remember Majella Flynn?'

Cliff went a shade of puce and shook his head.

Angela turned her head to look at him. 'Was she one of the Flynns from Castlehill?'

'The very ones,' said Scobie.

'Ah, sure, she was dragged up,' said Angela.

'I don't know her,' insisted Cliff.

Scobie winked at him. 'Ah, ye do. You were always chatting her up in Reds, asking her back to your place to show her your iguana.'

Angela giggled. 'Well, that's another word for it.'

Cliff was shifting in his seat. 'Ah, well, I don't remember much from Reds to be honest.'

Scobie laughed. 'I do. I remember plenty. He tried the same thing on with loads of young ones. Did ye ever score with the iguana thing?'

Cliff shook his head.

'Sure, even the Jaysus iguana tried to get away from ye in the end.'

Angela sat up now. She could see the sneer on Scobie's face. 'Now, mister, you're the last person to be slagging. Look at your own track record.'

'At least I wasn't the oldest swinger in town.'

'Scobie, what's got into ye?' asked Angela.

Scobie got up from the chair.

'Where are ye goin'?' Angela asked.

'Out,' said Scobie. 'I have to get out of this house.'

Angela shrugged. 'Grand. Me and Cliff need some privacy anyway.'

Scobie went to the door and pulled it open.

'We're goin' to ride for the rest of the night!' Angela shouted after him.

Scobie pulled the door shut. He heard his mother laughing. Ideally, he would have liked to change his shirt, but momentum kept him going on out the front door. Out into the cold night air. Back on track. Stephen's night and Scobie Donoghue was back in town!

The first port of call had to be McKeon's, his old stomping ground. It had closed during the crash but then reopened in the past two years with a new lounge and function room and kitchen out the back. The only scrap of food McKeon's used to serve was a ham and cheese toastie out of the plastic wrapper, fecked into a toaster. Now it was all pulled pork and rib-eye steaks. Scobie hardly recognised the place. He had to squeeze in the door past the crush of people. A lot of younger faces he didn't know. A few older ones he did. There was the odd 'How's Scobe' as he battled through to the bar, and then he had trouble getting served, as he knew not one of them behind the counter.

God be with the days of Cyril and the wife, Phil, who got a boob job in her forties and was the talk of the town. Cyril was a kind, hen-pecked-within-an-inch-of-his-life type of man, a publican through and through. He could take five orders at once. Watching him in action behind the bar was like poetry in motion. A real art. But the staff behind the bar now were as slow as a wet week, tying to make poxy cocktails. Scobie was losing the will to live until finally he got a pint and threw the first slug into him. He looked around, spotted Hammer in the corner, a fella he used to work with on the sites years ago. During the boom time. Hammer had swelled out and lost a lot on top, and looked old. He was in beside his wife, Mag, who looked equally ancient and pink-skinned, surrounded by family drinking and sweating, and Scobie decided to keep away.

He ordered another pint, and then he saw her at the far end of the counter. The young one from the other week. Looking very different now. Keelan, all eyes and tan and make-up and skimpy top, and she looked real good. She was drinking from a bottle and laughing with two lads both vying for her attention. Scobie was glad to see it. That she was okay, a normal girl out flirting and having the craic. Not walking around the town of an early morning looking like a drowned rat. Garda Delaney's face came into his head. Something in his eyes. He'd seen it before in fellas. Like they knew something you didn't and were one up on ye.

Scobie was distracted then by the Hog Hughes, who had stepped in from the smoking area and bumped into him. 'Be the Lord lamb of Jaysus, fuckin' Scobie Donoghue!'

Hog liked to shout no matter how close you were standing to him. Spittle tended to fly out of his gob.

Scobie grinned and nodded and shook his hand. 'How's Hog?'

Hog was fairly past it, but launched into Whitney Houston's 'I Will Always Love You'. Hog always had an amazingly powerful voice, but now it had gone totally off key because of years of drink.

'Ah, your father was some man, Lord have mercy on him.' Hog had been a younger player on the town's hurling team when Eddie was near to stepping down. 'He was some man for the hurl. Like one time, agin' Broadford, and whoosh – fucker chopped him, but Eddie stood up and whoosh, bang, straight in the balls. The lad never saw it comin'.'

Scobie was patient, and nodded and smiled at Hog, who seemed to long for those halcyon days of the 1980s, when whatever compulsion to drink that grabbed hold of him was still at arm's length. Scobie managed to scrummage his way past Hog and towards the back entrance to the smoking section. He was now in the vicinity of Keelan and her pals, and much to his surprise she broke off talking to the two bucks and turned towards him. 'How ye … Scobie, isn't it?'

'That's it. Sorry I didn't know ye the other day.'

'Ah, well, it's been a while.'

'You've grown, like.' Scobie winced at such an ol' fella thing to say.

Keelan smiled and leaned into him. 'About the other morning. I was a bit out of it. Ye know yourself. A bit confused about stuff.'

'He got ye home safe anyway.'

'He did. Yes. Garda Delaney was really looking out for me.'

Keelan's eyes spotted someone behind Scobie, and her expression froze. She took a swig of her bottle and planted it on the counter.

'See ye around, Scobie.' She nodded to the two bucks and they vamoosed through the crowd.

Scobie swung around to see Deirdre, Keelan's mother, who had just landed in the door. She stepped towards Scobie and they smiled at each other.

'Want a drink?' Scobie asked, turning to the counter.

'Gin and tonic, thanks, Scobie.'

Scobie got the order in and turned back to her. There was an awkward pause full of flashes of memories for both of them. It had been exciting and dangerous and, ultimately, embarrassing and mortifying, but now, 14 years on, what did it matter? Deirdre had always looked younger than her years, but now, even on her, the wrinkles showed when she smiled, and her face was fuller.

'You've met her ladyship,' Deirdre said.

'I have,' said Scobie. 'The spit of ye.'

For a moment he thought he should mention something about running into Keelan the other morning, but the girl had seemed fine just now, and he didn't want to be telling tales, so he left it alone.

'Some people think she looks more like her father,' said Deirdre.

'Ah, no. She's lucky. She takes after you.'

'I don't know.' Deirdre shrugged and nodded to someone she knew. 'How's Anna? Did ye have a good day? Ah, yeah, quiet. Ye know. See ye, Anna.'

Deirdre looked back to Scobie as he took a large swallow of his pint. 'So, what has ye back?'

Scobie hesitated before answering. 'Ah, I dunno. My time was up over there.'

'I heard ye had a woman an' all, very serious, according to your ma.'

'Oh yeah, well yeah … It was. We lived together for two years like, and I thought that maybe … But in the end, we just didn't make it.'

Scobie looked into his pint. Deirdre knocked back a good drop of her gin and tonic.

'How's Eamon?' asked Scobie.

'He's great. Top whack. Very busy. He's part of some midland task force, and he's on more Garda committees, but he loves it.'

Scobie raised his hand at one of the bar staff. 'Pint and a gin and tonic.'

Deirdre shook her head. 'Ah no, Scobe, I only popped in for the one on the way home from the church.'

'From the *church*?'

'Yeah, I help out there, ye know, the flowers and that. I enjoy it. I …' Deirdre looked away, her face sheepish. 'I've kind of got interested in the church again. Ye know, religion and that.'

'Really? Are ye serious?'

'Yeah. I've reconnected to something. The spiritual side of it. Like, I haven't gone all born again or anything weird. I just got back into prayer and finding some place away from the world outside in the church building. I find peace in it. Maybe it's like there's something else and not just us running around down here like headless chickens. There's something guiding the universe.' Deirdre reached for her fresh glass of gin and tonic.

Scobie didn't respond immediately.

Deirdre nudged him. 'Do ye think I've gone mad?'

Scobie shook his head. 'We all need something.' He took up his pint and drank. He could feel the alcohol beginning to properly swim around his system now. His system was calming. The anxiety chased back to the hills. He was out for the night now. He wouldn't be able to go home until he was properly Mickey Monk and away from himself. He knew that. He knew that because as he was drinking this pint, he was already thinking about the next one.

Scobie and Deirdre found a corner of the smoking area out the back. They agreed that they both felt like a different species to the youngsters that surrounded them. Lads with designer shirts and football-player haircuts and 1980s mullets, and the girls standing as near as they could to the overhead heaters with more exposed skin than could possibly be good for them on a cold winter's night.

Deirdre was on her fourth gin now, and was laughing at something she'd remembered. 'Remember the time we ended up in Taylor's playing pool with the Mole Mulvin and the Skunk Kelly and the guards were called?'

'You were locked. Ye hit the Mole Mulvin over the head with the Jaysus cue.'

'The fucker kept tryin' to feel me arse.'

Scobie smiled. 'You were wild that night.'

'I was.' Deirdre drained her glass and indicated the exit. 'I'd better ...'

Scobie nodded. 'Yeah, go on sure and I'll see ye.'

Deirdre suddenly remembered something. She whipped out her phone. 'Come here. I have to show you. I have shots of Jennifer and the two kids. Wanna see?'

'Does a bear shit in the woods? Absolutely!'

Deirdre opened a folder of photos. Her younger sister, Jennifer, beamed out from them, looking the epitome of motherhood with two little moppets crawling all over her. Floppy hair and cute as buttons, and Jennifer seemed to glow from every pore of her body.

Deirdre looked up from the photos. 'The only downside is that they call her "Mummy".'

'Oh, Jaysus. A fright. But it looks like life is really agreeing with her.'

'Yes. Married now to your man, Tom. House in the country. The whole nine yards.'

Scobie smiled as Deirdre continued to scroll down through the photos. Tom and Jennifer walking hand in hand with the two little ones. The sun was setting behind them and the fine-looking house topped it all off. Jennifer had made it. She'd got there. She was finally settled and happy. All the demons and drugs and drink and pent-up anger had been sorted.

'How the fuck did she do it?' he heard himself say out loud.

Deirdre shook her head. 'I don't know. She runs the wine business with him now. They have five shops. She even has a hint of an English accent.'

Scobie disappeared into the photo for a second. He hadn't thought about Jennifer in a while. She shot into his mind's eye. Like he was back in time, in 2009, a few months before he left for Oz. Her elfin face, full of mischief. Bold as brass, like. They were lying beside each other in a half-built house on the ghost estate where Scobie was night watchman. They were kissing after years of just being friends. He remembered her body. Her skin and the way she looked at him. A moment when she'd flicked hair out of her

53

eye. They had laughed a lot. He'd asked her to come to Oz with him. For a moment, it looked like she might say yes. But she was in love with someone else – this English lad, Tom. His heart still twinged a little at the thought of her, but he was genuinely glad she was happy.

Deirdre took the image away and put the phone back in her pocket. Scobie came back to the here and now and McKeon's bar on Stephen's night. He needed the next pint so they went back inside, but the staff had disappeared. The bar had closed. There was no Cyril or Phil to give you the late one. They stepped outside and Scobie spotted Hammer and the family getting into a taxi. He looked down the street and could see that a long queue had formed outside Club 52. He so wanted to join it, but there was no way José he was admitting that to Deirdre.

She pulled her jacket up around her neck. 'I'll be in trouble when I get home.'

'Wouldn't be the first time,' smirked Scobie.

Deirdre gave him a sharp look. He wished he hadn't said that. They stood for a moment. People roaring and shouting around them. Eating chips and kebabs and burgers and spice bags, and some were getting Moby Dick and others were trying to hail taxis, having given up on Club 52 – 'Ah, it's jammers … have ye seen the fuckin' queue?'

Deirdre leaned into Scobie as if she was about to give him a kiss on the cheek. Scobie went to give her one. Deirdre pulled her face out of the way and found herself punching him awkwardly in the shoulder. 'See ye around.' She turned on her heel and made her way back up the town. Scobie waited for exactly three seconds before high-tailing it to join the queue outside Club 52.

The bodies snaked up the street, through the arch of the yard gate of the club and right up to its front door. Scobie didn't know a soul, and he was by far the oldest in evidence. He craned his neck to see what was going on at the business end of the queue. The bouncers shook their heads and were admitting nobody. The word went down the queue like rapid fire that the doors were shut. Full to capacity. Girls were hysterical. Boys cursed and blamed each other for not leaving the pub sooner. Scobie felt a relief that he would hold onto some semblance of self-respect and not be the only one in there to be born before mobile phones were invented. He slumped out of the queue and back up the road. His dignity was intact, but that didn't solve the problem of where the fuck he was going to get distraction and another drink.

five

Deirdre

Deirdre walked on, feeling the cold of the night as the gin and tonics wore off. She hadn't been up the town at this hour in a long time. She passed a couple tearing shreds out of each other.

'Ye were looking at that bitch. I know ye were.'

'I wasn't fucking near her!'

She passed a couple laughing and sharing a bottle of beer and kissing. She was near enough to home now. The new estate, as it used to be called back in the day when she and Eamon had bought the house. Pre-boom and the really crazy prices. She'd be home in time for the race. No problem. A live horse race from Santa

Anita in Arcadia, California. She could watch it on her phone without anyone knowing. Keelan was in Club 52, the lads, Oisín and Paudge, would be engrossed in killing aliens in their bedroom and Eamon wouldn't be home for a good while yet. He was out at some golf club do. He'd got very involved with the club the past few years, just as she had begun to spend more time helping out at the church. It suited them both to have things they were interested in, as they certainly had lost all interest in each other.

Deirdre had met Eamon when she was 20, during the crazy World Cup summer of 1990, and he was just her type. Tall, sporty, straight talking and not full of the bull that a lot of lads went on with. Having lost her own father when she was 16, she had felt a need for someone she could rely on. Not the fly-by-night, devil-may-care, let's-get-locked merchants who would have you in stitches but then couldn't be serious about anything. Besides, Deirdre wanted children, as soon as possible. She wanted stability and her own nest, where she would have some modicum of control. She had dealt with too many 'pull the rug from underneath you' shocks and surprises. Her father's death. Her mother getting early-onset Alzheimer's. Trying to cope with her little sister Jennifer's increasingly mad and self-destructive behaviour. It had all been sheer chaos, and she'd been sick of it.

She first kissed Eamon, the new Garda in town, outside the local GAA club after a dinner dance, and the next Saturday they went to see *Pretty Woman* at the local cinema. Three years later they got engaged, but because of Eamon's job and financial concerns, they didn't actually tie the knot for three more years, and then, another three years later, Keelan, the first of the children, arrived, and Deirdre was full of joy and happiness. She took great succour in the order and routine of running a house. Her little kingdom.

She got a bad dose of postnatal depression after Paudge, the third and youngest, was born. She stared at the ceiling most mornings, and felt like her whole life was over. That her need for the familiar, the traditional, the ordinary and safe now seemed like cowardice. That she had fallen into a role to avoid the big bad world. To feel protected and to have some sort of illusion of control. She persevered, because school lunches and runs had to be made and Eamon deserved a good wife, even if the sex was now almost non-existent.

And then, one night out at the local, she found herself flirting with the young Scobie Donoghue.

It had been so mad seeing Scobie tonight. He looked so much older than when she'd last set eyes on him. There had been a comfort between them that they'd never had before. Deirdre had the guts of ten years on him, and had once been his babysitter, but now they felt very much the same kind of age. They were survivors who spoke each other's language, and all hint of the old sexual attraction was completely gone. Deirdre felt a tinge of sadness at that. He had once really wanted her, and that feeling of throwing it all away on a whim, risking her marriage and losing her kids, just for a quick ride with a young lad, it had been so fucked-up, but so exciting at the time.

When she'd decided to accept the ecstasy pill that Scobie had given her that first time they got it together, it was like crossing a threshold into another existence. Like she was making up for all the years of that other life she had chosen. She was transformed, reborn, as the great high engulfed her system and made her want to dance and drink and fuck and be disgraceful. The guard's wife was no more, but the next morning she felt awful. Guilt choked her, and she held Paudge tightly and smelt his head and kissed his little face and cheeks and swore that she must never again slip through into that world of abandon. She could never ingest any more mind-altering substances and go to bed with the likes of Scobie Donoghue. No, all of that had to be consigned to daydreams from then on. She had felt pathetic. The lonely housewife. What the fuck was happening to her?

The next week she'd found herself with Scobie in the back of his car, and she'd felt so young and free. They drove out into the bog with a bottle of vodka and they roared at the top of their voices and sang along to Eminem songs, and then he parked up and they made out in the back seat and she was completely turned on by the situation, away from the dull reality of the marriage bed in the nice safe house. This went on for a few weeks before they were spotted by a colleague of Eamon's and the chickens came home to roost, as they always do.

Eamon had taken it upon himself to forgive her. He had done the noble thing, and she'd felt so relieved and grateful, but as the years floated by, she got the distinct feeling that he had never really, truly been able to fully absolve her. He'd seemed less and less inclined to touch her or want her, and the saddest thing was she hadn't minded. She'd settled back into having the good steady family and raising the children and thrilling in all they did and thought and said. She masturbated the odd time with very little to imagine except Scobie's lean 25-year-old body pumping away behind her, and then she rolling over and sitting astride him.

Before Eamon she had only ever been with two fellas, both very disappointing experiences. She sometimes daydreamed about what might have happened if Eamon had thrown her out that time after Scobie. If she'd had to go it alone as the scarlet woman. She sometimes yearned for a time machine to bring her back. She should have walked out herself. She knew that now. Would they ever bite the bullet? She knew that Eamon must dream about it. An alternative existence, where he's happy, in love with the lady captain at the golf club, Paula Lynch, whose husband had been killed ten years previously in a car accident. Deirdre knew he liked her. She imagined them emerging out of the clubhouse on a night like tonight, giddy and merry, and then maybe a snatched kiss in the car park. Could she blame him? The clock was ticking past the 56-year mark for him. He must want to be desired by someone. Did she? That was a question that swirled around in her head some nights, or in the early mornings, when she'd lie awake, the unconscious still buzzing with crazy thoughts and images. To be in love with someone again in a 'heart leapt up in the chest' kind of way every time you saw them. Could she see this ever happening, or did sitting in front of the mirror in the morning dash any fantasy of one last romantic affair? She would examine every line and pat her skin where it used to be firm. She hadn't aged like some women she knew, but however hard she tried, she just couldn't imagine romantic passion and sex suddenly becoming a reality in her life.

She slipped in the back door at home and switched on the kitchen light. The lads must have ordered pizza, as there was a cold slice left over in the box. She absentmindedly picked it up and took a bite. She checked the time. She had ten minutes until the race. She could feel her pulse begin to quicken in nervous anticipation. This was a big one. This was huge. She tried not to think about Sister Senan handing over the parish funds to her to lodge in the bank. She tried not to think of the consequences of not winning.

'Are you sure you don't mind, Deirdre? Well, now, you're as good.'

But the money never went near the bank. Instead it was diverted into her Paddy Power account to go all out for a crazy accumulator. She stood to win big, and then she had sworn on her dear departed mother and the lives of her children that this time she would give it up and close the account no matter how much credit they offered her as an incentive to stay.

Deirdre sat at the kitchen table with her phone in her hand and clicked on the racing channel. They were under starter's orders, and her horse, Mugwump, number 15, wouldn't settle. Deirdre willed the horse to calm the fuck down and get in the starting gate, and then to take off and run like the wind.

This was the last leg of today's accumulator, which had been as follows: a third-division Croatian soccer match between NK Maksimir and Zagorec, which turned out to be a five-goal thriller, with Zagorec coming through with a goal in the last five minutes. The winnings from this memorable encounter all went on to a tennis match in Poland between the number 224 in the world, Germany's Yannick Maden, and number 240 in the world, João Domingues of Portugal. Deirdre was notified at around half nine that night, before she'd run into Scobie, that the bould João had prevailed in a five-set thriller after being two sets down. He will never know what it meant to Deirdre Freeman, kneeling in a chapel in the middle of Ireland, praying to God above that somehow everything would flip in her favour.

She had started on an Easter Monday, almost two years previously, with a three-euro each-way bet on the Irish Grand National, and only because her sister-in-law Jude was over visiting from England, and she loved a little flutter. Deirdre had picked out Brown Lad and he'd romped home, and she'd got a great kick out of the whole thing. It made her forget about everything in her life except the four legs of the horse and the jockey and his flailing arm and whip and the finishing line, and she'd felt a warm explosion in her belly like the universe was finally on her side and everything would work out for the best. Earlier that Easter Monday she had been involved in the mother of all mother–daughter fights with Keelan, who had come in very late the night before and was very hungover and rude, and seemed to regard Deirdre as some kind of embarrassment, someone who she was ashamed to be connected with. Keelan was commuting to Athlone College at that time, to do Event Management, much to her mother's disappointment, as Deirdre thought she had the brains for UCD or UCC and a business or accountancy course. Keelan just hadn't worked at the Leaving Cert and, even though she'd always been very quiet up to the age of 17 or so, now she'd started staying out late drinking.

That Easter Monday morning Keelan had called her mother the 'C' word in front of Jude. Eamon wasn't around, and Paudge and Oisín, teenage boys on their phones, barely looked up, but

Deirdre could feel Jude judging her because she had a fabulous relationship with her eldest girl, who was getting married the next year in Birmingham, so obviously Deirdre had failed somewhere along the line in the mammy stakes.

The relationship since then had slowly ground into a truce, where every now and again white flags were raised and talks were had but nothing disturbed the peace. Much like her relationship with Eamon. They had found a way to get by and live in the same house, but actually, if you could draw a heat map of the spaces they occupied within the four walls, it would confirm that they hardly ever spent time in the same room.

Brown Lad had given her a great lift that afternoon, and she didn't feel as much on her own or something. It had given her some excitement. That small element of risk. That thrill of hoping for something and the lovely feeling all over her when it came true. Most of all, it had soothed her. She wanted more of it, and a week later she started to place bets on other races and discovered a Paddy Power app, and she started to read up about the form and then the bets drifted into other sports, like soccer and rugby. She had always been a sporty girl, playing camogie in school, and been mad into the GAA and rugby, and had always been attracted to sporty lads. She had tried online bingo and the more fantasy-based games that the gambling industry had designed for the female market, but for Deirdre you couldn't beat live sport and the fact that someone real was existing to make you a winner or loser.

At last, Mugwump was settled and in the starting gate, and the race was about to get under way. Deirdre's heart beat in her chest. So much so that she put her hand up to massage it. She felt slightly faint and dry-throated, and her breath seemed short. She laughed to herself, how could she feel so awful but so completely alive, as the horses shot out of the gates and started around the first bend. She always felt like this at the start of the race or match or whatever she was betting on. The world was open and new, and the possibilities were boundless. This race was the universe to her now, the entire cosmos, because it was win or bust, and bust this time meant coming clean. There would be no more hiding places or wriggle room. She had maxed out credit cards and taken an overdraft with the bank. So if Mugwump came in and the accumulator paid off, she could at least clear her Paddy Power account and get the money back to the parish funds.

Mugwump made the second turn in joint fourth place and was looking strong and moving well, and was positioning itself cleverly out from the rails. Deirdre had a good feeling, and she hoped against hope and she prayed and she imagined that God was on her side because God had been impressed by the way she'd been coming to church and taking an interest in him, and he would make sure that Mugwump with a jockey named Billy Casper on his back would make it over the line in first place.

Deirdre felt a great sense of elation now that the crisis would soon be averted. Mugwump would not let her down. She could feel it. She made a pledge to herself to try and make some kind of attempt to build a bridge with Keelan. She had heard her creeping up the stairs at the crack of dawn on more than one occasion. She worried so much about her. Her room was locked all the time, and any time she did get a glimpse inside it was like a bomb site. She had become distant and withdrawn, and didn't seem to hang out as much with her old pals. This would all change as Mugwump took the last bend in first place. The old chats and laughter and hugs and smiles with her daughter would all come flooding back as Mugwump kept himself in front down the home stretch. But another horse was emerging from the pack: Pacific Heights, a twenty-to-one shot, seemed to have found the legs, galloping out of the chasing pack, and he was flying now and Mugwump was slowing. The jockey brandished the whip. Deirdre could hardly bear to look as Mugwump and the jockey desperately strained everything to hold on. The two horses were neck and neck, racing to the line, it looked like a photo finish, but no – Mugwump had it. He was declared the winner.

Deirdre banged the table with her fist. She stood and let out a silent scream of joy, releasing all the tension out of her body. Her head spun, and for a minute she felt like going to the sink to get sick, but instead she put her hands together and thanked God with all her heart, under her breath. She had just been delivered a massive get-out-of-jail card. She could now slip the money back to the parish funds, clear her online gambling debt and then close the account. No more betting. She would still have her bank overdraft and cards to deal with, but she'd find a way. The main thing was that she put a stop to all thoughts of gambling. Forever. The thought saddened her. She burst out laughing.

She went to the fridge to get some white wine, just a drop before bed. No more betting, she said to herself again. This time she meant it. A miracle had just happened. Lightning never struck twice, so any notions of doing one more accumulator were banished from her head. She sipped the wine, relishing the taste, enjoying her first few moments of being free. She would delete her Paddy Power account now, or maybe in the morning. She had been saved from herself, and she suddenly felt the need for another type of release. She thought of that night in her mother's house, all those years ago. Just another dull evening minding her Alzheimer's-afflicted parent, interrupted when Scobie Donoghue called around. She thought of their bodies up against the bedroom door, of his mouth and tongue, of clothes torn off, falling onto the bed. Deirdre put down the wine glass. She closed her eyes. God bless you, Mugwump!

six

Scobie waited patiently outside Taylor's, the last resort, 'only port in a storm' Taylor's, which was owned by Ollie Taylor, and his only rule was that he had to fill the place by any means possible. He'd sell booze to almost anyone, and he didn't particularly mind what they sold to each other. Scobie had already tapped the window a good few times but no dice. Many's the night he'd got a real late one. He was about to go for third time lucky, but before he had skin tapped against glass, the side door opened and out slipped a mulwoejuss mop of dyed-black hair over a puffy red face with a mouthful of missing teeth. The Mole Mulvin, all present and correct. He looked up and clocked Scobie, and it took a moment for the penny to drop.

'How is she hanging there, Scobie?'

'The Mole Mulvin, what's the story with ye?' Scobie had never been so glad to see Mole in his whole life. That's how desperate he was. He put his hand out and the Mole caught hold of it in a watery grip. Mole used to sell gear for Bomber Brennan years ago, before Bomber was put inside for breaking and entering and GBH.

'Is Ollie still peggin' out beer?'

Mole shook his head. 'He is in his shite. All over, red rover.'

Scobie nodded. 'So, Molesers, you don't happen to have any grass or anything knocking around your person?'

Mole let out a gigantic fart and then straightened himself up. 'Chance would be a fine thing. But come on with me and we might find some.' Mole wasn't the quickest on the pins. 'The hip is givin' me fierce hardship,' he said as they ambled along the road heading east. The road most people took when they left the town. The road to Dublin and beyond, to the USA, England and, since the crash of 2008, Canada and Australia. They walked on past the Mulrooneys' cottage. Derelict now. Two old bachelor brothers had lived there, and one of them, Jamsie, had lost his sight as a result of an assault by the Bomber Brennan. All history now, but Scobie remembered feeling fierce sorry for the two old men. They were never the same after the break-in. Like two wounded animals who hardly dared budge outside the front door.

'Jaysus, Mole, where are we headed?' Scobie asked, and for the third time Mole shook his head and refused to answer him.

'We'll be there soon.'

Scobie knew there was nothing in the vicinity except Tynan's timber yard, where his da, Eddie, had worked for 20 years. It had closed down this long time now. Scobie had spent many a summer's day with his da in the truck. He'd ride shotgun and let on they were in the westerns. That they were on the stagecoach or running with the Wild Bunch across the Mexican border. Eddie drove all over the country delivering the timber, but would bring Scobie on the short-haul journeys, around the midland counties: Westmeath, Offaly, Laois and Longford. Sometimes Shamie would come too, but he preferred to stay at home with his mother and build cars or trucks, Meccano and Lego and all that. He preferred his mother's company. Busying herself around the house with the radio on. He would ask her stuff about people and events on the news. He was happy to have the world out there. Beyond the four walls. He'd venture out there some day, but for now he was fine where he was. In the truck, on the road, he had to pretend to enjoy Eddie's slagging and teasing. Scobie knew that Shamie felt he was being continually tested in some way. Whereas Scobie absolutely revelled in the banter with his father.

'Ah Scobe, I heard you were useless in that last match ye played. Couldn't kick snow off a rope.'

'Well, I take after you so, Da!'

Nine-year-old Scobie cottoned on that this was a sign of respect and camaraderie, especially if you could answer back. He loved when they pulled into the various yards and building sites and men stopped what they were doing and the truck was unloaded and the banter was had. Scobie loved to stand with his father and the men and listen to the talk and nod as if he understood all that was being said. Back in the truck, he liked to sit with the window open and his elbow sticking out. Like a real grown-up man. He loved the chats about Eddie's hurling days and relished the long, easy silences, the Major cigarette smoke wafting his way, the bottles of Lucozade Sport and the ham sandwiches.

Mole stopped to catch his breath, struggling to collect the air. More tar in his lungs than on the road they stood on. Scobie was looking at the cracked sign that read TYNAN'S TIMBER YARD. The same sign that had been there since he was a boy. Scobie threw a glance in through the closed gate to the yard beyond. Mole recovered enough to start moving again.

'What the fuck are we doing, Mole?'

Mole waved him on. They approached the big gate, which Mole ignored, and walked on down the perimeter of the fence until they got to a certain point, where he lifted a wire and scrambled in under it. Scobie did the same.

Now inside in the yard, Mole turned back to him and said, 'Take her handy now. The lads do be jumpy. Guards have been around lately.'

Before Scobie could open his mouth, Mole moved on towards one of the big old storerooms where the timber used to be kept.

Scobie followed on behind him. 'I'm warnin' ye, Mole, there better be something at the end of this.'

They stepped inside the large galvanised shed with half the roof now missing. There were still stacks of timber lying around. Scobie spotted rat poison dotted around the place. He heard voices coming from the far corner. They were in darkness except for a small fire burning in a makeshift firepit, fashioned out of an old rusted half-barrel. Flickers of light from the flames illuminated a series of figures hunkered around it. When Scobie's eyes adjusted to the dark he could make out about ten human forms. They wore hoodies or long coats. Some were lying down, not moving. Some sat up, smoking. Two were preparing some kind of concoction with skins and kitchen foil and a lighter.

Mole whispered in the dark. 'Howsitgoin'? It's only me. Mole.'

There was no reaction from the faceless outlines. Mole gestured to Scobie to sit down beside him around the fire.

Scobie rubbed his hands and stuck them towards the bit of heat. Eyes looked up in his direction. The bits of faces he could make out were younger. Evacuees from the great Christmas ship that was happy families and goodwill to all men. Washed up here in a disused, rat-infested shed on the outskirts of the town.

Mole leaned into one of them, and there was a muttered few words. Mole turned back to Scobie. 'Any twine on ye?'

Scobie rooted in his pocket and produced a tenner. Mole took it and turned back to the lad, handing it to him. Scobie realised how cold it was. The modest few flames in the barrel weren't doing much. What the fuck was he doing here? Go home. Go the fuck home and have a quick shot of Cliff's whiskey and get into the nice warm bed and sleep and dream, but don't ever dream of this place or these people.

Mole turned back to him and held up a big fat joint, then lit it and inhaled deeply. He held the smoke in, exhaling with a wheezy cough that produced a death rattle in his chest. Scobie reached for the joint and took a blast off it. It was strong. He felt his face turn to jelly almost immediately. He was saying goodbye … bye bye … to himself and the world as he knew it. Bye bye. So long. See you later. He took another hit and handed it back to Mole. He saw a pair of the eyes looking over in his direction. He waved at the eyes. 'How's it goin'?'

The eyes didn't respond but stared at him. Scobie saw one of the bodies roll up their sleeve. They took up a syringe and injected themselves. Scobie was numb from the joint, but the sight of this still got to him. He'd heard there was plenty of the hard stuff going around the town, but to actually witness it? He nudged Mole, who was too stoned to respond. Scobie wondered how the likes of Mole was still alive. A man who had caned it for most of his life. Now the wrong side of 50. A man who used to train greyhounds and read historical fiction, but then it all fell away into booze and weed and bad memories of a priest who made him bleed once when he was eight in his own box bedroom with a poster of the Liverpool football team behind them on the wall. Mole was a shade of white now. His eyes completely dilated. Twisted. He slumped back into himself. He had disconnected. He had gone to his other place.

Scobie was drifting too. Hoping to get past this wave of weed that always felt like a high-wire act, teetering on the edge of the abyss, until a second wave arrived and he felt the calmness sweeping his body. But the wave wasn't arriving. Instead, he was feeling nothing but a high anxiety. So frightened that he couldn't move, even though he wanted nothing more than to get away from the eyes around the fire. One set of eyes in particular seemed to shine in the darkness. Looking straight at him. Luminous. Scobie's whole body tightened up. He saw them again. The kangaroo eyes in the dark. From that terrible night in Oz. A night he had banished from his head forever, but every now and then, he would see their eyes. Shining brightly. Kangaroos on high alert. Nervous systems highly tuned to feel the twang of danger on their antennae. No ease. No rest for these creatures.

Scobie was transfixed, and couldn't look away. His stomach twisted. He needed another smoke, or maybe another smoke might kill him. He wasn't sure. He looked down to the floor. Away from the eyes of the kangaroos. He needed to never see those eyes ever again. He gathered all his strength and got to his feet and managed to stumble along back into the timber yard. His eyes fixed on the derelict office, the broken window.

He had waited outside that office for his da one summer day. They were finished for the day. Eddie had gone inside to take a slash. He said he was only going to be gone for a minute. Scobie sat in the cab of the truck, waiting. It'd been 10 or 15 minutes, and still no sign. He wanted his dad now. Where the fuck was Eddie?! He'd had a mad notion to slide over in behind the steering wheel and start up the engine. The keys were there. In the ignition. He'd seen Eddie do it so many times. He knew what foot went on which pedal. What a surprise it would be for Eddie when he came back out to see his 10-year-old son behind the wheel. Then he'd rev up the engine and drive off. Leave Eddie standing. The other men would clap and cheer and slag Eddie, and Scobie would be the best son in Ireland.

He made his mind up then. Slid across the seat. Grabbed the hand brake with both hands and managed to release it. And then he waited another 10 minutes, until at last Eddie emerged from the office of Tynan's. Scobie put his hand on the keys and slowly turned them, and had to stretch himself out so both of his feet were able to reach the pedals. He released the clutch with one foot and pushed the accelerator with the other foot. The engine revved up. Eddie's face turned to thunder. Scobie was unable to keep his foot on the clutch. It slipped, and the truck jolted forward. Towards the office window. A woman inside saw this, and came running out. Eddie sprung up onto the truck and flung open the door and reefed his son out of the way as he pulled the hand brake.

'What the fuck were ye tryin' to do, ye little bollocks!' Eddie slammed the dashboard with his fist. For a moment Scobie thought that he was going to get it in the face.

'I told ye, I'll teach ye when you're old enough. Sick of fucking saying that to ye!'

Scobie shook his head. 'I'm so sorry, Da, I wanted to …' He couldn't get the words out right. 'I thought it would be brilliant if I could …'

Eddie slammed the dashboard again and shouted this time. 'No, okay? This is my livelihood. What would have happened if you'd have crashed it into that office?!'

Scobie was cowering now.

Then the woman from the office appeared outside the truck. 'Eddie. It's all right. No harm done.'

Eddie calmed down. 'Ah Jaysus, Eileen, I know. It's just I got a fright.'

Scobie was immediately fascinated by this woman. She was younger than his mother for one thing, and she wore red lipstick, and Scobie couldn't take his eyes off her. Eileen, who was the secretary in Tynan's, had a Dublin accent, and Scobie decided that she was very good-looking and he would like to marry someone like her one day.

Eileen looked in at him and smiled. 'He was only trying to show off to his da. That right, Scobie?'

Scobie nodded back to her and gave her a wink. She laughed.

Eddie shot Scobie a look. 'We'll get you home.'

Scobie was for it now. What could he do? He instinctively looked down and said in a small broken voice, 'I'm really sorry, Da.' He was playing to the gallery.

Eileen was stirred into action. 'Ah Eddie, go easy on him, he's a great lad. Aren't ye, Scobie?'

Scobie decided to say nothing and just nod solemnly, like he was in Mass at the Stations when ye had to let on to be all hurt when Jesus was nailed up, even though really ye wanted to burst out laughing.

Eddie's face finally relaxed, and his mouth curled into something resembling a smile. 'Okay. We won't kill him this time.'

Scobie kept the head down, but out of the corner of his eye he spotted Eileen smiling at his father. Her lovely red lips. He wondered about kissing those lips. He felt the stirrings of an erection. It was the wrong time and place to be getting the horn, as the older fellas in school called it.

Eddie revved up the truck and they pulled out of the yard. Eileen waved at them. Eddie raised the finger from the steering wheel and Scobie gave her a big wave back. They made it out onto the road and headed for home. Scobie relaxed. He had avoided the worst of it. He was all settling in to daydream about Eileen when the side of his face felt the clatter of something hard, and then he saw stars and a pain shot through his head. Tears welled in his eyes. To be crying in front of Da? No way. He fought them back.

Eddie didn't look at him or say a word. He lit a Major and turned on the radio. Scobie didn't mind the slap as much as the shock of it. That it was so unexpected. His father had promised Eileen that he'd go easy. Scobie didn't understand. That was the worst of it. Sometimes he just didn't understand his da at all.

Now, Scobie snapped out of his reverie when he heard something behind him in the darkness of Tynan's yard, a low, guttural growl. Like a wild dog. He was sweating, and his stomach churned with anxiety and all the booze he'd drunk, and the shit he'd just smoked was making him think of ravenous wolves or weirder monsters out for blood. He anticipated giant psychotic hounds from hell being let off chains, him having to make a mad dash towards the wire fence. He turned slowly to see what beast was behind him.

A hooded figure emerged from the darkness. Scobie narrowed his eyes. He could make out the hoodie being removed, revealing a young male face, his mouth twisted and contorted and his teeth bared as he made the low, guttural howling noise from the back of his throat. Like he was possessed by some devil. Scobie was in fight-or-flight mode. He thought about the best thing to do – turn and run, try and find the gap in the fence, or stay and take it on? He made a fist. The figure approached. Scobie clenched every muscle in his body. The second wave of the weed was hitting him at last. It was calming him. It was okay. He could defeat the beast. He would be okay. Then the face of the beast changed. Transformed from slavering animal to a thin, drawn male human being who looked like death but not a creature from the other world. The young man waved. He smiled. 'Scobie Donoghue. Long time no see.'

The face danced in front of him. Familiar. Who was it? A fog filled his brain. He tried to clear it. He knew the face, or a version of the face, a younger version, and then it hit him. The fog began to clear and he saw himself waking up, now and then, beside a woman called Julie, about 10 years ago. He remembered he would sneak along the corridor, but not to escape or run out on her. No, he'd sneak on down to the living room, where her young lad would be up watching morning cartoons, and Scobie would start the growling outside the room and then go full-blown monster by the time he entered the room, and the young lad would scream and Scobie would grab him and pretend to devour him. Robbie was the young lad's name. Robbie. A fair-haired, brown-eyed lovely boy, full of curiosity and innocence about the world around him.

Robbie had a longer face now, with a thin moustache and skin that was pockmarked and dry, as if he got no proper hydration.

'Robbie. Is that you?' asked Scobie.

'Yeah, that's me. I thought you were in Australia or the fuck like, ye know.'

'I was, Robbie. For 10 years but sure, ye know, back home now.'

Robbie was all smiles. 'Mad to see ye, like. Mad to see ye here, like, in this fucking place. I says to myself, "I'll go out now and do the monster on him like." The fucking monster, like, I loved it. The poor ma tried to do it when you left, but sure she was shit at it. She was trying to' – Robbie did an impression of his mother's very poor attempt at the monster, a low, lifeless attempt at a growl. 'Shit, like. How is that a monster, like?'

'How is she?' asked Scobie.

Robbie shifted his feet and shook his head. 'Dunno the fuck, like really. Don't know the fuck, like. She fucked off to England with this fella. Paul or Paulie, as she did call him. I called him a cunt.'

'She left ye here?' said Scobie.

'She left me with Gran. Ye know, I wouldn't go to England. If she was happy with Paulie, ye know, let her go. But I was staying.'

Scobie nodded and tried to fathom the reality that the little Robbie he used to watch *SpongeBob SquarePants* with was the same creature as this lad in front of him.

'She's not that well, ye know, kinda not right in the head. She's been to doctors, and this Paulie lad is all into helping her and all this craic, but I dunno. I suppose I was around 12 or so and she started to get fierce depressed and wouldn't get out of bed, or she'd be up like a mad yoke, spending money she didn't have and drinking and one-night stands and mad shit. No in-between, ye know. Up, down, up, down. So I was glad when she met this Paulie lad. She seemed to listen to him, but I dunno. There was something about him. I dunno. Anyway, just me and Gran now. Fucking love her, I do, but she's fallen out with me cause of me not staying at the youth centre place and being a bit, ye know. Love the buzz, man. That's all. Love the buzz. Sure, what else is there? Get me?'

Scobie nodded. 'Ah, yeah. Love the buzz meself, Robbie.'

Robbie laughed then. 'Who'd a thought the two of us would be having the buzz together? Mad shit, like.'

'So what do ye do with yourself?' asked Scobie.

Robbie shook his head and lit a cigarette. 'Not much, ye know. I was going to the centre that they do have there in the town and it was good, like, and I got into drawing and that craic. There was talk of college and that but I went on a massive sesh and fucked it up.'

Scobie thought of Julie and what a quiet kind of person she was when he had known her. They had dated on and off for about six months and she had asked little of him. Just turn up at the house whenever he liked. He felt an emotion coming up his throat. Was it the weed? Was it the drink? No, it seemed genuine enough. A concern and sorrow for Julie and her condition and hoping that he hadn't added to it. She was very into him. He had known that. She had understood why he needed to go to Oz, had never tried to persuade him to stay, because she had put him first above her own heart. He looked at her son standing here in front of him and he felt a sudden need to take him back home and mind him. That he could get him away from the weed and whatever other shit he was taking.

Scobie felt the cold again and shivered and pulled his coat up around him and indicated the road beyond. 'Are ye heading on home or anything?'

Robbie shrugged.

Scobie took a step towards the wire fence but then stopped and turned back to Robbie and said, 'Like, ye can phone me or – ye know. I'm around, like.'

Robbie laughed again. A strange little internal laugh which he held at the back of his throat like only he alone would find the thing funny or worth laughing at.

Scobie shook his head. 'Okay. I sound like a fuckin' gomie, but Jaysus, ye need to stay away from places like this.'

Robbie laughed again, and he said with a real straight face, 'So do you, Scobie.'

In the same moment, a car engine cut the silence of the night air. Scobie and Robbie turned their heads towards the blue light spilling through the large metal gate. A figure emerged from a squad car. The lock was turned. This someone had a key. The gate slowly swung open. Scobie and Robbie stood like statues. Guard Delaney walked towards them behind the beam of a torch. They shielded their eyes.

Robbie swore under his breath, 'This fucker.'

Delaney ambled on down towards them like a man on a Sunday morning stroll. Scobie saw a pair of piercing dark eyes looking at him and a flinch of recognition across the face. Delaney stood beside Robbie, who automatically moved his legs apart and held his arms up, so Delaney could pat him down. The search didn't yield anything. Delaney wore a broad smile on his face.

'Seeing as it's Christmas, Robbie, I won't detain you. Get home to your granny. Go on. Clear off.'

Robbie didn't need to be told twice. He slipped out through the open gate and tore off down the road. Delaney turned towards Scobie. 'Now, Mister Donoghue, what has you out here?'

Scobie was tongue-tied, still far too high to be talking to a guard. He saw Delaney's shit-eating grin and the 100 per cent confident look in his eye, and he dearly wanted to tell him to fuck off.

Delaney took a step closer to Scobie. There was a moment of silence. Scobie felt compelled to stay put until this man dismissed him. The power of the uniform, or was it the aura of Guard Delaney, the 'cool as a cucumber', 'I'm in complete control' way he had of going on. Delaney smiled then. A friendly, gentle sort of smile. Like an old pal would give another pal if they'd messed up a bit and needed help. He put his arm around Scobie. He held him very firmly. Gently applying pressure. 'Angela is a very nice woman. I'm sure she'd love to know that you've been hanging out with the lowest of the low, taking pills.'

Scobie shook his head. 'I wasn't taking …'

Delaney nodded. 'I know. Probably just puffed a bit of weed.'

All the energy seemed to drain from Scobie's body. He felt like crashing and lying down and going to sleep.

Delaney patted him on the back. 'Okay, we'll get you home. Back to Mammy. She's a decent person. She deserves more than this, Scobie.'

Scobie knew that he was right. Tears welled up in his eyes. He had never cried in front of a man before. He wasn't about to start now.

Delaney moved past him on into the building. 'Back in a second.'

Scobie heard him shouting, then the others emerged. Scurrying into the yard like rats. Scurrying on into the early morning light.

seven
Angela

It was icy 'brass monkeys' cold, the kind that got into your bones, no matter how many layers you had on. A late-January early morning, which always made Angela insist that both Scobie and Cliff had porridge before they went out, and plenty of scalding-hot tea.

'Set ye up for the day,' beamed Angela.

She was in high form watching her two men as they headed off to work together. The lads piled into the car, Scobie behind the wheel, and headed off to the site with the radio blasting out pop music and celebrity gossip.

'Put on the news and turn that shite off,' protested Cliff.

Scobie only turned it up louder, and sang along to Lewis

Capaldi's 'Before You Go'. Then he broke off to say, 'I see Sheffield Wednesday were knocked out of the cup, Cliff. Three–nil.'

Cliff scowled. 'Just 'cause we're a proper football club with proper roots in the community who don't buy success.'

'Yis can't buy a result,' laughed Scobie.

Cliff shook his head sadly. 'I want to cry when I think of the state of our national game. Money, the root of all evil.'

Scobie ignored this, swaying his head in time to the music and taking the turn into the site way too fast, skidding and sending up a load of gravel.

'Jesus, Scobie, health and safety.'

'Ah, live a little, Cliff!' Scobie parked up and hopped out of the car.

Niallers and a lad from Donegal, Bob Bonner, were just finishing their tea in the Portakabin.

'Ah lads, we better get goin', the foreman's son has arrived.'

'Feck off.'

'How ye doin', Scobie.'

'Hey, Bob, have ye got that tenner ye owe me from the weekend?'

'Ye can't take feathers off a frog, Scobie, nor knickers off a bare arse,' Bob replied.

'It's some load of shite ye do talk above in Donegal.'

'Ah sure, what would ye expect from a cow but a kick!'

Last cigarettes were lit, safety helmets were donned and gloves were put on, and the day's work began.

After the Stephen's night experience, Scobie had taken to the bed and hardly got out of it for about three days. Even when he had sweated all the toxins out of his body and drunk gallons of water, he still felt very anxious. His stomach was tight and upset, and he could barely even eat the ma's shepherd's pie, which was his favourite go-to comfort food. There was nothing for it. He hightailed it out and landed in the waiting room of the local GP, Doctor Byrne.

'So what's wrong with you, Scobie?'

'I don't know. It's like some sort of pain in the stomach.'

The doctor felt around Scobie's abdomen and listened to his heart. 'How are you after food?'

'Not good, like I'm all tight or something.'

The doctor nodded. 'Okay. Are you experiencing regurgitation of food?'

Scobie nodded. 'Yeah, like it wants to come back up. Like it's not digesting properly.'

Doctor Byrne paused for a moment. 'You may have a condition called GERD. Gastroesophageal reflux disease.'

'Jaysus, what does that mean?'

'It's basically too much acid splashing up into your oesophagus, the tube that connects your throat with your stomach, and it's getting inflamed. So you need to cut out alcohol, spicy foods, dairy. I can give you a website address to look up.'

Scobie nodded, but all he could think of was that the man had said no alcohol. Jaysus, surely he must just mean spirits, like not beer. Surely beer would be okay?

'How are you otherwise?' asked Byrne.

'Like what do ye mean?'

'In yourself. Are you sleeping?'

'Well, to be honest, I'm not sleeping at all much. Up until four

or five most nights. During the day I feel, I dunno. It's hard to …'
Scobie felt stupid now, and warm around his face, as if he was
blushing.

'Go on Scobie, it's only us.' Byrne said, smiling.

'I just don't feel, how will I say it, it's like I don't know if I'm
coming or goin'.'

Byrne let this hang for a moment. Scobie couldn't meet his
eyes. 'I feel bad in the mornings when I wake, like real worried
about all sorts of shite, and I don't feel like gettin' up nor nothin',
and it's a struggle to be honest, doc. It's like I'm wading through
shite and muck, and I feel real hollow.'

'Why do you think that is?' asked Byrne.

'I don't know, doc. Just life seems to have gotten much harder
or something.'

'How long have you been experiencing this?'

'Since for a few years. When I was in Oz, it would happen out
of the blue, but like …' Scobie felt a tightness in his throat, like
his body wanted to stop him from saying any more.

'Go on,' said Byrne, smiling again encouragingly.

Scobie trusted Doc Byrne enough to open his mouth and continue to speak. 'I remember years ago, as a kid, being in here with
you and I felt it then and I wanted to tell you but I didn't.'

'What age were you, Scobie?'

'I dunno. Around eight or nine. I can't believe that I'm – I've
never told anyone this. I could do with a bit of help, doc.'

Byrne joined the tips of his fingers together and glanced out
the window in classic doctor pose. 'Okay, I'm not keen on them,
but maybe some anti-anxiety medication would help.'

Scobie perked up immediately. 'Okay. Sound.'

Doc Byrne took a pen in his hand to start writing a prescription. 'I'm giving you Xanax for six weeks and no longer, to help take the anxiety down. Okay? But I won't give you a repeat prescription. It's just to get you over this hump. Understood?'

Scobie nodded. 'Thanks, doc.'

'I'll also give you some antacid tablets for the GERD. The main thing is to start to look after yourself a bit better. Stick to the new diet. Anxiety is often connected to what you're putting into your body.'

Scobie had a flash of a giant keg pouring out the entire contents of all he had drank in his 25-year 'drinking' career. A vast deluge of liquids of all varieties cascading and splashing down into the earth and flowing down the bogs and fields of the midlands into the River Shannon and causing it to overflow.

Scobie thanked the doctor, left the surgery and went to the medical hall to get his tablets.

Once Scobie had started to get some proper sleep, he was able to really start to focus on what he needed to do. He had stumbled over a thing on a self-help website saying he should write down the changes he needed to make in his life. So he wrote into his phone, *I need some work and routine and a wage. I am off all Persian rugs of any kind. I will follow the doc's orders and stay off all spirits and shots. I will allow myself a few nice pints in the pub but try to cut out any drinking at home.* He also wrote into his phone, *I never want to be in a place like I was on Stephen's night. That kind of thing is pure mule. Beyond the beyond. Like why the fuck was I there?* It was a question he didn't care to dwell on just now. He was okay, and was luckier than most, especially when he thought of those zombies out in the gutted building of Tynan's. He thought of Robbie, of his growl and his sunken eyes, but he shook the thoughts out of his head. He didn't dream anymore either, or at least he couldn't remember any of his dreams, and for this he was very thankful.

On New Year's Eve he had hugged and kissed his mother and allowed Cliff a brief embrace to start off 2020. 'Eh, Cliff. I was just wondering whether the offer of a job on your site still stands?'

Cliff nodded and smiled. 'Of course. We're crying out for a lad with your experience.'

Angela beamed from ear to ear. Scobie mentioned to his mother that he was taking the antacid tablets, and that he had to get almond milk instead of milk milk, and to cut out garlic and tomatoes and spicy stuff. He didn't mention anything about taking Xanax. He wouldn't be long on them anyway. As the doc had said, just a little help to get himself back on track.

Scobie now had four weeks of solid sleep under his belt – up at seven, out the door with Cliff by ten to eight, and then on to the site. A new housing estate on the far side of the town. Made a millionaire out of a lad called the Miller Monaghan. He'd been a few years ahead of Scobie at school and inherited land from his elderly parents. Miller sold the land on to some developer, and now, hey presto, the houses were going up. All three-bedroomed, all bought off plans. There were whispers that a cuckoo fund from England had swooped in to land nearly 80 per cent of them. Outbidding first-time buyers who will end up having to rent for life.

Scobie didn't think it was right if it was true, but the houses had to be built. He soon got back into the swing of the work. He plastered and mixed cement, and it was cold but good to be out and breathing air and talking shite, and the lads were a good bunch. No shorthand from any of them. No big smart-arse either, sucking all the air out of the room. He was glad to be working with Niallers again, and their awkward exchange when he'd bumped into him in Lidl was forgotten after a few days grafting on the site, back in each other's groove again, like the old days.

Bob Bonner was dead sound, and he talked faster than any human being Scobie had ever encountered, with a thick Donegal accent that was sometimes impossible to decipher.

'Ach, what about ye there, me darling duck? Howsitgoin', and don't you be worrying about that, hi, no bother, hi.'

Bob was in his mid-thirties with a big open face, and loved nothing more than to stand his round and be the one to buy a load of packets of crisps on a Friday evening in McKeon's because they'd eat no dinner until the chippers after the pub was over.

Scobie did his best to keep the drinking to Friday nights. He'd go toe to toe with Bob and the other lads, pint for pint, but he never went near shorts or shots. Bob was one of eleven children from a frenetic Donegal farm, and was fiercely close to Mammy and Daddy, who still worked the land and reared cattle. Bob came in the middle somewhere, and seemed on balance to be one of the saner ones in the family, judging from the stories he told. He had a big heart and was mostly upbeat and friendly and, 'Ach, now, come here and let me tell ye', but he could take a 'wild turn', as he'd say himself, and display outbursts of pure, almost comical, bad temper. Anything could set him off. Anything to do with Fine Gael or Fianna Fáil sent him into an apoplexy, 'Because them bastards own half the houses in Ireland, Scobie, so why would they want a rent cap on the fuckin' things when they're the ones to line their middle-class pockets? Ah, it just sickens the bollocks of me now so it does to tell ye the truth, people sleeping out on cardboard boxes.'

Most of the younger lads avoided or were completely apathetic to politics. They tended to sit back and scroll on their phones and laugh at TikTok videos and Instagram memes and the like. But Bob liked the bit of back and forth with Scobie, and had loads of useless information at his fingertips to distract the lads from their phones.

'Did you know, boys, that the earliest-known dildo was found in Germany in a cave over 30,000 years ago?'

'What was it made out of?' asked Niallers.

'Wood or bone, maybe ivory,' replied Bob.

'Did ye ever use one,' asked Niallers, 'or a vibrator or anything?'

Bob shook his head. 'Don't need one.' He tapped the table. 'Mahogany, lads, honest to God. She couldn't keep up with me last night, and that's the truth.'

Scobie said, 'I found a rabbit in a house one time when we were in finishing off a shower unit. This girl was getting married the next week, so I didn't think she'd need it. Then the fiancé dumped her on the way to the church. I had to sneak it back into the drawer.'

Niallers shook his head. 'Ye stole her rabbit? What do ye mean? She was having sex with a rabbit? That's mad.'

The lads suppressed their laughter. 'Well ye've heard of bestiality, Niallers,' Scobie said. 'Ye know, dogs and horses and sheep? Well there's some people into bunny rabbits.'

Niallers shook his head. 'Well that beats all, lads.'

Scobie and Bob burst out laughing. 'I don't know where we ever got you from, Niallers,' said Scobie.

'What? What are yis on about?' asked Niallers.

Scobie downed his pint and grinned as Bob said, 'It's a vibrator. It's not an actual rabbit, ye fucking eejit.'

Niallers took the abuse in his stride. 'Ah sure, how would I hear about the likes of that?!'

'Would Aine not use one, Niallers?' asked Scobie.

'She would not. Mind you, we're that fucking worn out with the two lads, I can barely raise a smile, never mind anything else.'

'Playing snooker with a rope,' shouted Bob.

Niallers and Bob were the right sort of boys to be hanging around with, thought Scobie. They were steady and more or less happy in their own skin or whatever you'd say. Scobie envied their certainty about what was important in life.

Bob, happily drunk at the end of the night, would talk about the future. 'I do love the bones of every one of them, the family, like. And I want to go back one day, set up me own wee firm, like. And I'll bring the mot with me. About time I asked her, lads. I'm serious. Ye know, get married, the whole thing. It's shoot dog or shite the licence.'

Niallers, who was completely in love with his two sons, said, 'I can't think of a time before they came along, like.'

'I can,' laughed Scobie. 'When you used to go to Reds every weekend and walk home on your tod.'

'Feck off, you. I only had to get lucky the once. With Aine. I wouldn't swap that.'

'You're just like the bro, a one-woman man,' remarked Scobie.

Bob drained his last pint. 'Right, boys, move your arses there now, I'm starvin'. It's the chip, batter burger, onion ring special for me tonight!'

Scobie and Niallers followed the lead and drank up, and they all barrelled out the door. Scobie looked across at Club 52, but he no longer had any compulsion to slip in there. He had a new ritual. Chips and burgers with the lads, or maybe even a kebab to eat on the way home. Then into the bed by two, and a little Xanax sent him off lovely. Away into a deep sleep and a great floaty pleasant buzz just before he dropped off.

Scobie did adhere to the gluten-free, non-dairy diet advised by Doc Byrne at first, except of course for the pints and takeaway of a Friday. But as the days and weeks crept into February, he started to slip back into old eating habits and the gastro thing would flare up and he'd have to horse down the antacid tablets. He was also trying to imagine life without the Xanax, as he only had a week of them left.

One night he decided to try and go without just to see what it would be like. He would save them for emergencies. He got into bed and settled down and felt okay and tried to think good thoughts. He saw Shamie Jr in the pool in Melbourne with his armbands on, Uncle Scobie trying to teach him how to swim even though he had been only four and a half at the time. He saw them on St Kilda Beach, where he accompanied the boy on his very first ride on a roller coaster, an old-fashioned rickety wooden structure that rattled loudly. Shamie Jr had screamed with pleasure, and they got hot dogs and ice cream afterwards, and that night, when Scobie tucked him in, the boy had said it was one of the best days he had ever had.

In bed Scobie drifted further down the lane to sleep, holding, in his mind, Shamie Jr's hand as they walked along the boardwalk at St Kilda. A sofa materialised up ahead and they sat down. Scobie looked out at the beautiful azure sea, but when he looked down at Shamie Jr he was gone. He had morphed into Robbie, small and wide-eyed on the sofa as he had been on one of his birthdays, when Scobie had given him a book about dinosaurs and his eyes had lit up and he hugged him. Really tightly. Scobie felt now the warmth of that hug, but it didn't last. A wave of unease swept up through his arms and chest. Drifting away from sleep and back into the conscious world, he was hugging Robbie, but the boy was now older and colder – dead. Wide, empty, frighteningly vacant eyes. Scobie let go of him. He woke fully, bang smack back in the real world, then leaned across into a drawer to retrieve the Xanax.

The next morning, Scobie looked up while wolfing down his porridge, and instead of Cliff opposite him he saw a young Robbie wolfing down his own porridge. Robbie had always mimicked the way Scobie ate before skipping down from his chair and racing into the living room, which to him had been a tropical jungle, where all manner of dinosaurs roamed, and he would talk to himself in different voices embodying the various characters in the story until Scobie arrived in to join him in Jurassic Park.

Scobie was frozen for a second, spoon paused in mid-air between dish and mouth.

Cliff snapped him out of it with another one of his terrible attempts at an accent, this time American. 'Earth calling Scobie. Come in, Scobie. Do you read? Over.' Angela laughed and Cliff went on, 'Remember that, Ange? Mork calling Orson. Come in, Orson.'

'Oh yeah, I used to love that. Nanu nanu!' Angela laughed.

'Oh yeah, nanu nanu,' mimicked Cliff, putting his finger in the air and bending it the way Robin Williams had in *Mork and Mindy*.

Scobie just sighed and carried on eating. 'Jaysus, can a fella not get a few minutes in this house? A bit of quiet?'

Cliff and Angela made faces at each other and nodded their heads and put their fingers to their lips and made loud shushing sounds, and again Cliff attempted some kind of foreign accent. 'We so sorry, sir, for making noise. We stay mucho quiet from now on.'

They laughed like children, and Scobie got up and left the porridge behind him.

He went on out of the house and waited for Cliff in the car. He tapped the steering wheel. He wondered could he chance another Xanax. He was feeling queer as fuck. Cliff got in beside him and belted up and nudged Scobie. 'Sorry if me and your mam are a bit giddy sometimes.'

Scobie started up the engine. 'Ah, sure, yis are only having the craic.'

'I was thinking of taking her away for a few days. Ye know, one of those mini breaks in a spa hotel down in Galway or somewhere.'

'Fair play, Cliff, sure she'd love that.'

They reversed out onto the road. Scobie switched on the radio and changed the station to RTÉ One, so Cliff could get the news. Cliff acknowledged this gesture with a smile. There was more on the flu virus story from China and how it might be spreading to other areas of the country. They were calling it the coronavirus. Scobie kept his eyes on the road as they drove on through the town. He had to pull up for a truck unloading outside the local Centra when he spotted a figure ambling along, approaching the shop, hoodie up, smoking a cigarette. It could have been Robbie. Scobie wasn't sure. All them young lads could kinda look the same. Scobie thought about rolling down the window and calling his name, but he decided against it. The young lad disappeared inside the entrance to Centra, and Scobie drove on to the site for another day of labour.

Scobie started, as always, by cleaning his tools and then scrubbing the wall with a good tough hand brush before mixing the PVC glue in a paint tray.

Bob was working alongside him around a fireplace, talking 90 to the dozen. 'Aye and then we went for a wee drink afterwards to this little pub across the way and it was grand until this shower of drunken Dublin southsiders came in, off their tits, like, high as kites, bein' terrible loud, and one of them kind of bumped into herself goin' to the toilet and I turned on him and I swear to fuckin' Christ I could have decked the bastard, but I didn't and we drank up and left but I wondered afterwards, like. Did she want me to hit him? Like a real man. Like, in me younger days I used to get into plenty of scraps, it was a way of standing out from the crowd. Ye know, like, ye'd get a reputation for being a bit of a fighter, so ye felt like a man or what used to be what being a man was all about. Ye know what I mean?'

Scobie grunted, not really in the humour for this non-stop broadcast from Donegal. He'd have preferred the radio and his own thoughts.

'Like, I know ye can't be goin' around hitting people, even if they're acting like pricks, but then what are we? Are we men?'

Scobie kept slapping plaster on the wall, grunted an 'I dunno', but his thoughts kept drifting to Robbie, his sunken eyes, his broken body hurtling into a vortex of homelessness and hardship.

The rain continued to fall for another four days. It had turned into sleety shitty scuttery rain by the Thursday morning, and Scobie hadn't slept great the night before, and his Xanax supply was zilch, as was his big claim to himself that it would be a great challenge not to crave them so much. That it would all come down to his willpower. That it would be grand, just like giving up the smokes. It had all proved wishful thinking of the most deluded kind. He was going up the walls, wound tight, irritated by everyone, drinking sugary tea at the break with Bob and Niallers.

'It's like a flu or something, but people are dying from it.'

'Where's that, Bob?' asked Niallers.

'Some place in China.'

'Ah, grand,' Niallers said, relieved, as he was very susceptible to flus. 'May it stay the fuck over there.'

'Well, it looks like there's a case in Europe. In northern Italy,' piped up Bob, enjoying Niallers' discomfort.

'Ah no, do you know something?' said Niallers. 'If I was in charge, I'd shut all flights from Italy. Like, we're an island. Stay the fuck away. And if you're Irish over there ye may stay there for the time being.'

Bob added, 'Do you know that the last major pandemic was the Spanish flu, which infected over one-third of the world's population and killed over 20 million people?'

Niallers was now beside himself with worry. 'Jaysus, that couldn't happen again, not nowadays, like, could it?'

Bob said, 'It could. Like, SARS was pretty serious that time. Like, we're due a big virus.' He turned to wink at Scobie and recruit his help in continuing to freak out Niallers. 'What do you think, Scobie?'

But Scobie wasn't coming out to play. He threw the remains of his tea on the ground and shrugged as if he had barely heard anything that had been said.

He was like a hen on a hot griddle and mad for work. Like it was distracting him. The rain continued to pour outside, but Scobie was inside, warm and dry, and he sang 'Umbrella', the Rihanna song, as he plastered the ceiling of an upstairs room, thinking about the email he'd got from Doc Byrne suggesting all sorts of mindfulness and meditation and links to stress management sites and yoga, when Scobie had no intention of doing any of it. Imagine. *Hi lads, can't come for pints, I'm just off to me meditation yoga class.* Fuck's sake, no way José.

Scobie worked up a great sweat that afternoon, thinking that maybe if he really tired himself out he'd get some sleep that night. He was irked then when Bob's rapid-fire Donegal voice box made noise behind him, interrupting his solitary activity at the wall.

'She went off at me for no good reason, like, disgraceful behaviour altogether. I found it really upsettin', to be honest. I

have always tried my best with that woman, but it was absolutely—'
Scobie walked away from him to the other wall to continue plastering. Bob took high umbrage, but Scobie shrugged.

Bob followed him across the room. 'Hi there, sir, thought we were mates. That's wild ignorant there now.'

Scobie threw his plastering trowel to the floor and walked away.

Bob was more amazed than angry or hurt at the behaviour. So not like Scobie. In 10 minutes or so Scobie arrived back in the room. 'I'm sorry, Bob,' he said.

'Are ye okay, Scobe?'

'I am. I just have a kind of headache,' lied Scobie. 'Sorry.'

Scobie always drove them to work, and Cliff drove them home. It was a pattern they had fallen into. So that evening Cliff took up his place behind the wheel.

Scobie approached the car, opened the back door, threw his tools in and thumped the roof. 'Go on there, Cliff,' he said. 'I feel like a walk.'

'What, are ye serious? It's shite out,' said Cliff, looking up to darkened skies spitting with rain.

'No bother, go on. I'll be home in time for the tea.'

Cliff revved up the engine. 'Don't be late. I'm starving. She's doing the shepherd's pie this evening!'

The car moved on. Scobie felt a relief to be on his own, away from Bob and Cliff, the constant noise and verbiage. He walked on into the town, around the back road behind the church and through the church grounds to the road beyond. He wasn't going directly home.

The spits of rain turned to a heavy shower, so he ducked in under the big tree at the side of the school field, into Dinny's Hole, surveying the rain dripping off the branches above, trying to remember what type of tree it was. They had been told in school. An evergreen, a coniferous tree, one that kept its leaves all year round. Not leaves, needles. He looked around at Dinny's Hole. He had probably stepped on every single blade of grass that grew here, chattin' up girls, thrilled at the reality of kissing them, or playing five-a-side with the country lads before they had to run to catch their bus. Darker thoughts took over then, that those carefree, I-couldn't-give-a-shite-about-anything days were all so far gone, and that there was only tomorrow and the next day and the next, leading to what? To what?

Just then Scobie noticed three bodies that had appeared down the way underneath one of the other big trees, huddled together, heads with hoodies, one of them smoking and then handing over what was presumably a joint to the lad beside him. Scobie's eyes focused in on them. He thought he recognised one of them. Robbie. He looked up to see that the rain had eased off. He ventured out from underneath the tree, which he suddenly remembered was an ancient yew. Was it Robbie? He'd have to get closer. He walked towards the young lads to get a better view. The lads looked up but didn't flinch. They kept sharing the spliff. Scobie could see clearly that it was Robbie now, even younger-looking in broad daylight than he had appeared on Stephen's night out at the timber yard. Scobie had no idea what he was going to say to him, so he said the first thing that seemed perfectly natural to say.

'Any chance of a smoke, boys?'

The other two lads scowled at him and shook their heads with a 'what's the mad ol' fella at' expression on their little acne-ridden, malnourished faces, but Robbie grinned and offered the spliff to him with an 'It's all right, I know him'.

Scobie got it off him and took a blast. What harm? Might help him sleep tonight. He took a second pull and exhaled the smoke, handing it back to Robbie.

The two lads sloped off. Robbie took the last few tokes out of the joint before dropping it on the grass and stamping it out.

'I was only wondering how ye were, Robbie.'

'I'm grand. Not a bother.'

'That's good. I've not been out to the yard since. Have I missed much?' Scobie said with a hint of a grin.

Robbie shook his head. 'Naw, me neither. Your man Delaney has clamped down, so we had to find somewhere else.'

'Oh right, so where's that then?'

'Ah, that would be tellin' now, Scobie.'

Robbie took out a cigarette and offered Scobie one, which he refused. As Robbie lit his smoke Scobie noticed a little shake in his hand and that his wrists were white as snow and really thin.

'So how's the granny?'

'She's good. I've been goin' back to the youth centre, so she's happier with me, ye know?'

'What do ye do down there?'

'Ye do shite, like talkin' about the world and who you are, and there's a gym and computers, and basically it's a place for us that can't stick school, ye know? Like, I do a bit of drawing.'

Robbie took out a folded sheet of paper from a sports bag on his shoulder. He unfolded the paper to reveal a giant monster-type creature riding a motor bike, graphic comic style, sketched in black pencil. It reminded Scobie of a heavy metal album cover. There was great detail, down to the tattoos on the monster's arms.

'That's cool, Robbie.'

Robbie shrugged and put the drawing back in the bag.

'Like, ye really have a knack for it. I mean, you could do something with that.'

'I know, they're all sick telling me that down below, so ye know.'

They were silent then. Scobie could feel the weed working on his inner cortex, a dampening down of the nerves. The sky was beginning to clear a little, but neither of them felt like moving just yet.

'Any girls at the centre?' asked Scobie eventually.

Robbie nodded.

'Any of them you like?' asked Scobie.

'Naw, I mean there's a girl called Ruth, who's cool and kinda deadly, ye know, she's into things I like, but she dropped out there last week. It was the anniversary of her mother's suicide so she didn't cope well. I miss her, like.'

'Sorry to hear that,' said Scobie.

Robbie didn't react.

'She'll be back, and maybe then you can tell her that you like her.'

'Who said I like her? I mean she was a mate, not anything else.'

'Okay, I dunno. I think ye like her.'

'Fuck off, will ye? And don't be brownin' me now.'

'Go for it, Robbie. Ye should be at all that, like. You know, chatting up girls and all that.'

'Are you married or have a girlfriend?'

'No, I'm not married.'

'Wow, a big hit with the women so.'

'Feck off, I was in my day.'

'Ye were with my ma, so ye must have been desperate.'

'Your ma was a fine-lookin' woman, and I still have it, or I like to think that I still have it.' Scobie laughed that this admission had just popped out of him. 'Ah no, I was kinda almost married in Oz, but I'm back here now, living with the ma and her husband, who is decent but he's not my da, and I have no fucking idea what I'm at really.' Scobie breathed out, like it was a relief to say that to someone.

Robbie looked over at Scobie. 'Were ye in love and all that?'

Scobie nodded. 'Ah yeah, stone mad about her. Ella was her name.'

'Bet she was a dog,' laughed Robbie.

Scobie whipped out his phone and flicked through until he found a photo of her. It was from the day she graduated to be a primary school teacher. Scobie arm in arm with her, bright big smiles and shiny eyes. The sight of her set off an ice-cold lead weight falling into his stomach.

'She's not bad now, for an auld one, like,' said Robbie.

Scobie laughed and put the phone away. He hadn't expected to be hit like that at his first sight of her in so long. He remembered the night well. They had gone out to celebrate with her classmates and ended up in some bar with live jazz, and Scobie felt a bit isolated as they all went on about stuff that had happened in the college and plans for the summer.

A lot of them were much younger, in their early twenties. He let on to be listening and laughing, and he did shots with them. Ella had smiled lovingly over at him at some point and Scobie had given her a big trademark 'How's it goin' there, darlin'?' wink and raised his glass. He brought her out to dance. He held her close. He said all the right things. But he felt displaced. Like he didn't quite occupy the same space as her now. Like he could sense the end of something. He had felt a terrible surge of anxiety then. In his stomach. He could feel it creep down his arms and he got dry-mouthed and panicky and had a terrible feeling of dread, like there was nothing up ahead but darkness. He would fight it with drink. He would chase it away with drink. He could drown this creepy cunt of a feeling with a load of drink and good riddance and fuck ye. I'm grand. He would drop back into his body again. The body of Scobie Donoghue. The craic master. Everyone's friend! 'Now we're at it!' That night at the jazz club he lifted Ella up in his arms, out on the floor. He swung her around and she screamed, and he had screamed, 'It's pure mule! Pure fuckin' mule!', just like he used to.

Robbie put up his hoodie and turned to go. 'See ye around.'

Scobie watched as he ambled away down the field. He found himself heading after him. The weed had definitely helped things.

'Hey, Robbie, sorry, but ye don't have any more grass to spare?'

Robbie shook his head. 'I don't deal it.'

'I know, Jaysus, just as a favour to me, for old times' sake and the dinosaurs, ye know.'

Robbie grinned at this, but said, 'Sorry, but I have enough for myself. That's it.'

Robbie walked on. Scobie got a vision of his bed tonight, tossing and turning and the gnawing in his brain.

He went after him again. 'Just a nodge would do. I've not been sleeping. A bit anxious or something. Ye'd be really helping me out.'

Robbie stopped and shook his head. 'Well, the last thing ye should be doin' is smoking weed if you're anxious. Fuck me. Go on. Go home.'

Scobie was annoyed now. How dare the little bollocks dismiss him like that? 'Hey, Robbie, for fuck's sake, come on and help me out.'

Robbie stopped again. 'Okay, Jaysus, for fuck's sake. I can get ye some pills, anti-anxiety. Strong fuckers. It'll cost ye. But I won't give ye weed. Meet me here tomorrow at four.'

'Oh, right, that would be brilliant. Thanks, Robbie.'

Robbie turned on his heels and walked away. Scobie watched as he disappeared out onto the road. He felt relief flood through this body. Just one night to get through and he'd be grand. Good man, Robbie.

That night he tossed and turned and kicked and jerked around the bed in that state between sleep and being awake. He dreamed of this kangaroo-like animal covered in blood running away from him and he running after it like he was trying to catch up with it, until the thing turned its head and let out a fierce noise of pain that seemed to reverberate in Scobie's head and he sat up in the bed and put on the light and thought of Oz and that terrible night he had spent in the outback. He could still sense the smell of fear, and he banished it from his mind, telling himself again that he must never even begin to think of that night. Told himself he had to get through this night, and then tomorrow he'd be okay. He'd procure the pills from Robbie and in return he'd try and do something for him. He'd try and encourage him to stop messing, stop smoking and being around God knows who and try and give the centre a real go, and the art. He could still see that lovely light he had as a young lad. It was still there, flickering away. Scobie would try and help to bring it out.

The next day he waited under the ancient yew. Robbie was late, and he cursed him from a height, but just as he was ready to turn tail and bolt for home, the boy in the hoodie loped his way into the field and produced a small plastic pouch of pills.

'Xanax. They'll be fifty quid to you,' said Robbie.

'Where do ye get them?' asked Scobie.

'For me to know and you to find out, boss.'

'Thanks a million, Robbie, and, like, listen, I want to give you my number.'

Robbie shook his head. 'I don't deal, I told ye. This was a once-off.'

'I don't mean to get anything off ye. Just so you have it so tomorrow morning when I ring ye you'll know who it is.'

'Why the fuck would you be ringing me?'

'To make sure you go into the centre,' said Scobie with a grin. 'That drawing ye showed me was fuckin' brilliant, and I want to see more. Like, could ye do me one? For my wall.'

'Are ye serious? Nah. Well, I missed last week, so I don't know, but there was this national exhibition thing. I was supposed to be getting work together to present to it. Ye know, so maybe …'

'Well, I think you owe it to yourself, 'cause you have a great fucking talent, like. Not that I'd know fuck-all about it, but imagine how proud your granny would be, not to mention your ma.'

'My ma doesn't much care what I do.'

'Well, get her attention. Make her care. Send her a drawing. Come on, Robbie, I see a great thing in you.'

Robbie looked up at Scobie now. A smile crept across his face, and he burst out laughing. Scobie laughed too.

Robbie shook his head and pointed at the plastic pouch of pills in Scobie's hand. 'Look at you, all fuckin' givin' the advice and all. Well, if I go to the centre and cut down on the weed, you need to stop taking those yokes.'

'I will. I promise ye.'

Robbie shrugged. 'Give us that number then.'

Scobie gave him his digits and Robbie punched them into his phone.

Later that evening, Scobie skipped through the door at home in great form, kissing his mother on the cheek and fist bumping Cliff and full of chat and gossip and craic, and his mother's heart was warmed and her worry lines receded. Scobie was back with them. Not the moody, withdrawn lad that had taken his place for the past week or so. Scobie went up to bed that night, completely relaxed, his nerve endings salved, and there was no dry mouth or feelings of anxiety creeping up his arms. He floated off to sleep on a magic carpet overlooking the tall, strong ancient yews, and the whole town receded below into the distance until the houses and people were all just tiny specks and of no consequence to him at all.

eight
Deirdre

Deirdre lay, wide awake, in the bed. Eamon snored lightly beside her, lying on his back. He was wearing his old-man blue striped pyjamas, but in fairness he had looked after himself. He was still lean around the middle, and his skin was clear and healthy-looking. He looked younger than his 56 years. Stephanie Darby had remarked to Deirdre after Mass the previous Sunday that she wouldn't mind being arrested by him and locked up in a cell, as long as he was doing the interrogating. She meant it as a compliment, as most of the husbands sported sizeable paunches and very little hair.

Deirdre had laughed and played along, saying, 'I'll have to keep my eyes on you, Stephanie.'

Deirdre had stayed behind after the Mass to help Sister Senan with the altar and the flowers. As she was arranging red carnations she looked up at the long stained-glass window behind the altar, which portrayed the crucifixion. She knew every detail of it. She had been staring at it for as long as she could remember. Christ's gaunt but stoic expression, gazing up to the heavens. The Roman soldiers underneath, looking up at him, and the spear in his side. Deirdre sometimes tried to imagine the reality of nails being hammered into flesh and the absolute sheer agony he must have felt as he waited to die.

Deirdre didn't set foot in the church for a few years after the kids had all done the confirmations, but about 14 months ago she'd been in a bad state one Saturday evening. Eamon was away and the gambling had taken hold of her. She had lost heavily that day and realised how pathetic she had become, relying on the bounce of a ball or the nose of a horse to bring her some relief and peace. She started to walk, half thinking that she'd go to a school reunion party that had been organised in one of the pubs, just so she wouldn't be on her own. Maybe have a few glasses of wine and relive old times, when she was Deirdre Jackson, average student, excellent camogie player and fancied by a fair number of the lads in her class.

She had passed by the church and spied Sister Senan carrying a box of Christmas lights that she was barely able to manage. Deirdre could see how the little octogenarian bird of a nun struggled to make it to the front doors of the church. She scooted in and offered to help her. Inside, as Deirdre helped her put up the lights, she was hit by the peace and silence of the place, and the sister's warm smile. She knelt with Sister Senan then and they said their prayers together. Deirdre felt the comfort of this, and for a moment forgot about the money she'd lost and the trouble it would cause and abandoned all notions of attending the school reunion. After that, helping out in the church became a weekly stint.

Eamon stirred in his sleep to lay on his side, so his snoring subsided. Deirdre eyed the alarm clock. It was only six thirty. She could still feel the vibrations of yesterday's shit show in her system. On the surface the Saturday would have seemed like the most boring, mundane day of anyone's life. She had brought the lads to training. Cleaned the oven. Stopped off to do the weekly shop in Lidl. But as she walked the aisles she listened to a race in Haydock Park, and just as she was shovelling pizzas for the boys out of the freezer, her horse was approaching the finishing line, and she let out a little squeal as it got home in first place! Her latest crazy accumulator had got off to a great start. She thrilled to the secret life she led. While all the other people shuffled around filling up their baskets with crap, she was living life on the very edge. Lose one of the five bets on this accumulator and she was really and truly in the shit. No more credit on the cards. No more hiding and ducking and diving – she would have to come clean. She had ridden her luck so many times, but this was the final last chance dance.

Deirdre had brought the groceries home and unpacked them, then started to make lasagne for the tea, glancing at her phone constantly to get the latest scores from a basketball game in Russia on the Paddy Power app to keep the whole thing afloat. The terrible dread of fear, followed by the relief that filled her up as the

PBC Lokomotiv won by 10 points, made her do a dance around her kitchen. By the time Paudge and Oisín had come in from training, dumped their filthy jerseys and boots in the utility room and gone up for showers, the third part of the accumulator had come in, thanks to an own goal by Larsson of Malmö FF.

Laying her head on the pillow that night with Eamon asleep beside her, she got notification from a race in Australia. Her horse, Captain Fantastic, had fallen at the third. The inevitable had finally happened. She was broke. She was completely fucked. Her Paddy Power account was so far in the red that she wouldn't be able to bet with them. She needed cash from somewhere. Enough to keep gambling. To keep the show on the road. To give herself one more go at it. She could still get out of this. She had tossed and turned all night. She had to get up out of the bed. She needed some coffee. She needed to think. She slipped off the mattress, put on a dressing gown and crept out of the room, down the stairs and into the kitchen. She filled the kettle and put coffee in the cafetière.

She heard the back door opening. She looked up to see Keelan standing in front of her. Both women froze, as if someone had pressed pause. Deirdre could see that her daughter was definitely not sober: her make-up was smudged and her mascara had run, not to mention her hair, which had fallen asunder, and her mouth made a funny shape, like a kind of stupid grin, which infuriated Deirdre. The grin of someone who had all the brains but didn't try. The empty vacuous grin of a young woman who could have got out of the town and walked through the gates of Trinity into a cobblestoned future full of interesting people and knowledge and career and travel. All the things Deirdre hadn't done. But look at her now. Standing there in the kitchen in the early morning out of her box, with no plan for her future. Sleepwalking her life away.

Keelan put her hand on the kitchen counter and indicated the cafetière. 'I'd have a cup if it was going,' she said, still grinning.

Deirdre nodded and stood over the kettle as it boiled.

'Where were ye till this hour?'

'Club, and then Amanda's house.'

Silence then, except for the kettle. Deirdre continued to stare at it, the steam beginning to emerge from the spout. 'I couldn't sleep. Me head was full of stuff, ye know, so I just decided to get up.' Deirdre looked to her daughter. Her eyelids seemed heavy, her pupils dilated. She seemed more out of it than Deirdre had first realised.

'Do you want to know what I was thinking about?'

Keelan shrugged and moved away to flop down at the kitchen table. She opened her clutch bag and started looking for something inside in it.

'I was thinking about you and what you're going to do with yourself,' said Deirdre.

The kettle was nearly boiled now. Keelan didn't respond. She kept rooting in her bag. Deirdre wondered if she had heard her. 'Like, ye can't mope around this house for the rest of your life.'

Keelan found what she was looking for. A stick of lip balm. She began to apply it.

'Do ye hear me, Keelan?'

Keelan nodded, but applying the lip balm was all she could concentrate on.

Deirdre sighed and waited for the kettle to finally boil, then poured water in on top of the coffee in the cafetière. She felt like going across the kitchen and pushing the girl off her chair and onto the floor. She had an uncontrollable urge to hurt her in some way. To wake her up. Or was it that she really wanted to hurt herself? To give herself a good kicking. But that wasn't physically possible, so Keelan, her own flesh and blood, her little woman, as she used to call her, her little shadow, when she was a young one. She'd have to do.

Deirdre wanted to go across and slap her face. WHAT ARE YOU DOING! STUPID BITCH! WHAT HAS HAPPENED TO YOU? I USED TO KNOW EXACTLY WHERE I STOOD WITH YOU BUT NOW YOU'RE LIKE THIS FUCKING STRANGER WHO HATES AND RESENTS ME! WHY?! But then something else hit Deirdre, the problem in hand. She needed cash money. About five hundred quid would be enough to bet on one more big accumulator. She would ask her only daughter for a loan. That's what she'd do. Ask her now while she's a bit out of it. Might be easier. Deirdre gathered herself. She plunged the cafetière and let it settle for a moment. Then she poured out the coffees. She handed one to Keelan. 'Now, get that into you and get off to bed.'

'Thanks,' said Keelan. She sipped her coffee. She looked at her phone. She laughed at something.

Deirdre watched her. Biding her time. 'Keelan, could I ask you something?'

Keelan was still engrossed in the phone. She was typing.

'I was just wondering could you spot me a few bob?'

Keelan looked up at her. 'What's that?'

'I just need some cash, Keelan. No biggie. Just until tomorrow.'

Keelan frowned, she was tired now. She needed to lie down. 'Eh, how much?'

'Five hundred.'

'What the fuck? What do you want that for?'

'I'll tell ye when you're sober. Come on. Can you do it?'

Keelan put her phone into her bag. She tried to stand, but her hand-to-eye wasn't great.

Deirdre stepped in to help Keelan, grabbing her arm and guiding her to her feet. 'Just give me your card. I'll run down and get it. What's your number?'

Keelan's stupid grin appeared on her face again. She shrugged. 'I don't have it.'

'What do you mean? It's five hundred. Surely to Jaysus you have five hundred in your account.'

Keelan shook her head and winced. Deirdre realised that she had a vice-like grip on her daughter's arm.

'I spent it. I blew it all.' Keelan couldn't help laughing.

Deirdre squeezed her arm tighter, wanting to cause real pain now.

'Jesus Christ, you stupid bitch, what did you spend it on?'

Keelan wrestled her arm away from her mother, looking now pale and frightened, like a little girl who'd just been scolded harshly and wanted to retreat upstairs to the sanctuary of her room and away from the big bad world of adults.

Deirdre realised she needed to keep her temper in check. 'I'm sorry, love. Just I'm concerned that you seem to have no sense of responsibility for anything.'

Keelan let out a laugh from the bottom of her throat. Deirdre detected a bitterness in the sound of it. Keelan took a step away from her mother towards the door. She stopped and looked back. 'Maybe you should ask Scobie Donoghue for the money.'

Deirdre had to wait a moment to make sure she had heard correctly. 'Excuse me, but why would I possibly ask Scobie?'

Keelan shrugged and smiled. 'Let's just say because of your shared history.'

'What the fuck are you talking about?'

Keelan's smile disappeared. 'Pathetic. We were only kids and you carrying on with fuckin' Scobie.'

Deirdre felt as if she had been punched in the stomach. She felt sick. Her face felt hot and flushed, burning with shame. 'Where did you hear that?'

Keelan waved her away and went to the door.

Deirdre thought about going after her and demanding to know who told her, but she didn't want a scene. She didn't want Eamon waking up. She didn't want any of this. All the pain and tribulation and effort and emotion spent on them, and this is how they treat you. Fucking children. In that moment she regretted ever having any of them. Especially Keelan. So she said something. Words formed in her throat and she let them go, aiming to get them out before Keelan left the room.

Just as Keelan was about to cross the threshold, the words flew through the air. 'You're a fierce disappointment to me. Do ye know that, Keelan?'

Keelan was stunned. Her eyes stung with tears. She was too hurt to respond. She disappeared from Deirdre's view, her footsteps on the stairs. Deirdre was alone in the kitchen. She didn't regret any of those words. Not for now, anyway. Because Keelan had given her an idea. Of course Scobie Donoghue would give her the cash. No better man. Scobie would come through for her. That was what she'd do. She eyed the clock. Nearly seven. Time enough. She knew that Angela and Cliff were away, so that would make it easier to slip around there. She went back upstairs and managed to grab jeans and a top out of the room and bring them down out onto the landing. She looked towards Keelan's door, an old worn sticker for Hogwarts School still stuck on it. The young one who'd loved books and made them queue overnight to get the last of the series – where had she gone?

Deirdre went downstairs and changed in the kitchen. She took one last slurp of coffee, put on a coat and hightailed it out the back. A cold gust of wind blew as she crossed the green at the far end of Castlepark estate, causing her to shiver and making her wish that she'd brought a scarf. Some people were up and about. Lights were on in houses, the odd car trundled past. Deirdre whipped out her phone and called Scobie. It rang for what seemed like ages. She had crossed the green and was heading for his front door on St Colman's Road by the time his croaky voice could be heard in her ear.

'Hello?'

'Hey, Scobie, I'm outside your door.'

Deirdre could hear nothing but silence now, as if Scobie's head had not arrived back fully into the conscious world.

'Please, Scobe, I just need to ask a favour.'

'Eh, Jaysus, Deirdre, what the fuck like, it's only Jaysus seven o'clock of a Sunday morning?'

'Scobie. Lookit, can you let me in or not?'

Deirdre entered the front yard and approached the door of the house. She glanced up, and could see the curtains opening above and Scobie looking down on her. He waved. She saw him pulling on a jumper.

Deirdre sat at the kitchen table while Scobie handed her a cup of tea and a carton of milk from the fridge. Deirdre poured the smallest drop of milk into the tea, barely browning it.

'What's the point of that?' asked Scobie.

'What's the point of anything?' said Deirdre, and then she smiled at the worried look on Scobie's face. 'I know. It's a bit mad, turning up at this hour. Your ma's away, isn't she?'

'She told the whole town,' said Scobie.

'Oh yeah,' said Deirdre. 'I met her last week on the road and she was that excited.'

'So what's the story, like?' asked Scobie.

'Oh, right, well, I need a favour that I can't ask none belonging to me, and I thought of you because I know ye so long and we've had our moments and I know how much Jennifer valued your friendship. What I'm trying to say is that you've always been decent. A good man, underneath it all, so ...'

Deirdre hesitated now. She took a sip of her tea. She noticed a slight reddening of his face at the compliment. 'I need to borrow some money, don't ask why, please. I just do. Five hundred. I need it this morning. You'd really be helping me out. I'd pay it back to you next week.'

Scobie looked slightly bemused. 'I don't get it.'

'Look, I'm not going to explain the whys and wherefores, I just need you to help me out or not.'

Scobie shrugged. 'Well, okay, grand, I'll just go upstairs and look under me mattress.'

Deirdre shook her head and stood up. 'Okay, that's fine. If you can't help me, that's fine.' She felt closer to the edge than she wanted to be. She knew that Scobie was aware that all was not quite Kool and the Gang with her.

'Are ye all right, Dee?'

Deirdre shook her head sadly, and her eyes met his and then looked to the floor, like she was exposing something vulnerable of herself to him that she clearly didn't want to name. 'Please, Scobie,' she said under her breath, 'could you manage it?' She was tired now. Her head filled with Eamon's sleeping body and Keelan's crushed expression in the kitchen. She felt like crying. She didn't try to discourage the emotion. Scobie could sense her upset. This might be no harm.

'Okay, fair enough,' he said eventually.

Deirdre grabbed Scobie's arm and squeezed it, saying, 'Thanks so much, Scobie,' and she felt so relieved. 'I'll wait here if you want to go down the town to the cash machine.'

Scobie sighed and went to put on his shoes in the hall. 'I'll need it back, Dee. Like, by Wednesday at the latest.'

'Absolutely. You'll have it by tomorrow. I promise.'

Scobie pulled on his coat and slid open the glass doors. 'I'll see ye in a while.'

'Thanks so much, Scobe. Take your time. I really appreciate this.'

Scobie ducked out and shut the sliding door after him.

Deirdre took out her phone to check out other gambling apps. She must make a plan now for a new accumulator. A Super Sunday. The day she'd finally get ahead of it all and lay it to rest. This was it. She'd go to the church first and say a prayer and light a candle. Everything would work out. Dear Jesus, please let everything work out.

nine

Scobie cursed the fact that Angela and Cliff had taken the car so he was going to have to bomb it down to the main street to get the money out. He set off down the road and heard the birds and the church bell ringing, and he thought of Sundays and trying to mitch Mass by hanging out behind the school sheds smoking fags and trying to act the hard in front of the other lads and hoping in the back of his mind that God wasn't looking down and ready to fuck him up in some way because he was missing his show across the road. His mind raced. What did she need the money for? Should he give it to her? But he couldn't help feeling a certain surge of something inside of him. Another body needed his help, and it gave him an energy. A way of stepping back outside of himself and concentrating on someone else. It was a relief.

The night before he had sat in his da's old armchair half-dozing and watched the news and Eileen had told the nation about the first case of coronavirus to be detected in the Republic. A man had travelled from the infected part of Italy but he had been isolated and contained. Scobie had enjoyed the blissful silence of the house as Cliff had swept Angela away for the whole weekend to a spa hotel in Connemara. It was like he was bringing her to a five-star resort in the Maldives the way Angela reacted to the news. She wasn't used to being surprised like that. It touched her deep down, and Scobie's heart gladdened to witness that. Cliff could be a bit of a tool a lot of the time, but he was absolutely on the ball when it came to making Angela happy.

Scobie had pigged out on the meat-feast pizza, a large bottle of Coke and wedges, not caring whether his GERD burst out through his hole when he'd devoured the lot. He had watched Saturday-night-type shite on the telly. The kind of thing that has Ant and Dec and members of the great British public. Stuff he hadn't seen in ages. He had turned over to *Winning Streak* to see all the families roaring and shouting with their shitty home-made signs, and the contestants forced to make small talk with Marty and then get cash and prizes for doing fuck-all. You didn't even have to answer a Jaysus question.

Later on, he had watched a film with Leonardo DiCaprio out in the wilderness where he fights a bear and has to survive through all sorts of shite and Scobie had seen it before but he'd been drunk so he wanted to see it properly. It's the kind of movie that Eddie would have loved, and for a while Scobie had felt him there in the room. Like being all alone in the house had encouraged Eddie's ghost out of the woodwork. Scobie was a bit spooked going up to bed after the movie was over, like he could hear sounds and creaks around the house. He realised that he had never been home alone before. He got into the bed and wrapped the duvet around him, took one of Robbie's pills and closed his eyes.

He had called Robbie every morning of that past week and badgered him until he got out of the bed and took himself into the centre. One morning Robbie didn't answer, so Scobie drove around to the granny's house on the way to work and rang the doorbell until Robbie, mule thick, came out to the doorstep. Five minutes later Scobie had him in the front seat of the car and dropped him off at the centre. That evening Robbie sent a drawing to him. A caricature of Scobie, complete with pint in his hand and a mad bleary-eyed head on him with no teeth. Scobie had been delighted to get it. He felt that he'd done something proper for someone. He felt like he was needed.

Scobie strode along the roads, which were still shiny from last night's rain, and he slowed his pace and took his ease. Why should he rush like a half eejit? He saw that the Centra was opening up, so he went in to get some milk and bread. Inside he was tempted by cans of Coke, Mars bars, packets of Doritos, all the supplies he'd need for a day of scratching his hole and more endless channel-hopping, which always seemed to end up with him watching some programme about the Jaysus Galápagos Islands. Scobie would turn to porn then on his phone, going through his favourite sites, and he'd be excited at the first bits of action but then he'd get bored and click on something else, and if the threesome wasn't doing it for him he'd click onto MILF and then he'd eventually finish, but there was no great pleasure in it. Just scratching an itch. He definitely had the itch that morning, and as he paid for the stuff and hightailed it to the bank machine, his head was full of the fact that a woman he had once had sex with was waiting for him inside in his house. He thought that he recognised a certain wild look in her eye, one he had encountered before. The wild look that meant she was on the run again from something. The last time it had been from her marriage. This time, God knows.

Scobie reached the front door and let himself in, and saw Deirdre sitting in the exact same spot as he'd left her.

'All right. Sorry, I had to stop off in the shop.' Scobie dumped the goods on the kitchen counter.

Deirdre got up with a smile. 'No problem, Scobe.'

Scobie took the ten fifties out of his pocket and offered it to her.

Deirdre put the money in her purse. 'Thanks so much, Scobe.'

He reached to plug in the kettle. 'You'll stay for another cup, sure.'

Deirdre eyed the kitchen clock, but sat back down. 'Okay, grand.'

Scobie boiled the kettle. 'Good to see ye anyway.'

Deirdre smiled, but there was an awkwardness now. 'So, anything planned for the day while the cat's away?'

Scobie leaned against the kitchen counter. 'Naw. Nothing planned.'

'No girl on the go?'

Scobie shook his head.

'That's hard to believe. I always thought that you'd settle at some stage. That some woman would be mad enough to take you on.'

Scobie laughed.

'What happened with the women down below?' asked Deirdre.

Scobie turned to fill the cups from the kettle, then placed them on the table and sat in front of Deirdre.

'Things changed. She started training as a teacher and … I dunno. We did try and spark it up again. Like, we went to this wedding of an old friend of hers. An excuse for a blowout. Nothing to do but relax for three days and have the craic with each other. It was brilliant. Ella really let her hair down. We took ecstasy and danced ourselves stupid and smoked grass to come down and drank all the way through the night and into the early morning, when we talked about having a baby. High as kites, and went at it, ye know, the full monty, and Scobie-Wan Kenobi's little sperms were strong swimmers. Hit the target first time out of the traps! Three weeks later, Ella reported the results of her home pregnancy test. We were expecting.' Scobie paused. He glanced across at Deirdre, amazed that he had got into this.

She smiled. 'What happened, Scobe?'

He was suddenly gripped by a deep emotion chasing up from his stomach, past any acid in his oesophagus, up into his throat, causing it to constrict. His mind shot back to the time in the hospital with Ella when she had miscarried the baby. He'd held her tight and she'd cried as much as anyone had ever cried in front of him. His mother had broken down at their father's funeral, but this was a grief rooted in something so primal that it was frightening.

Eventually Scobie was able to speak. 'She lost it. Normal miscarriage, but … ye know. Ah, we were never the same after it.'

'I'm sorry, Scobie,' said Deirdre. She moved across to him and put her hand on his shoulder. Scobie placed his hand on hers and he turned to face her. She leaned down and they hugged each other tightly, both drawing a different kind of comfort from each other.

Scobie placed his hands slowly around her waist. He could smell her hair, and for a moment he thought about making a move, just for the distraction of human touch and something other than the slow monotony of the day. She imperceptibly squeezed him that little bit tighter, and he responded by ever so gently increasing the pressure of his hold on her. He dared to move his hand down an inch or so. She took a breath. He was thinking about moving his face and kissing her. He felt her hand move down to his ass and she gave it a grope and Scobie moved his lips across to her cheek and kissed it and was about to go for her lips but then they both heard something behind them. Car doors shutting and voices and keys in the front door. Deirdre sprang away from him and grabbed her bag and Scobie didn't understand what was happening. Why were they home? The front door was opening.

Deirdre gestured at the back sliding doors of the kitchen. 'How the fuck do you open this?' she snapped at Scobie.

He moved and reefed open the doors and slid them back and Deirdre was through them and around the side of the house and Scobie pulled them shut again, just in time to face Angela and Cliff appearing, like unwanted ghosts, into the kitchen.

'All right, son?' Angela said.

Scobie replied, 'Ye gave me a fright.'

'Sorry, Scobe,' said Cliff. 'Bit of a change of plan. Put on the kettle there and we'll explain.'

Scobie turned and, for the third time that morning, filled the kettle. His head raced with Deirdre and what might have been, and just as well it didn't.

His mother picked up the cup that Deirdre had been drinking out of and shook her head. 'Jeez, at least finish one cup before ye make yourself another one,' she said, and then she came over to him and put her hand on his arm. 'Everything all right?'

Scobie nodded. 'Sound as a pound,' he said, and then he turned back to make the tea. 'Now, would ye mind tellin' me what the Jaysus ye are doing back so soon?'

ten

Angela

The hotel in Connemara had been very comfortable, with a jacuzzi and saunas, and they both had treated themselves to massages before a three-course dinner and drinks in the bar afterwards. They had climbed into their king-size double bed, a bit tipsy, and taken the clothes off each other's backs, and they had kissed and stroked each other and very slowly brought each other into a beautifully intense state of arousal. They had sex and laughed, and Angela kicked her legs up and down in the bed with sheer happiness.

'Riding at the age of 62. Ye can't bate it with a big stick.'

Cliff had laughed and kissed her mouth.

Angela had been serious then for a moment. 'You were so good that time, ye know, when I was going through the menopause. When I had no want of doing any of this.' She leaned over and kissed his chest. 'I felt so past it. Dried up. No juice. And thinking the very fucking depressing thought that this was it. For the rest of me born days.' She kissed him again. 'Thanks, Cliff. You have a great heart. I'm very lucky.'

'I'm not bad in the sack either.'

Angela slapped him playfully across the chest.

Cliff grabbed her hand and kissed it. 'No, seriously, Ange. I'm the lucky one.'

They had drifted off to a lovely slumber then, arms around each other, until one of their phones rang suddenly. The ring tone entered Angela's ear and vibrated her bones and sent the message to the brain inside in her skull that she'd better wake up, as someone was trying to contact them. But she was at perfect rest, and no amount of noise was going to wake her up. The phone went silent for a minute or so, but then vibrated and sounded its generic electronica tone once again, and this time her brain paid more attention, as someone calling twice in quick succession must really need to talk to one of them. The brain decided to act. *Wake up, Angela, the phone is ringing.* She stirred, and her eyes opened, and she realised that it was Cliff's phone, so she gave him a poke.

He lifted his head, his hand reached for the phone and pressed the loudspeaker button, so Angela could hear an older English female voice speak with a great urgency.

'Cliff, is that you? This is your cousin, Daphne.'

'Yeah, hello, Daphne. What is it?'

'It's your mam. She's had a serious heart attack. She's been rushed to the hospital. I'm sorry to phone so early.'

Angela gripped Cliff's arm. She checked the time. It was six o'clock.

'It's just she was asking for you. You know, as she was going in and out of consciousness. All she kept saying was that she wanted to see Cliff. She wanted to see her boy one more time, as she is convinced that she isn't long for this world.'

So they climbed out of the bed, paid the hotel bill, jumped into the car, and hightailed it back home, barging into the kitchen, both amazed to see Scobie up at such an early hour of a Sunday morning.

There was nothing for it only Cliff would have to get over to Ethel as soon as possible. Angela got out the laptop on the kitchen table to book a flight. Scobie went back up to bed. Cliff fried up some bacon. 'I mean, I suppose this time it's a genuine case,' he said. 'Like she really is in the hospital. I don't trust that Daphne.'

'Of course she is, Cliff. Come on. The poor woman's had a heart attack.'

'Well, remember the last time she phoned about the supposed fall down the stairs, which turned out to be a slightly twisted ankle? And there was that time she kept ringing about the reno-vations to the kitchen, as she called them.'

'That you'd have to come home to oversee them,' Angela added. 'I mean, she was only getting a new washing machine in.'

Cliff placed the bacon on two plates with two slices of toast. 'I just can't help feeling that Mam is setting a trap. That she's brought on the heart attack in some way in order to snare me back into her.'

'I'll go with ye if ye want?' said Angela.

Cliff thought about this for a moment, then shook his head. 'No, I wouldn't do it to you. This is a journey best undertaken by me on me own. I could be gone for a month, though, Ange. I mean, she's got no one else, like.'

'Well, if you're sure.' Angela didn't press it too much, as her one and only experience with Ethel at the wedding had been enough.

'I dread the thought of it, but I suppose duty calls,' said Cliff.

'Seriously though, Cliff, she might, you know, pass away, like. You'll have to prepare yourself for the possibility.'

'Nah. She'll live for spite.'

They sat and ate their breakfast, and Angela booked a flight for him, as he was hopeless with computers and all of that.

Upstairs Angela helped him pack his suitcase. She folded socks for him, suddenly feeling a tide of emotion come over her. She sat on the bed and took Cliff's hand, and when he enveloped her in a big tight hug, she laid her head on his chest.

'I just hope this lockdown thing doesn't happen. I mean what if you can't get back, or ye get the virus thing, and ...'

Cliff shushed her and kissed her forehead. 'Don't worry, Ange. It'll all be fine. You have Scobie here to mind you.'

He trailed off, and Angela stared at their wedding photograph on the dressing table. They sat for ages after that. Just there on the bed, in each other's arms, the packing abandoned, in silence. Just them, because soon it wouldn't be.

The next morning the whole household grimaced and raised their heads off their respective pillows and blinked in the five-in-the-morning reality and dressed themselves. Scobie, who was going to drive Cliff to the airport, wolfed down some Frosties, while Angela made a sandwich for Cliff to take with him.

'Ye couldn't be paying for the shite they'd give ye in the airport.'

Then Angela leaned in and gave him a long, tender kiss.

Five minutes later she found herself sitting in silence in the kitchen, in the empty house, and she yawned and wondered whether to go back to bed or just stay up. But it didn't really matter what she did, as there was no avoiding the hollow, lonely feeling she had inside. She drank some coffee and tried to think of things to look forward to. The bridge club was having a big night during the week, and she loved the craic of it and the chat. This shone some sunlight into her, until she thought of the dark clouds of the pandemic looming over everything and all the mad talk going around about what was waiting in the wings.

She tried to think of her son and how it might be good to spend time with him on her own. Maybe they'd get more time to really talk with Cliff not there. When she thought about it, all their chat consisted of jokey pleasantries or gossip. All good craic, but they had never broached the loss of the child in Oz, and she had continued to notice a gradual, almost imperceptible retreat into himself. Like there was something else occupying his head that no one was privy to, not least his mother. He kept on reminding her of Eddie, and how he could be, or at least how she picked up on it. A change in the air around him. Like Scobie was here in the house but somewhere else at the same time.

She decided to catch up with a load of laundry that needed doing. She went upstairs to gather up the stuff. She had rarely been alone between the four walls of this house, which she'd moved into as a young bride of 21. Was it weird that she'd lived here, in the same place, with two different men? Cliff had never said anything about getting their own place, but sometimes she caught sight of Eddie around the place, and it disturbed her. She'd feel his presence. She'd hear his laugh. She stood on the landing now. They had stood there that first evening in the house, she remembered. Holding each other and feeling so full. Their own place. The future lying in wait for them.

She saw Eddie's handsome, strong face, his blue eyes, and she remembered the first time she'd seen him. Outside the chippers down the town one lunchtime when she was 17 and doing the Leaving. He was from the country, and had left school at 14 to work the farm, and he was all tanned and lean from the outdoor labouring, and she got a sexual tingle in her lower body that she had never experienced before. That night she touched herself thinking about him, and was so ashamed and guilt-ridden that she got up early to go to the half-seven Mass and confession afterwards.

'Bless me, Father, for I have sinned. I had bad thoughts about this lad.' Bad thoughts my hole. Angela laughed to herself, sitting in the car. They were wonderful thoughts. Magical thoughts. The first time they'd kissed was something that she would never forget. The smell of the cigarettes on his breath, and the tang of beer and chewing gum. He was a divil for gum, a nervous workout for the jaw. They had gone to see Gina, Dale Haze and the Champions at the Copper Beech nightclub in Edenderry, a good 20-odd miles from home, but it was the biggest venue around the midlands at that time, so Eddie got a lift organised with a pal, as he had no car. They sat at a table at the back, got up to dance with everyone else near the end for the encores and then poured out of the place, from the heat and sweat into the cold of winter, and he offered his arm to keep her warm as they walked up to the town hall to get the lift back. That's where it happened. On the town hall steps, in the doorway. In the freezing cold. They kissed and kissed for 20 minutes. Glad that the pal was late picking them up.

Angela went downstairs and loaded the washing machine. She thought of the first time that Cliff had tried to kiss her. On their third date, they'd gone out for a drink into McKeon's, and she could tell that he was nervous, like he was desperate to seal the deal. He was on a mission to get some kind of snog or bust. He had the haircut and his aftershave was a little too strong, and he drank more quickly than normal. He was also very self-conscious, as Scobie and Shamie were up at the counter making faces and watching them, deliberately trying to put him off. Angela liked Cliff, but her patience was being tested that night, as he couldn't sit still and he tried to tell stupid jokes and at one point attempted to hold her hand in a way that was toe-curlingly inappropriate – that was not how the evening was going. The romance had drained from the occasion the longer it went on.

After closing they were walking along the main street when he suddenly made a lunge for her but kind of missed and kissed her nose and cheek and Angela started laughing and he got thick. For the first time, she saw a temper in him, and she liked it. A bit of the real Cliff showed himself. The polite, overpowering like-me-please demeanour suddenly went up in smoke, and Cliff stood and fumed at her. 'Well, you needn't laugh. I've not done this sort of thing in a long time and ... I ... I'm sorry if I fucked it up, but there's no need to laugh. I'll say goodnight to you.'

With that he turned and walked away in the other direction. Angela went after him and caught up with him and grabbed his arm and they looked at each other and she apologised and then he leant in and kissed her. She was surprised at her body's response to the kiss. It shot around her and lit her up, and she wanted another one.

Every year, on the anniversary of that date, they celebrated that first kiss. Cliff insisted on it. Eddie had never remembered their first kiss on the cold town hall steps. Or if he had, he'd never let on. He wasn't able to show that he cared. He was locked into something deep down inside him. Angela hoped and prayed that Scobie hadn't gone the same way. That the smiling, cheeky little boy with the craic and ability to get on with anyone hadn't turned into Eddie. He would have been such a great dad. Angela pondered this now as she switched on the washing machine. She thought of her son and dreamed of visiting him in his own house with his own family some day, a little Scobie and a little Ella bursting out the door to greet her as she walked in through the front gate. Because she still very much clung to the hope that they might get back together. She just knew, deep down, that they belonged with each other.

eleven

Scobie and Cliff travelled in silence. Too sleepy to chat. Scobie let him listen to Radio 1 news, more fears about the virus, how out of control it was getting in Italy. Now it was Cliff who didn't want the news. He turned the dial to classic hits. 'Message in a Bottle' by the Police came on. Cliff turned it up. 'I saw them back in Manchester in '79 just before this went number one,' he said.

'Sting's a bit of a bollocks now, isn't he?' said Scobie. 'With his save the rainforests and tantric sex and all that.'

'Ah, he was great in his day.' Cliff paused, and then touched Scobie's arm. 'Look after her,' he said.

'I will surely,' replied Scobie. 'Don't worry, like.'

Cliff nodded, and his eyes drifted to rain that was flecking the windscreen. Then, out of nowhere, he said, 'My mother is a sad woman.'

'Well, she can't be too sad now if she got rid of you for so long,' Scobie said, smiling.

Cliff shook his head. 'She was determined to be ... I dunno ... at odds with the world.' Cliff was quiet then. Lost in thought. Scobie concentrated on the approaching airport roundabouts.

Then Cliff spoke again, like the words just escaped from his mouth. 'It's like something happened to her way back when and she was never really able to get over it.'

'Well, anyways, I hope she gets better, Cliff. I mean that,' said Scobie. He threw his eyes across to Cliff, but his attention seemed to have passed on to the sky and an airplane circling above them, getting ready to land.

Scobie got back to the site later that morning with Cliff safely dispatched on the 07:30 Ryanair to Leeds.

'The cat's away, the mice will play,' laughed Niallers.

Bob was shook from a two-day weekend binge. 'Meself and the woman made it up on Saturday and we went on a fierce tear, boys. Like, honest to God now, but it was like throwing buns at a bear. Didn't touch the sides now. Pints and pints, she kept up like, fair fucks to her, got up on Sunday and went for the cure and went at it all day again!'

Bob had to stop to puke at lunchtime. Scobie went through the motions, doing as little work as possible, as he was bolloxed from the early start. He got home that evening to an envelope sitting on the kitchen table with his name on it.

Angela was frying a couple of chops. 'That was dropped through the letterbox for you.'

Scobie took the envelope, knowing immediately that there was cash inside in it. He went upstairs to change. He opened the envelope, which sure enough had the €500, with a short note – *Thanks again. Deirdre.* Scobie thought of the two of them the day before, how they had touched each other, that wild look in her eyes and what had it meant. Scobie lay down on the bed, closed the eyes for a minute, but the smell of the chops wafted up. He stirred himself and went downstairs.

Scobie had texted Deirdre a thank you and no bother, but received no reply, so he got on with work and living with his ma, and they developed their own routine. The days passed, and the nine o'clock news was avidly tuned into. The government announced that the Paddy's Day parade was to be cancelled, and Angela got a fright at the Lidl the next day, as toilet paper was almost sold out.

'The Jaysus virus can't be stopped by having a clean hole,' remarked Scobie.

'People are getting ready for the worst. There's all sorts of talk flying around. The army is going to be brought in to keep us locked up in our homes and all this,' said Angela.

Then Cliff phoned from Sheffield. Scobie could tell that the news wasn't great by the expression on Angela's face.

'For how long, Cliff? I mean, I hope she appreciates what you're doin'.'

Scobie left her to it, and went inside to boil the kettle. He reckoned she might be in need of a good strong cup of tea once she got off the phone, and he was right.

Angela accepted it gratefully and reached for her special old Quality Street tin, which always had a stash of biscuits and chocolate bars in it.

'So what's the story?' asked Scobie.

'Ethel is doing much better, but she's insisting on going back to her own house, so Cliff is going to have to stay on another while to look after her.'

'Ah, he won't be too long,' said Scobie, just for something to say.

Angela sighed but said little else, and not even a Fry's Chocolate Cream could lift her mood.

Scobie woke to the news the next morning that the first death had occurred in Ireland from coronavirus. A woman in the east of the country. Scobie was more worried about his supply of pills running low again. He didn't want to be getting on to Robbie to get more. No, all his texts and calls with him now were about how well he was doing at the centre, and that he had drawn a load of stuff for this national youth exhibition in Dublin. Scobie had stopped calling him every morning, as there seemed no need. He felt very pleased with himself over Robbie, but he knew that the day would soon be upon him when he would run out of tablets, and then what? His whole system shuddered at the thought of it.

At work Bob approached himself and Niallers. 'All right boys, are you on for a major session this Thursday night? We have to mark Armageddon. All restaurants, hotels and bars are shutting down. I mean, they're using body bags in Italy, lads.'

Niallers went pale. 'Christ lads, this is like a horror film or something. Like it's like 9/11 but like multiplied by a hundred.'

That Thursday evening, they piled into McKeon's after work and the place was wedged. The young staff were run off their feet and under fierce pressure. Bob roared for porter in at one young lad, a rabbit caught in the headlights, cowering behind the Guinness pump and trying to keep up with the orders.

Bob turned to the lads. 'It's like the last chance saloon. I mean, I know the offies will be open, but like it's not the same at home out of a can.'

Niallers sighed. 'Only break I get from home is comin' in here of a Friday with you boys.'

Scobie laughed, eyeing up a group of three girls, all in their twenties, sitting around a table. He had an excited whatchama-callit, giddy, a kind of devil-may-care feeling that screamed *the world is on the brink so let's just have the craic, baby*! One of the girls looked across at him and raised her drink. Scobie raised his pint, giving a wink back to her.

Bob nudged Scobie. 'Are ye going in there, sir? Not the Mae West lookswise but sure I'd say you'd get up on yourself if you could turn quick enough!'

Scobie laughed. 'Oh yeah. Gee is gee, Bob!'

Niallers made a face and shook his head in disapproval. 'Ye can't say that, Scobe.'

Scobie grinned. 'What the fuck, Niallers?'

'Like ye just can't say gee is gee anymore,' said Niallers.

Scobie said, 'Why the fuck not?'

''Cause it's offensive,' insisted Niallers.

'To whom?' asked Scobie.

'To women,' said Niallers.

Bob roared in at the young lad behind the counter, 'Sorry, but have ye gone up to James's Gate for those pints?'

Scobie said, 'It can't be offensive, as there is no women in our company, and anyway, not all women would give a shite about whether I said gee or not.'

Niallers shrugged. 'Well, some might. A niece of mine says that terms like that are derogatory, out of date, and it's up to men to call other men out.'

'Good man, Niallers,' said Bob. 'Whatever, come on, lads, and get stuck in.'

They raised their glasses and Scobie said, 'To the last pints before the end of the world.'

They gulped the stout back, Adam's apples bobbing, and the three glasses were a third gone in the first swallow.

The next few hours twisted, expanded and contracted as they always do in the pub, in a sort of weird space-time continuum during which the lads watched a conspiracy theory video on Niallers' phone claiming that the virus was created by Bill Gates to implant digital microchips into people to track and control the world's population.

'Well, that explains you, Niallers, anyhow,' said Bob. 'I knew you couldn't be for real.'

The Hog Hughes then came over to serenade them with his full-throated version of 'Nothing Compares 2 U', and he sang it with his eyes squinted shut and the veins on his big red forehead throbbing until the lads thought he was going to burst.

'Good man, Hog, Sinead is shitting herself,' laughed Scobie.

Hog clapped him on the back. 'Did I ever tell ye about the soccer match we played once above on the canal that time it froze over? Ah, it was classic. Magic days, lads.'

'Ye told us, Hog,' the lads assured him, so Hog moved on through the mêlée.

On the way back from the jacks, Scobie bumped into the girl who he'd winked at earlier on. She had curly hair, a big smile and a figure that Bob had described as 'two tonnes of fun'. The girl was flying it on the back of a load of Bacardi Breezers.

'So what's the story? You from the town?' asked Scobie.

'Yvonne Casey from Greendale Park,' said the girl.

'Scobie Donoghue, how's it going? So we may squeeze as much craic as we can out of tonight, Yvonne.'

'I'd squeeze more than craic tonight if I get half a chance,' said Yvonne, letting out the loudest foghorn of a braying laugh that Scobie had ever heard.

Scobie flinched, and then she slapped him on the arse. 'See ye later, so, for the squeeze.'

Yvonne moved on back to her table, and Scobie had to admit that her confidence was kinda sexy, even if he wouldn't fancy her in a million years. But then he was in a Gobi Desert situation, and sometimes any oasis will do.

Scobie arrived back to Bob, who was full of it. 'A lovely wee girl. A heart as big as her arse!'

'Ah boys, come on now, ye can't be saying that,' protested Niallers.

'What do ye mean, can't say it?' protested Bob. 'I mean, what the fuck is going on when I have to watch what I say in the pub?'

'It's only craic, Niallers,' said Scobie.

'Chill the fuck out there, Mother Teresa,' said Bob.

Niallers shrugged and finished his pint, then turned to go.

Scobie grabbed his arm. 'Ah, Niallers, sorry. Come on. She's a big girl, that's all.'

'People called me a stupid cunt when I was at school 'cause I was slow,' said Niallers.

'And you're still a bit slow,' said Bob.

'No, I'm dyslexic, but like, I didn't know, and I was hurt, like. I mean, words can hurt ye, like.'

Bob said, 'But I'm not saying it to her face, I'm only fuckin' using her to slag Scobie. I mean, come on.'

Niallers reached for his coat. 'I've had enough. I just want to go home. Goodnight.'

Niallers pushed his way on through the crowd towards the door. Scobie and Bob looked at each other and shrugged.

Bob drained his glass and looked at his phone. 'I have a missed call from herself. I'll just go and give her a shout back.'

Bob made his way to the back door to make the call, and Scobie was going to slag him about being under the thumb and all that, but he couldn't be bothered. Instead he ordered another two pints and watched the faces crowding into the bar. He could hear Hog in the distance singing a Kenny Rogers song inside in the bar. He spotted Keelan with a group of young people at the far end. Scobie wondered how her mother was. Whether he should try to text her again. No. Just leave it. It was none of his business. He'd done his good turn with the loan of the money.

Bob appeared back inside and grabbed his coat, saying, 'Sorry,

Scobe, but I have to skedaddle. Herself's been called into work so she needs me to mind her wee nephew she was babysitting, so. Ah, for fuck's sake, like, but what can you do?'

Scobie nodded. 'Well sure, if you're needed.'

'I am. Duty calls. Brownie points. Ye know yourself.'

Scobie grinned. 'See ye, Bob.'

'See ye, Scobe.' Bob sighed and went on.

Scobie knew well that Bob was only letting on to be pissed off and put out, but really he was delighted. Bob was needed. Scobie drained the last of his pint, feeling a hard stone in his stomach. He heard that deep braying laugh coming from the table to his right. Yvonne and her two mates were doing shots, and he felt a stirring, because he knew that it was there on a plate if he wanted it. Pure, guilt-free sex with someone you don't really fancy can be just the job. Pure animal, like. Pure mule. It would chase the bad feeling to the hills. So he sidled over to the table. Yvonne looked up at him, batted her eyelids in an exaggerated cartoonish way that sent the girls into flitters of giggles. Scobie lapped it all up, winked at the three of them and wondered might he have more than one taker.

'You're all three of ye looking very well tonight, if you don't mind me saying.'

'We don't mind at all. It's always nice to hear that, isn't it, girls?' said Yvonne, and the girls nodded, but there was a lull for a moment.

Scobie dived in to fill it. 'So it's like the end of the world tonight, girls. Which one of ye wants to go out with a big bang?!'

The girls did not react to the line the way Scobie had hoped or envisioned before he said it.

Yvonne waited for a moment, and then a weird grin appeared on her face. 'You're not being, like, ironic? No … you're actually saying that. Yeah, okay.'

Scobie was a bit taken aback. 'I'm just saying that it's the last day before the pubs go dark, so, like, let's party while we can.'

Scobie didn't see Yvonne nudging the girl beside her before turning to him. 'So you reckon we all want a big bang from you, is it?'

'Well, now, I wouldn't take it for granted but,' said Scobie. 'Come on, I mean, you could do worse.'

Yvonne shook her head and looked him squarely in the eye. 'Sorry, Scub, or Scobie, or whatever you call yourself, please leave us alone. I was just having a laugh. I wasn't serious about it.'

Scobie was confused now. 'What? Ye slapped my arse.'

Yvonne said, 'I was high as a kite. I'd just taken a pill.'

Scobie was dumbstruck.

Yvonne added, 'You're too old, man. Jesus, you must be over forty. Like, fuck off with ye. We had the bit of craic, now go on and leave us alone.'

Scobie got up slowly from the seat. He was full of shame, and wanted to shout at them that they were fat ugly bitches that the tide wouldn't take out, but he didn't say anything. He realised that they were at least 15 years younger than him. Scobie made his retreat, moving back towards the counter to order another pint. He surveyed the crowd, seeing faces of people he used to know long ago, before Australia. When he was Scobie-Wan Kenobi, and everyone loved him. But now none of them seemed that bothered with him. He would rather drink at home. He'd have to get into practice of drinking at home anyway, as that was all anyone was going to be doing for the foreseeable. So he turned and hightailed it out the front door of McKeon's.

Out on the street he thought about going for chips, but he couldn't be bothered with that either, and instead he ambled on up the street to the market square, where he and Shamie used to dodge around the stalls every Saturday morning, hoping to run into girls they fancied and try and chat them up. Scobie suddenly became aware of a car parked at the far end of the square beside one of the town's many abandoned buildings. The headlights flashed twice like they were signalling to him, or was he losing his mind. Then the driver's window rolled down and a hand waved. Scobie squinted into the darkness at the car, trying to make out the figure behind the wheel. The hand gestured again. There was no one else around, so it had to be at him. Scobie walked on towards the car, a Kia Ceed, and as he got closer the hand disappeared back inside the car and the window rolled up. Scobie was close enough now to recognise who it was. Garda Delaney leaned across to open the passenger door. Scobie walked around the car and sat inside beside Delaney, shaking hands like they were old mates who were about to go off on a weekend trip together. Delaney was dressed in his civvies, in a smart, trendy denim jacket that made him look younger or something.

'Thanks, Scobie. Sorry for this, but I've been wanting a discreet chat with you. Do you have a few minutes?'

Scobie shrugged. 'I suppose, yeah, sound.'

'Have you been looking after yourself since the last time I saw ye?'

'I have, Guard, been to the doc to get a bit of help and just, ye know, keeping the head down and getting on with work so, ye know.'

Delaney remained impassive and offered Scobie a stick of spearmint chewing gum.

Scobie took one, even though he didn't want it.

Delaney unwrapped his and popped it in his mouth, chewing methodically. 'So I heard a few stories about you, Scobie Donoghue.'

'Ah now, people do be great at telling tales,' said Scobie, trying to make light of it.

'I had a few drinks with Sergeant Freeman one night, and he sort of offloaded some stuff, about the wife at home and how she's, well, I can't divulge anything about that, but just to say she's got a problem, and then Eamon told me about you.'

Scobie felt his heart flutter.

'Like about your involvement with Mrs Freeman, and how they were able to get over it, but—'

Scobie said, 'Ah now, that's all ancient history. I mean it was a big mistake and—'

'I know, Scobie,' said Delaney.

Scobie went on. 'I mean, I was young and mad for it.'

Delaney grinned. 'Weren't we all?'

There was a silence then. They watched as Hog Hughes left McKeon's, stumbling across the road to the chipper. Delaney continued to chew his gum in the same methodical way. Scobie just wanted to spit his out. He was beginning to feel more than a little uneasy about this whole situation. What the fuck did Delaney really want to talk to him about?

'I used to be stationed above in Dublin. Summerhill.'

'Oh right, rough enough there, I'd say,' said Scobie.

'Dog rough, Scobie. Drugs. Gangs. The whole shebang, and they fucking hated us. I mean really hated us. We were the enemy who'd jailed their das and grandas, and yet there was a kind of mutual respect or … no, I won't say respect, more like an understanding. Like we got each other. We knew the world far better than any politician or ordinary middle-Ireland Joe or Josephine. We understood the nuances, ye know? The cat-and-mouse. And some of the stuff I've seen is …' Delaney paused, shaking his head. 'I mean, to actually hold a man in your arms who's bleeding to death is … Anyway, sorry.' Delaney took a breath. 'Mind you, drugs are through the roof down here. As you know from being out in that yard.'

Scobie shrugged. 'I've not been back there. That was a once-off. Never again.'

'I know. You're not the type. Anyway, the yard is a no-go area for them now. But it's a losing battle. We do our best. But more and more of our young people are being blighted by the scourge of this shit.'

'Ah, yeah, like, it's much worse than in my day,' said Scobie.

'Absolutely, Scobie. So I was wondering had you heard any whispers about where they might congregate now.'

Scobie hesitated. 'Me? No. Jaysus, I haven't. I mean, how would I know that kind of thing?'

Delaney turned to Scobie. 'How well do you know Robbie McNamee?'

'I don't really, like. I was havin' a thing with his mother and we got on really well. He was only a young lad.'

'Ah right. Okay, so you have some sort of bond with him?'

'Well, I wouldn't say bond, but like we're still able to talk. He's a vulnerable young lad, really.'

The rhythm of Delaney's gum chewing increased in intensity. 'So, I'm going to ask you to do something for him.' He stopped chewing the gum, then reached for a tissue and spat the gum into it, wound down the window and threw it out. 'Try to find out where they're going. So we can move in and shut it down. It would really help, Scobie.' Delaney tapped his hand on the steering wheel. 'Robbie might know, or one of his friends.'

There was something about Delaney that made Scobie feel safe and afraid all at the same time.

'Well now, Robbie is well out of all of that. He's back at his art and doin' real well so,' spluttered out Scobie.

'But he might have heard something,' said Delaney.

Scobie rubbed his face with his hands and laughed, to release the tension. He was feeling cooped up in the car. 'Listen, this is all a bit fucking too much for me at the minute. I have my own problems, like.'

Delaney let this go, as if Scobie hadn't said anything. 'The best way of helping that young lad is by helping us.'

Scobie looked out across the square. Hog was singing outside the chippers. A load of young people were laughing at him, but he didn't care, just kept belting out Madonna's 'Material Girl', complete with very unsteady sub-David Brent dance moves.

Delaney popped another chewing gum in his mouth. 'Because you were trespassing on private property that night out in Tynan's. I could have had you for that but I let it go, so you owe me one, Scobie. I'll be in touch.'

Delaney switched on the engine of the car and Scobie reached for the door handle to get the fuck out. He was shaken by the whole encounter. The car drove off down the town. Scobie walked on through the square, past the chippers and the gang outside and Hog, who'd quietened down and was now stuffing his face. Scobie felt in bad need of another drink. He didn't trust Delaney. He wanted to tell him to fuck right off, but he had to admit that he was knocked off his stride by him. There was something in his eyes. The way he spoke. So carefully. Like he was in control. Calling the shots. Scobie felt jumpy now, and nowhere near able to face the bed. He needed a drink, a good pint of Guinness and a whiskey. He'd head to Taylor's bar. He'd try and gather his head there. Maybe Delaney was right. Maybe he could try and find out the new druggie hideout. Maybe this was a new mission for the Scobemeister General. Back from Oz to deliver salvation to the town!

twelve

cobie stood at the counter waiting for a pint from Ollie Taylor. He eyed the clock behind the bar, which was always set to a later time. It said it was nearly twenty past eleven, which meant it was only actually ten past or around about, and he reckoned they'd serve until twelve. The place was fairly packed, and the decibels were rising as the last pints before the lockdown were sunk. Scobie thought about calling Robbie, but he didn't want to be badgering him with questions and seeming like some kind of Garda tout. No, he'd leave him. There was a trust there now that he didn't want to fuck up, and anyway, he had suddenly just thought of the obvious candidate who might know the answer to his question.

'Is the Mole about?' he asked Ollie.

'He is, of course. Outside smoking,' grunted Ollie, who was throwing out drink to beat the band but nevertheless in foul humour. 'Fucking ridiculous, closing us down. Fucking ruin us, they will. It's all a cod.'

Scobie nodded and paid for his pint then took a good swallow. He thought of the Freeman house and wondered what kind of 'problem' Deirdre had. He had always wondered how that marriage had lasted all the years. Scobie picked up his pint, drank from it and waited for Mole to hobble across the floor and take his customary stool at the edge of the counter beside him.

'Scobie, how's the form?' he said as he climbed up onto the stool and caught his breath.

'Not a bother, Molesers,' said Scobie.

'Not a bother, I wouldn't say that. Fuckin' disgraceful. I mean it's only a flu and they're shutting the boozer. Ah, it's not right.'

'Where will ye go now, Molesers?' said Scobie.

'Ah, I dunno. Stay at home with the cat. Sheba. That'll be the height of it.'

'Surely ye'll go somewhere, like the yard or some place.'

'No way José. That bollocks of a guard clamped down on it.'

'So is there a new spot?' asked Scobie.

Mole shook his head. 'If they have some new place else to go, they ain't tellin' Mole about it anyhow.'

Scobie took this in and swallowed his pint. He signalled for two more off of Ollie. He reckoned the Mole wasn't too far away from being locked, and then he'd reveal all.

Mole's demeanour brightened up a little. 'Thanking you,' he said.

Scobie left the Mole and went for the jacks. Inside in the toilet he faced the wall and started to piss. A body slipped in beside him, clapping him on the back. Hippo Hynes, who Scobie hadn't seen in years. He had less hair, more weight around the face but the high-pitched voice hadn't changed.

'Scobie, ye legend ye, it was only a matter of time before they got sense and threw ye out of Oz.'

'That's right, Hippo,' said Scobie.

'I'd say ye had some time down there,' laughed Hippo. 'The right *buachaill* for it.'

'Oh, you better believe it, Hippo,' said Scobie as he continued to empty out.

Hippo said, 'I was mad to give it a go, not long after you left, applied and everything, but Liz just didn't want to leave the old mammy, ye know.' Hippo leant his head against the wall and went silent. Like the life he could have had in Oz was flashing before his eyes.

Scobie shook the lad and zipped up. 'See ye, Hippo, and listen, Oz isn't all it's cracked up to be either.'

Hippo nodded. 'Maybe not, but I would have liked to have seen it for meself.'

Scobie squeezed through the drinkers back to Mole, who was halfway down the new pint already. Scobie grabbed up his and did a good job in catching up with him.

Scobie leaned into Mole. 'How's the Skunk?'

He hadn't thought to ask him before about his wingman. The Skunk Kelly. The two of them had been joined at the hip since they were kids.

'I don't know, to be honest. We had a falling out. He had a bit of a health thing that scared the shite out of him and a sister of his moved back to the town and got him, ye know … he got sense or something, and he doesn't be drinking or drugging anymore, so.' The blood had left Mole's face. His eyes were completely dilated. Twisted. He gave his head a little shake and said again, 'I don't know.' Mole slumped back into himself. He had disconnected. He had gone to his other place.

'Come on, Mole, I know you know. Where do they go now? Where's the new hang-out?'

Mole blinked and grinned. He indicated towards the optics behind the counter. 'It'll cost ye another pint and a brandy.'

'No bother.'

Mole leaned across to Scobie, making sure no one was in easy earshot. 'They do be in a house above in St Colman's Road.'

'That's where I live, Mole,' said Scobie.

'Oh, right. Well, that's where they do be. Number 27 Colman's Road. Now, what about me drink?'

Scobie ordered the pint and brandy off Ollie. He was flabbergasted. Number 27, what the fuck like, the old Jackson family home, where Deirdre and the sister Jennifer grew up. He had noticed the FOR SALE sign out front of it ever since he got back from Oz. The house he had spent many a teenage year in, dancing around to 'Where's Me Jumper' with Jennifer, laughing with their ma, Molly, who was always the best of craic until she got Alzheimer's, and she only in her sixties. Fierce sad. Scobie's head flashed with images of the inside of that house. The living room where he gave Deirdre an ecstasy tablet, which she took into her gob, gyrating around the room like a woman who had just been cut loose from 10 years of duty and baby-minding. He thought of the kitchen, where Jennifer told him she was leaving for London that first time, and his heart broke just a little.

Scobie paid Ollie for the drink and slipped off his stool. 'See ye, Mole.'

Scobie bid his retreat back out to the bar, where he was stopped by Dano Doyle, who used to drive the trucks with Eddie.

'Young Donoghue, I was only talking about your father there a while ago.' Scobie knew he couldn't get stuck here or it would be all 'Did I ever tell ye about the time me and your father ...' Long yarns about the old days that Dano had no problem dragging out with no discernible point to them.

Scobie gave him the big nod and a 'Howareye, Dano, sorry, have to run, see ye again.'

Scobie, not waiting for a response, vamoosed out the front door, twitching with a nervous excitement at the thought of completing his mission. He was going to check the place out, make sure Robbie wasn't in there. He was doing all of this for the good of the town. But in the back of his head, a new beat was beginning to gain a rhythm. This new rhythm was spelling out words and putting them in order. He might be able to score some more pills down in the house of fun. He might be able to score some pills down at the house of fun. He might be able to score some ... He shook himself and tried to shake the words from his *ceann* as the pace of his walk quickened, past the Centra and Tommy's tattoo parlour and on by Sweet Dreams café, run by two lovely Polish women, and he kept on bombing it along and arrived up into his road in record time.

He went on past his own house and saw the light was off in the upstairs window. Angela was asleep. He crossed the road like he had done so many thousands of times in his life, all through school and beyond, over to hang out in Number 27 with Jen, who was on her own with the ma, as the da died when they were young and Deirdre, the older sister by nearly a decade, had moved out to marry the local guard.

Scobie approached the darkened house, which needed a good coat of paint, glancing into the coal shed to the side of the house, where he and Jen would hide sometimes to smoke fags. Angela had told him that the house had been put up for sale by a hedge fund who had taken over the distressed mortgage of the family who bought it off the Jacksons when Molly died. It had been empty this past six months or so.

Standing outside the back door, he could hear music on inside at a low enough volume, gentle techno to chill out to. He wasn't thinking now, just following his animal curiosity, and usually when he did that, when he ignored common sense, he ended up in the absolute shite, but sure when had that ever stopped him before? He put his hand to the door and gave it a gentle shove. Open sesame. Inside the darkened kitchen, lit only by two candles, he could make out five figures in a cloud of smoke, sitting around a table strewn with cans and bottles and all manner of drug parapher- nalia. They all seemed to be lads, and thankfully none of them were Robbie, and they barely registered his presence. He glanced around the place, and despite the gloom he could make out that it had been spruced up and modernised since he'd last stood in it, but would need a major deep clean if they ever wanted to sell it.

Scobie stopped at the table and addressed one of the lads. 'Hi, sorry to bother ye. I'm a mate of Robbie's. He's not around, is he?'

The lad looked up and took him in. It was one of the fellas who had been with Robbie up in Dinny's Hole. He shook his head.

Scobie was very pleased to hear this, but he needed to get on with business. 'Anyone sellin' anything? Just looking for some Xanax or anything like that.'

The lad pointed over at a slightly older-looking boy with a full goatee rather than bum fluff on his face, sitting in an armchair and rolling a spliff.

Scobie went across to him. 'Howsitgoin', I'm a mate of Robbie's, just wondering if I could score some Xanax or something like that, something stronger if you had it?'

The lad looked up with a big grin. 'You want to score?' He laughed to himself. 'Okay, I can get you that. I'll text ye, but it's a hundred now for two packets of twenty-four pills.'

Scobie was going to argue over the price increase, but he couldn't be bothered. A lightness and relief coursed through his brains. He handed over the money to the lad. 'So you'll text me tomorrow and I get it then?' he asked.

The lad nodded and pocketed the cash. He took out his phone and Scobie gave him his number. The lad took the details and continued with the joint.

Scobie moved on into the living room. Three people were sitting on a couch with a one-bar heater on in front of them. He couldn't make out who they were, as the only illumination was the bit of streetlight that escaped through the drawn curtains. One of the shapes on the couch stirred, then stood up and extended a hand towards Scobie.

He saw a lit joint in the hand, and then heard a female voice he recognised, saying, 'Scobie Donoghue. Good man yourself, want a smoke?' Keelan stood before him, grinning and pretty stoned.

Scobie couldn't help being a bit shocked to see her here. His head swam, thinking, should he ring Deirdre this minute? But instead, he took the joint from her and let a couple of quick tokes into his lungs.

'How long have ye been coming here?' asked Scobie.

'Not sure. A couple of weeks. Some of them were on a sesh,' said Keelan. 'One of the lads was able to pick the lock of the back door.'

'I didn't hear anything and I only across the street,' said Scobie.

'Ah, they do be very quiet. Just a chill sesh, ye know.'

'Oh, I know,' said Scobie.

'Oh, I know you know, Scobie Donoghue,' giggled Keelan. 'Are you goin' to sit down?'

Keelan moved back to the sofa and shoved up to make space for Scobie. One of the bodies got up and left the room. Scobie sat down beside her.

'Do you know Robbie?' he asked.

'Yeah, a small bit. Not really my crowd, ye know. Just drop in for a quick smoke on me way home.'

'Was he here tonight?' asked Scobie.

'Not since I've been here. He's not been around for a week or so. Maybe he's gotten sense.'

'Maybe he has,' said Scobie, then, 'Jaysus, Keelan, you shouldn't be ... if your ma knew that you were ...'

Keelan burst out laughing, took a last pull of the joint and put it out in a small plastic ashtray on the floor. 'I'm only visitin' me granny's house. I remember it so well as a kid. Molly playing her records with her lovely big laugh before, ye know, she got the Alzheimer's.'

'She was a great lady,' said Scobie.

Keelan closed her eyes and lay back on the sofa. Scobie glanced back in the direction of the kitchen. They were doing more than smoking weed in there.

'I hope you're not ... doing anything else.'

'Fuck no. I stay in the front room. The kitchen is where the fucked-up shit does be happenin'.'

Scobie was again seized with a compulsion to drag her from the house and bring her home to Deirdre. He felt completely out of his depth. He tried to gather his thoughts. His head swam a bit with the weed. He suddenly felt completely knackered. After a while Keelan's voice cut the silence.

'I heard something about you the other day.'

'All good I hope,' said Scobie.

Keelan smiled and arched her eyebrows. 'Well, it was interesting, anyway. Left me fierce nosey.'

'What about?' asked Scobie.

'About all sorts,' Keelan said, turning to look at him. 'You and Mam had some sort of mad fling, as far as I can work out.'

Scobie shook his head and held up his hands. 'I don't kiss and tell.'

Keelan made a face as if she was gagging. 'Oh that's so gross. I can't imagine her, like, doin' it or anything. Anyway, it's shit at home at the moment. Real shit. Something's happened. My ma's done something stupid, but I dunno what it is. Dad does what he always does, which is to say nothing and then suddenly fly off the fuckin' handle and shout and roar and … I'm thinking of asking Auntie Jen can I visit her in England for a while. Get the fuck away.'

'Deirdre won't like that,' said Scobie.

Keelan shook her head. 'Well, I spent a long time tryin' to do what I thought they wanted me to do. Have a nice reliable fella who played football and knuckle down to the study and do well in school. I got a great Junior Cert. I mean, there was great things expected, so that no matter how fucking miserable Mam and Dad really were with each other, the good girl Keelan was doing them proud. One day I woke up, Scobie, and I just didn't want to be that girl anymore. Because it wasn't fair. I was doin' everything for them, so I thought fuck that.' Keelan stirred herself and sat forward on the couch. Her face changed colour then, ashy, and her cool 'fuck it, laid-back' demeanour crumbled. She curled up in a ball on the couch like a small child. Tears filled her eyes. She started to cry, like she might never stop.

'You're all right.' Scobie had no idea how to react. It came out of nowhere.

Keelan wiped the tears away, blinked her eyes, looked up at him and said, 'Ah Scobie, it's all such a mess. I don't know what to do.'

'Go home and talk to your mother,' urged Scobie.

'I can't.' Keelan straightened herself up, grabbed her bag and coat and stood to leave. 'I just can't.'

Keelan disappeared from the room. Scobie sat perfectly still for a moment. Then he made his own way through the kitchen. There were only two people left. One of them was about to snort something off tinfoil. Scobie couldn't look. He got out the back door as soon as he could, crossed the road back to his own place, climbed the stairs, hearing his mother's gentle breathing inside in her room, then slumped onto his bed and conked out.

thirteen

Keelan

Keelan lay awake feeling groggy and tired from the night before, listening to the rest of the house. Her brothers would be at GAA training, but she could detect murmured voices downstairs. Eamon and Deirdre were home and talking, which was a very rare event. It was around lunchtime now, so she was beginning to get hungry, but she couldn't quite face the two of them for the moment. Her father seemed to be staying away from the family home more and more this past while, and Deirdre had been completely in her own world, like she was walking around in a trance. Deep down, Keelan knew that the marriage was too far gone to ever get back on any meaningful track. They'd tried counsellors and all that, and part of her wanted them to split up finally, to do whatever might make them happy, and another part of her, a small little-girl part, just felt like crying at the thought of that. It made her feel lonely and abandoned out in the dark woods, and especially now. Fuck, fuck, fuck, she needed them now!

She roused herself into a sitting position and managed to make it over to her dressing table, which was piled up with make-up, moisturisers, perfumes and cotton wool and all sorts of crap, and she made a promise to herself to clean it up. In fact, she would try and do a job on the whole room. She stared at the reflection of herself in the mirror, surrounded by lights just like in a Hollywood star's dressing room.

She looked at the photos stuck on the frame around it. Herself and her best friend Nicola at her eighteenth. All smiles, eyebrows, orange tan and Fat Frogs, thinking about getting off with Jason McCarthy before the night was over. The photo beside it, of herself and her brothers with big, excited heads on them at Dublin Zoo looking at the seals being fed. She must have been nine or ten, face all red and squinty from the brightness of the sun, but God love that little girl, she hadn't a care in the world.

Keelan thought about getting back into the bed, but she doubted very much that she'd ever be able to sleep. She'd check outside again. It had been at least a good hour since last she'd dared sneak a peek through the curtains. She stood to the side, carefully putting her fingers around the drapes and pulling them back ever so slightly. She was able to see across the road and, much to her relief, his car was gone. He had given up. She checked her phone. The last call he'd made had been an hour ago. The last one of 12 since last night. He hadn't left any message. He had texted almost 15 times, and they all read simply, *Call me. Please.*

She sat and combed her hair, which she'd always found so soothing. Liking it even more when her mother did it, although that hadn't happened in a while. Her thoughts were hijacked now by those first few sightings of him, when her father brought him home that first time to introduce him around. He was new in town, so Eamon had made an effort, inviting him to the house for dinner. She had turned up late to the table that evening, a bit jarred, and Eamon knew she was, but said nothing, which only added to the fierce tension, and Keelan remembered feeling so grateful that Peter was there, because that kept everyone civil. He seemed a real shy sort of fella, and he stayed on drinking tea, and for once Keelan hadn't left the table with Oisín and Paudge, as it was such a relief to have someone else there other than the ma and da at odds with each other. He told them very matter-of-factly about his failed marriage, how the wife had lost a child.

The next time he came around was a Saturday night. He insisted on ordering pizza, so Deirdre wouldn't have to cook. Oisín and Paudge were delighted, because he bought a meat-feast special, with as many wedges, chicken wings, takeaway shite and Cokes as you could manage. Keelan was supposed to be going out afterwards, but she was late to meet Nicola and the girls, so Peter offered her a lift to McKeon's. It was pissing rain, so she was glad to take him up on the offer.

She would always remember the short journey in the car. He asked questions that didn't seem like small talk. It was like he was really interested. Stuff about what she wanted to do with herself and all that. When they pulled up into the square, they kept chatting even though she was going to be dead late. Keelan convinced herself that it was on account of the rain, waiting for it to clear, but really it was him. She wanted to stay with him. He was so easy to talk to.

The next time he came over to the house was a Tuesday or Wednesday, but they didn't even get to sit down for any food. Deirdre was really stressed and wound up, and there was no dinner made so Eamon was embarrassed, and when Keelan tried to cook burgers but burned them he snapped at her and she got upset. The two brothers disappeared into their alternative dimension of video games to kill as much stuff as they could. Eamon tried to apologise to her, but she just wanted to be left alone, and Peter put on his coat to leave. He stalled in the hallway, asked Keelan if she wanted to get out of the house for a while. She said okay.

They went for a drive and he suggested they go for a drink in a nearby village, into a pub she'd never set foot in before. He had a Coke. She just had a glass of Orchard Thieves. It was great to be free of the rest of them. He told her about his job, where he'd been posted before in north Dublin, the things he'd seen, and she didn't think he was showing off or anything.

'Jesus, I haven't lived really,' said Keelan. 'I still haven't managed to decide what I really want to do with myself.'

'You have time, Keelan. Don't sweat it. You'll find it. I was adrift meself for years,' said Peter. 'Hadn't a clue what I was at. I did things to please other people. Ye know, you have to find what's right for you.'

He had dropped her home, and all night she lay in the bed and thought of him and his kind, concerned manner, and the generosity of taking the time out to talk to her.

Bringing herself back into the present moment, Keelan put the comb down and pulled on a jumper and sweatpants, then listened out for any noises down below. All seemed quiet. She hadn't heard the front door or a car departing, though, so she thought they must be still down there. Brooding in separate rooms, probably.

She thought of the night he drove them out to Twomey's pub in Broadford and she drank a few more than she usually had with him. She'd had a terrible fight at home on account of her wanting to leave college, so she was mad for a proper session.

He had suggested they go back to his place, which was one of the apartments down Father Maguire Road, and when they were settled on the sofa drinking wine she had stared into his great brown eyes that kinda looked right into her, and she remembered asking him his age and he told her he was 39, and she had laughed and said he was too old. And he had said, real innocent, 'For what?' and she had launched straight in, kissed him on the mouth, and they kissed again, properly, and then he drew back and said that he couldn't. Had insisted on driving her home.

He had stayed away from the house for a while after that. She didn't see him until one night there was a big fight outside Club 52, so the squad was called. Himself and another guard broke up the fight, and he insisted on driving her home. She had been mortified in front of her friends because he ordered her into the car, but then he didn't drive her home but back to his place. He said he was mad about her, and they slept together for the first time, and Keelan finally discovered what all the fuss was about. She had had her first proper satisfying sexual experience, and it was just intoxicating, not to mention the extra excitement of meeting up in secret, sneaking back to his place.

Quite soon after this, he had arranged a special night in a hotel in Dublin, which was all sex in the afternoon and lazy evening pints in McDaid's, but then the next day getting ready to go out he had made a remark about her appearance, saying she was showing off too much, and Keelan told him to fuck off and chill out, but for the whole evening he was off with her and they ended up sleeping with their backs to each other. Then for a week after he didn't contact her and Keelan really missed him, like life was so much emptier without him, so she gave in to it. She started to dress a bit differently, only wearing things that he liked, and gradually this seeped into other areas until one morning she woke up and realised that she was doing everything to please him, and the worst thing was that she didn't care. She wanted to be doing it. She loved him, or at least she thought she did.

Keelan heard a pair of footsteps on the stairs. On the landing. A knock on her door. She said nothing. Another knock, a little louder.

'Keelan, love, are you awake?' It was her mother's voice.

Keelan realised she couldn't hide forever. 'Yeah.'

'Can I come in, love?'

'Yeah,' said Keelan, who stood now and began to fix her duvet.

Deirdre entered the room. 'Leave that, love. Myself and your father need to talk to you.'

Keelan took this in as she continued to fix the duvet. They were breaking up. She was sure of it. She'd been waiting for this.

'What about?' she asked.

'Please just come downstairs before the boys come home,' said Deirdre.

Keelan let go of the duvet and followed Deirdre out of the bedroom and on down the stairs.

Eamon was waiting for them in the lounge, sitting on the sofa in front of the TV with a cup of coffee. He looked very composed, like a man who had done diplomatic talks with the Middle East and was now out the other side, hoping for a brighter, more peaceful future.

'Hiya, love,' he said.

Keelan nodded and took a seat in the comfy chair opposite, the one Oisín and Paudge always fought over. Deirdre sat in beside Eamon so it looked like some sort of weird, relaxed job interview.

The parents glanced at each other. Eamon cleared his throat. Deirdre patted his hand. She'd get the ball rolling.

'Listen, Keelan, I need to tell ye something. I've been gambling. Ye know, like losing heavy money.'

There was a pause. This was not what Keelan was expecting. She shook her head. 'What do you mean?'

Deirdre went on. 'Like, I really kinda lost the run of myself. I've dug into credit cards and bank accounts, I even asked Scobie Donoghue for money, I was that desperate. I mean, I feel so awful about the whole thing.'

Keelan tried to gather her thoughts. 'I don't understand. Why the fuck would you be gambling?'

'It's hard to explain. It was like, if I won that everything would be okay. Do ye get me? It was never about winning money. I know that now. I was just so down and ...' Deirdre felt herself getting upset.

Eamon leaned forward to take over. 'Your mother has signed into a Gamblers Anonymous programme, and she'll have a considerable amount of money to pay back, but look, the main thing is she's stopped.'

'Just wanted to tell you before the boys,' said Deirdre.

Keelan nodded. She looked to the two of them. Their faces were not at rest. It was like they had only got through round one, and there was more to follow.

Eamon took up the baton. 'We also wanted to let you know that your mother and I have decided to separate.'

Deirdre followed up. 'It can't come as much of a surprise to you. We think it's by far the best thing to do. The lads are old enough now, and hopefully it won't hit them too hard.'

Keelan again nodded impassively. 'Wow. A double whammy.'

Her cold, rational mind knew that they were right, it wasn't much of a surprise to her. It would probably be a relief all around the house. Including the boys. Not to have to pretend anymore. The tension would now be released. All of this made sense, but the little girl who lived down deep inside Keelan felt like she had just been struck in the heart and was beginning to bleed. Abandoned and lost in the dark woods, carrying a terrible burden of her own.

Keelan formed words in her mouth and let them out. 'Okay. Well, I'm obviously really sad to hear this but ...' She trailed off. Her eyes filled with tears. She could no longer be in the room. Deirdre got up to move towards her, but she wasn't able for that either. It had been too long since mother and daughter had embraced or felt close, and all she wanted was to be out of the room and away from them, up the stairs. They were calling her name but she didn't stop until the door was shut and locked behind her. Face into pillow.

She thought of her childhood, treasured memories. A holiday in Bettystown, the seagulls in the sky and hunting for crabs in the shallow rock pools with other children and making a short, intense little friendship with a girl from Gorey, who told her that her mammy couldn't have babies so she was adopted. There was the treat of a knickerbocker glory in the Neptune hotel – 'Don't eat it too quickly or you'll be sick,' Mam had said as she'd gulped down the dessert, and then afterwards they lifted her up, a parent holding each arm and bouncing her in the air, the sea in front of them, and Keelan cried now thinking of this. She reached for a hanky to blow snot from her nose, and wished for a joint to smoke to make it all go away.

fourteen

Scobie stood with Bob and Niallers finishing off a cup of tea, and they glanced over at Nigel, the new foreman, who was giving one of the lads a pain in his hole about how the lunch break was now over, and for them all to get back to work. Cliff's replacement was from Dublin, and, as Bob remarked, 'He's a bit of a smart-arse bollocks.'

Nigel had greeted Scobie that morning by saying, 'Ah, would ye look at himself. Like the back of my bag. State of him.'

In fairness, Scobie had been very tired and hungover from the night before. Hangovers were definitely getting harder since he'd turned 40. In his twenties, sure, he'd thrive on them. Up out of the bed, into the shower, down for the fry, out the door to the site, still a bit half giddy with the drink rolling around in his system but not a bother on him. But now it was a different story, and especially today, as he was jumpy as fuck and hadn't heard anything from the lad about the pills he'd been promised.

That morning it had been particularly difficult to lift his body out of the bed. All he could think of was Keelan's tears from the night before. He forced himself out to the bathroom and splashed water onto his face, belched, grimaced and managed to get downstairs to fill a bowl with Coco Pops. He was sitting at the table to eat them when Angela appeared down into the kitchen and turned on Tubridy on the radio.

'Ye must have been late, I didn't hear ye comin' in. Was there many down the town?'

'Fairly packed all right,' said Scobie.

'Do ye want an egg?' asked Angela.

'No thanks, Ma, a bit of toast will do.'

Ryan was welcoming teachers and lecturers to listen to his show, as the schools had closed the day before. He told his listeners that he went into a Centra shop and the lads there asked him to tell people to stop panicking. The trucks were still rolling, delivering supplies, so there was no danger of any shortages. Ryan then went on to remind people of the date, Friday the 13th, but that seemed immaterial now. The misfortune was already happening. Cabin fever may become a serious issue as more people are asked to stay at home. Angela boiled the kettle and listened avidly. She liked Tubridy. Scobie could take him or leave him, but today he had been grateful for Tubridy's ability to distract his mother and allow him to eat his breakfast in peace.

Nigel approached Scobie, Bob and Niallers with a half-smile. 'Yis are an *off-aly* lazy bunch of fuckers, come on now and no slackin'.'

'Hey, Nigel, come here and tell us, what's the story, like? Are we closing as well as everything else?' asked Bob.

'Yeah, Nigel, have ye heard anything?' Niallers pitched in.

Nigel stopped to put his foot up on a piece of wall. He rested his elbows on his knee, enjoying the fact that he had news they needed.

'Well, I'll tell yis. The rumours are that we'll be shut down at the end of the month. That's two weeks, lads. That's what I heard now, off a very reliable source.'

'They'll have to pay us,' said Niallers.

'They will surely,' said Bob.

'Well, that will be up to the government to do dat, sozin' anyways now yis know, so – chop chop!' Nigel clapped his hands together.

Niallers and Bob dispersed to their work. Scobie picked up his tools and followed on with them.

Bob grinned from ear to ear. 'God bless the Chinese lads for that virus – no work and some pay? I'd call that a result.'

Scobie went upstairs into one of the houses, looking forward to losing himself in the plastering of a wall. His mind raced. Where the fuck was that lad with his pills? The rhythms and actions of the work soothed him for a short while, but then the familiar compulsion to crawl the walls began to take over. A nightmare from last night slipped into his brain again. A long, dank corridor, then into some abattoir, where there's a long line of carcasses hanging upside down. Dead kangaroos, eyes missing, blood dripping onto the floor. He tries to run through them but they seem to go on forever, and somewhere in the maelstrom of panic, still in the bad dream, he told himself that this is just a dream, but another voice echoed around the abattoir that no it wasn't, and that really scared the bejaysus out of him, and he woke seriously relieved that he was landed back into his single bed, staring across at Shamie's empty bed, and above it posters of Jeanette, the perfect girl, and the large red Corvette.

Scobie slapped glue up onto the wall and was wondering just how he'd get through another night without any chemical assistance when his phone pinged. He grabbed it up. It was a text from the young lad, *Meet me up under the trees in Dinny's Hole in 15*. Scobie dropped the brush and was gone down the stairs, but before he emerged outside, he took a good gander to see where Nigel might be, and saw him walking into the site office across the way. Scobie had to make a move. He bolted for the last house in the row under construction and was able to walk through, skip over a half-built wall at the rear, jump to the ground and sneak back along until he reached where the cars were parked. He slipped into the car and turned on the engine, not daring to look up, then backed out of the parking space and drove off the site, turning left up the town, past the schools and parking up beside the field. He stayed in the car for a moment. There was no sign of anyone under the trees as yet.

Scobie felt an apprehension, like he was doing something wrong. He'd only ever spent one night in a Garda cell, and that was enough. He'd been arrested for trespassing into one of the show houses when he was supposed to be doing security back in 2009. He used to bring a crowd after the pub to the half-built estate and they'd have a party in the house. Mad craic, and cheaper than a nightclub when the crash hit and everyone was broke. Scobie remembered staring at the graffitied walls of the cell all that night and thinking about how locking up men is kind of mad. Counterproductive. Doesn't ever solve the problem, just creates more misery and frustration with the world at large. He had had a sore back the next day from the hard bed, along with a terrible hangover, and he swore he'd never set foot in a cell again.

He looked across and saw the lad with the hoodie loping along. Scobie hopped out of the car and approached him under the giant yew tree. The young lad handed over a paper bag with two packets of pills inside.

'Just to give you the heads-up. They're not Xanax. But they work far better. Trust me.'

'Okay. Sound,' said Scobie, and he turned and bolted back to the car. He sat for a moment and took one of the packets out to read the label. Klonopin. He'd never heard of it, but he didn't care. He tore the packet open and swallowed down two pills with a slurp from a bottle of Coke. Then his phone pinged. A message from Delaney, *Meet you out at Tynan's in 20 minutes.*

'Fuck me,' muttered Scobie under his breath. He let out a big sigh.

He closed his eyes to get himself together. Then, ever so slightly, he began to feel the effects of the Klonopin. Inside he felt a gradual softening of his tight belly, as well as a calm and ease with himself and the world slowly begin to take hold. Scobie was then full of a 'fuck it, yes', a slight elation and tummy-tickling wave of 'everything is absolutely fine', and he was grateful to that young lad from the bottom of his heart, because with these little mothers on board he could cope with anything! Even a meeting with Delaney.

Scobie would now be dead late back to work, but what could he do? He reached the outside of the rusted iron gates of Tynan's yard and parked up the car. He imagined the gates opening, his da's truck appearing, and seeing himself as a 10-year-old boy up in the cab with Eddie behind the wheel, Major cigarette in the gob until the ash burned down to his lips. There was the sound of a car approaching, and he looked in the rear-view. It was Delaney in his civilian jalopy, the Kia Ceed, pulling in behind him. The engine cut out but the radio stayed on. Scobie didn't hesitate. Time to get it over with. He got out of the car and sat into Delaney's passenger seat.

'Hello, Scobie,' said Delaney, offering him a stick of chewing gum.

'How are ye, Guard,' said Scobie, declining the gum. 'Thanks, you're grand.'

'Just call me Peter.'

'Oh, right, sound as a pound, Peter.'

Delaney smiled and turned off the radio.

Scobie shifted in his seat, keen to say his piece. 'Listen, I did find out where they do be all hanging out.'

Delaney broke into a big smile. 'Good man. I knew ye would.'

'It's the house up opposite me own in St Colman's Road. Number 27. Mad, like. It's been lying empty for six months and that's where they go. Now I want to tell ye that Robbie was not there. You know he's a good kid. He's back on the straight and narrow as far as I can see, so I just want to make that known to ye.'

Scobie was feeling a great kind of high off the pills, and he was aware that he might be speaking too quickly. He tried to remain still. Delaney looked across at him, his mouth tight.

'Any of them could be at it, I'm afraid, Scobie. You have a sentimental attachment to the lad but you can't trust him.'

Scobie opened his mouth to respond. 'Yeah, but I know he's got loads of talent, and given the right encouragement he could get off the fuckin' path of … shite, ye know.'

Delaney didn't respond immediately. He sat with a funny-looking smile on his face. 'I asked a colleague one time what's the biggest problem about being a guard, and he replied "Other guards". Like some of us are more naturally suited to the job than others.'

'It must be full on, right enough,' said Scobie.

'It can be, or just mind-numbing paperwork and stamping passports, but I'm dedicated to it. I want you to know that, Scobie,' said Delaney.

'Sound. Yeah.' Scobie nodded.

'Do you have kids?' asked Delaney.

Scobie shook his head and smiled. 'No, not that I know of anyway.'

Delaney's voice took on a quiet intensity, like he really wanted Scobie to hear him. 'I have a daughter,' he said. 'A four-year-old, but I never see her. The mother and I were a three-night stand, you know the sort of thing. When the child was born, she gave me an ultimatum. She wanted me to live with her and the baby, be a family together, or else I'd never see the child again. I just couldn't do it. I didn't have any feelings for her. She was adamant, and so she took the baby back to Kilkenny to her mother. I've never seen the child since the day she was born in the Rotunda Hospital.'

Scobie shook his head in sympathy. 'That's a shame, but like, if ye don't mind me askin' ye, why the fuck are you telling me all this?'

Delaney turned and looked at Scobie in a way that demanded eye contact. 'I know what it means to have your own flesh and blood in the world. I've known that feeling of losing them. I've met parents who've lost kids to drugs, and I think we have a duty to try and help.'

Delaney let this sit. He stared straight out in front of him.

Scobie shifted in his seat. He watched Delaney's jaws working on the gum. He felt like he was going to explode. He had to say something. He needed to promise something.

'Of course, I'll keep at him, ye know, see does he drop the act or … tell me anything useful.' Scobie had no idea where these words came from, but he desperately hoped that they would do the trick and satisfy the man.

'Okay. Go on. We'll talk soon.' Delaney put his hand on his keys and started the engine. Scobie jumped out of the car and with some relief landed back to his own. He felt like he had betrayed Robbie in some way, but he had to say something.

As Scobie drove back towards town, thoughts of his own child flooded into his head. He wondered what they'd look like now if they'd gone full term and been born and lived. They'd be a mad little two-year-old, a mini Scobie-Wan Kenobi or little Ella belle. Who knows? He thought of the day about four months after they'd lost it, when he decided to cook a special meal to try and get them back into the romantic swing of things, and maybe they could try again, because he knew Ella really wanted a child. She had thrown herself into work, into weekend yoga retreats, into friends he didn't really know. So he had cooked a few steaks and waited for her to come home from work. But she didn't arrive for ages. And when she did, she was tipsy and grouchy. Nothing he could do was right. Scobie allowed her to throw the shite at him. He knew she needed to get angry with someone.

'Listen, Scobie, the two of us have been a big mistake, and I just can't live the life I now want with you. It's impossible. I wish you'd just pack up and fuck off back to Ireland!'

Scobie was hurt. He lashed back at her. 'Why can't ye just make more of an effort to get over it? We can try for another one. For fuck's sake, like!'

Ella went quiet. She looked up slowly. 'I don't think you ever really wanted a baby.'

Scobie averted his eyes away from her. 'I swear to Jaysus and my late father that I want nothing more than to have a child with you.'

Ella burst into a bitter laughter. 'You'll say anything so as you don't have to deal with me or my pain. Real fuckin' shit scares the living daylights out of you. Anything to avoid strife. Fucking Irish disease. Hail-fellow-well-met bullshit, needing to be liked at all costs! If you didn't want a child why the fuck didn't you come out and say it?'

'Okay! Okay! I didn't really want the child! I hate myself for it, but part of me felt a relief when it … Because maybe I'm just not ready or able to be a father.'

Ella let out a scream, then drew her hand back and clattered him full whack in the face. He was knocked back, and she instinctively reached out to him to take his hand. He put his arms around her and squeezed her tight. They clung to each other, and she whispered his name, and they made sounds that meant nothing and everything, and they collapsed to the ground and tore at each other's clothes and kissed and squeezed and licked and sucked and tried to fuck themselves better.

Afterwards they lay in each other's arms for a while as the darkness gathered outside. They didn't speak. Scobie gently stroked her upper arm. She had always liked that. It made her feel calm. But that evening it didn't seem to be having any effect. She stirred herself and moved away from him, then went into the bathroom, and Scobie could hear the shower water. They began to sleep apart and live their lives apart, and Scobie went back to Crazy Girls and found another Cindy until one early morning, a few months later, he wandered home dead drunk and collapsed at the front door, and he woke to Ella looking down at him. He told her that he would move out, and Ella nodded and stepped over him to go to school.

As he neared the building site, Scobie felt a terrible lead weight in his stomach. He wished he hadn't gone down that particular rabbit hole in his head, but the ongoing effect of the pills seemed to tip the balance back in his favour.

Scobie arrived at the site, parked up the car, and tried to slip back into the house where he was working without being seen, but Nigel spotted him as he was about to jump back over the low wall.

'Where the fuck were you?'

'Sorry, Nigel, I got called away. My mother needed me for something. I hadn't time to let ye know. I am so sorry. I swear to God it was an emergency.'

'Go on, I'll fuckin' believe ye this time. Thousands wouldn't. Don't let it happen again. I'm serious now, pal.'

Scobie nodded, giving Nigel the thumbs up before heading into the house to get on with the work.

fifteen

Keelan

Keelan decided, after mulling it over for most of the day, that she would try and call Nicola. She had texted her best friend loads of times already, but with no reply. Keelan hadn't left the room or her bed for over 24 hours, and now it was late evening, and her head zoomed back through the mortification of the night of Nicola's twenty-first. They hadn't spoken since, and that had been three months ago – the longest that they'd ever not spoken since they were in third class and fell out over a doll.

The twenty-first had been on in the Bridge House in Tullamore, and Keelan had known she was going to be late for it, because she had absconded with Peter to a cottage in Kildare that he said a mate of his had loaned him for the afternoon. Peter was especially attentive and loving that day, cooking steak and opening wine, and there was a fire. She was delighted, but hoped this didn't mean he was expecting her to stay all night. She had to get to the party. They started to make out beside the fire, and she totally got into it while keeping an eye on the time. Then he suggested that they get a bit more adventurous, that sexual experimentation in a safe environment was healthy and vital in moving a relationship forward. Keelan agreed. She had seen too many couples who had let the sex go off the boil, her parents being a prime example. She asked what he might be thinking of, joking that she was no fan of *Fifty Shades of Grey*-type carry-on. He laughed at this, then took up his laptop and suggested they watch some porn together. Keelan wasn't mad on the idea, but she didn't want to let him down, and she was anxious to be seen as 'with it', and not some ordinary square little sergeant's daughter.

So he opened his laptop, and a couple of clicks later she was watching a good-looking girl and boy making out on a bed and removing each other's clothes. They kissed and caressed each other, and Keelan didn't mind it at all, and Peter glanced at her and gave her a kind of shy smile, as if this was a new thing he was trying for the first time. They watched for a while until the couple started to have sex, and then Peter put his hands around her and slowly undressed her, and Keelan responded and reached out her arm to try to turn the porn off. What was the need for it now? But Peter grabbed her arm, and it was clear that he wanted to continue watching. The screen was now full of close-ups, and had become much more graphic, and as Peter kissed Keelan's neck and breasts, his eyes never left the screen. Keelan couldn't settle into it. She was definitely not turned on, and was now becoming uncomfortable with the whole thing, so she asked him to stop, but he ignored her. She asked him again, but he was gone somewhere else, his eyes at the back of his head, like he was lost in something. She eventually had to push him away, and rolled out from underneath him and stood up.

He shook his head and sighed, disappointed in her. He thought she was in love with him. She promised him that she was. He said that he needed her to show him. That he found it hard to trust, as he had been so badly hurt in the past. He reminded her of how his ex-partner had left him so suddenly, taking their child.

Keelan could see how genuinely upset he was. She sat back down on the sofa beside him. He stroked her hair. They looked into the fire for a while. She eyed the clock. She would now be very late. She suggested that maybe it would be better to just end the evening, as she had to get to Tullamore. No hard feelings.

Peter nodded, and said that maybe it was time to call a halt to their relationship. That they were at different points in their life experience. That she'd be better off with someone her own age. Keelan felt a stab in her heart and panic rising in her chest. No, she couldn't be without him. He was strength and security and she loved him. She begged him not to break up with her, and he held her then, and whispered in her ear that what they had was real adult passionate sexual love. With no boundaries. He would never leave her. He couldn't live without her. Keelan felt the words soothe her whole body. All the shit at home and feelings of abject inadequacy disappeared, and she kissed him hungrily on the mouth.

He opened up the laptop and pressed play and the porn came back on. The loud grunts and cries of pleasure. She slowly allowed herself to get into the sex. She opened her eyes every now and again to see that he was continuing to watch the screen. She felt disconnected from him, as if she was some sort of empty vessel, but this seemed to be the way he needed it to be, so Keelan pretended she was one of the actors, on the screen, disassociating from her body and making it into a performance, a kind of role play. To please the man she loved. Because she knew that he would look after her. He wouldn't let anything hurt her.

Keelan turned up to the Bridge House after 10, and Nicola was annoyed with her and wanted to know where she'd been. Keelan was tipsy, having drunk several vodkas as soon as the sex was finished. He had dropped her to a taxi rank and thrust three €20 notes into her hand to pay for the fare across to Tullamore. She spent the whole 40-minute journey thinking back on what had just happened and convincing herself that it was okay. Relationships were all about give and take. She was doing her bit. She dressed the way he liked her to dress. She was always available whenever they got a chance to see each other. She didn't see any other friends any more. Even the party tonight had been a problem until he relented and, much to her relief, granted her permission to go, seeing as it was her best pal's twenty-first.

But the porn was a new thing. She would have to get used to that. Her head battled to justify all the little quirks and habits that had become the norm in this first great 'can't live without him', most serious love affair of her life. But towards the end of the journey, as the taxi driver blathered on about the pandemic, she suddenly felt a terrible sense of unease creeping up on her. The sensation of lovemaking had been so confusing. On the one hand she loved being with this man, his touch, his body, but then the disconnect of it made her feel so small and insignificant. His eyes never meeting hers. The way he changed his position or action in tandem with the porn on the screen. She couldn't wait to get to the Bridge House. She needed a drink. She realised there were tears rolling down her cheeks, and the taxi man asked her was she okay and was it boyfriend trouble.

Keelan laughed and kissed Nicola and disappeared onto the packed dance floor. She just wanted to dance and drink and get lost, and she found two lads who she knew would have weed so they smoked a joint out the back near the food bins. She floated inside to dance some more and hugged Nicola, who was now drunk enough herself not to care, but there was this Amanda Shanley one that she never liked, a right stupid bitch, and there was a spilt drink and insults flew and Keelan started shouting at her. How she and the rest of them were just small-town ignorant bogger girls with no idea of real life. And she suddenly turned and barfed her guts up all over Amanda and fled the scene and wanted the main street of Tullamore to open and swallow her up.

She dialled Nicola's number and was prepared to wait, as she never picked up until about the tenth ring. Keelan leaned across the bed and reached out to part the curtains of the bedroom window. Much to her relief, she could see no sign of his car. The ringing stopped and Nicola answered.

'Hello, Keelan.'

'Hi, Nicola. I hope ye don't mind me calling ye. I meant to do it so many times, but I was so fuckin' embarrassed, like.'

'Yeah, it was bad all right.'

'I'm so sorry. I was going through a lot of shit then. I'd really like to talk to ye about it.'

'Yeah, the thing is I don't really want to know about it, Keelan. Like, you've been a shit friend to me for a long time now, and I've kinda moved on and that. So, like, I hope you're doing okay, but like, we're done.'

'Ah, no, Nicky, no. I'm not doing well at all. I need to talk to ye. I really do. I *have* been a real shite friend to ye, I know that. But please, please, I need ye now. Something's after happening to me.'

There was a long pause on the phone.

'Nicky, are ye still there?'

'Yeah. Listen I have to go. I can't be your friend anymore. Go back to smoking the weed or whatever it is you like doing.'

'Ah, Nicky, sorry, I've been on the down low, I know that, from you and all the girls, but it's just so much has gone on and I couldn't tell ye before but now I can. Can I call around to see ye?'

'No, Kee, ye can't. Ye can't just not give a flying fuck about someone and then expect them to be your friend. You were nowhere to be Jaysus seen when Cormac broke up with me, and you fucked up my twenty-first. I've had enough of it. Okay? Goodbye. Have a nice life.' And she was gone.

Keelan lay back in her bed. Her eyes filled with tears. She tried to turn over and get some sleep, but she couldn't. All she could see was that last time she spent in his flat, and the laptop was set up and he was behind her and the porn was much more hard-core now. It was rough and sadistic, and the girl was submissive and the man squeezed her throat. As usual, Peter expected her to re-enact what was happening on-screen. His arm around her throat, squeezing it so tightly, and her eyes watered and she felt like she might pass out until she managed to get free of him. Out onto the road, early morning, wrong shoes for the wet, looked like she'd been dragged through a hedge backwards. Ran into Scobie Donoghue before Peter pulled up and hauled her back into the car. He had been nice as pie then, putting her to bed, and no wild dog disgusting suggestions to humiliate her. Bastard! She stayed away then. That had been the night. No matter how much he pleaded and professed his love she kept strong, even when she found out that her body had betrayed her.

She heard Deirdre outside her door, knocking first politely, and then with greater urgency.

'Please, love. Let me in. I need to talk to you. I'm so sorry. I love you. Please let me in.'

She so wanted to let her in. She was lost in the woods, and the big bad wolf was somewhere in the darkness, and she needed her mam like she needed her the morning she did the first test. She had never felt as alone as that morning. So alone that she'd told him. A moment of weakness. A huge mistake. She did another test then, hoping against hope, but it gave the same result, so she went to the doctor to get it confirmed. Her mind filled with the two competing realities, first a beautiful newborn, apple of your eye, bundle of new baby smell, and then the images they march with on the streets, of blood-soaked foetuses being dumped into bins.

But there was never any real debate. She could never keep it. She told him that, very plainly. She would not have his baby. And he'd gone mad. She would be a murderer, he'd said. And she would have it, he would make sure of that. From then, she was terrified of Peter Delaney, the big bad wolf deep in the woods.

Her mother kept saying her name outside the door. Let her in, Keelan told herself, let her in and tell her. Tell her you're pregnant but you're not keeping it. Let her in! Keelan climbed out of the bed and moved across to the door and opened it, then fell into her mother's arms. They held each other tight.

'You must think I'm an awful fuckin' eejit,' said Deirdre. 'It was mad, ye know, how you can get caught up in a thing.'

'What's done is done, Ma,' replied Keelan.

They wanted to squeeze each other until they hadn't a drop of breath left in their bodies. Holding on for dear life. Their first physical contact in two years. Keelan would tell her. In a moment. She would tell her. But for now, she just needed to hold her.

sixteen

The weekend was a quiet one at home with no pubs to go to. Scobie and Angela watched the telly, which was so boring that Scobie actually started work on a shelf in the kitchen, which he had promised to do for the longest time and had never got around to it. Cliff called every night at the same time, just as the nine o'clock news and weather was finished, and Angela would take the phone into the kitchen and talk to him for an hour. What they found to Jaysus talk about Scobie could never fathom, as each day was extremely uneventful.

The main message she had to report that night was that Cliff would be away for some time yet. Ethel was more or less bedbound, and it was going to take time to arrange a nursing home, and what with the uncertainty of lockdowns and travel it was hard to know when he could get back home to Ireland. Ethel even came on the phone, which was a first, to say how grateful she was to Angela for loaning Cliff to her. Angela took all this in her stride, but after the phone call she went to bed early.

Scobie nearly thought about offering her one of his magic Klonopin tablets. They really were amazing little chemical miracles. Scobie felt no more awful anxiety, no more pit-of-the-stomach tension building up. He did find, however, that he was taking two at a time now to get the desired effect. He didn't care. They were doing the job.

Scobie raised his glass to the light, admiring the rosy colour that you got inside a pint of Guinness, looking up to the heavens and thanking almighty God for Ollie Taylor, publican, keen hare courser, purveyor of underage drink, perpetrator of tax evasion and buying booze from the IRA in the eighties. Ollie had acted fast, and as soon as the pubs were ordered to close, he got busy designing a makeshift shebeen-type set-up in the back yard of the pub. He got his brother Shay-shay to knock up a class of a counter with three kegs – Guinness, Carlsberg and Smithwick's – installed underneath, and optics and bottles of spirits attached to the wall behind. In two days flat himself and Shay-shay had the place operational, and the word went out to regulars, who would have to form a close-knit community of secret boozers.

Scobie had run into Ollie that morning, when he had raced into the Centra to get Lucozade, and Ollie tipped him the nod and said that he could bring one other. Scobie would have preferred Niallers, but he knew that Niallers would fuss over the legality and the risk of spreading the disease and we all have to do our bit and all that, as he listened to the radio and TV coverage every day and paid great heed to Leo's speeches. On the other hand, Scobie knew well that the renegade Donegal head that was Bob Bonner would love the prospect of sticking it to Leo and company trying to tell him what he could and could not do. Sure enough, Bob was over several moons on his way to Jupiter when Scobie let him know about it, but he had to inform the Queen, as he called her, and she flat out thought it was a bad, irresponsible idea, and that he could do what he liked of course, he was a grown man, but it was clear that a very dim view would be taken.

Bob had to opt out gracefully, which left Scobie with no one, but that was never going to put him off. So here he was, taking a long, lovely swallow of the stout, made all the more sweet by the fact that it was illegal and covert. Indeed, Ollie had been very strict about the limited inner circle of only loyal clientele who could be trusted.

'It's like Jaysus Fight Club,' Ollie had said. 'The first rule of Fight Club is you don't talk about Fight Club. The second rule of Fight Club is you don't talk about Fight Club!'

When Ollie had pulled the pints behind the counter he was beaming from ear to ear. He was beating the law and the powers that be, and nothing gave him greater pleasure than that. He whipped his phone out of his shirt pocket and read a text. He had slipped across to the back door of the yard and looked out. That was the third rule of Fight Club. You texted Ollie when you were about 30 seconds away from the door, and he texted back a yay or nay, depending on how many were inside.

Ollie had opened the door and the Mole appeared, looking as unsteady on the pins as ever, but not quite the wild man from Borneo, as he had pulled a comb through his thatch of thick hair. Scobie raised a glass to him. Mole nodded back. 'Mad times, Scobie,' he'd said.

Then another body had stepped through the door behind Mole. It had taken Scobie a moment to recognise him. It was Robbie, the hoodie down, and he waved across before coming over to join Scobie up at the counter. Mole dragged one foot after the other, at a snail's pace, to follow on after him.

'What has you in here?' asked Scobie.

Robbie indicated Mole, who was huffing and puffing behind him, then lifting his saggy arse cheek onto a bar stool. 'I met this man outside, so I decided to tag along. Me and Gran in the house, 24/7, like. Needed the break.'

Mole signalled to Ollie. 'Pint and a Powers for me, and a pint of cider for the young lad. His shout.'

Mole had needed a moment to settle. He looked around at the new set-up. 'Not bad, I suppose, but I mean, it's an infringement on our civil rights anyway. I mean, ye can read all sorts of stuff, Scobe. I mean there's the fuckin' 5G mobile phone signals and how they could be transmitting the virus or be reducing our defences to it.'

'Too much time on t'Internet, boy,' said Scobie.

'No, Scobie. It's all about depopulation of the world so Bill Gates can get fuckin' microchips into all our brains,' insisted Mole.

Scobie glanced across to Ollie. 'Ollie, is there any house rule on being put out for talking absolute shite?'

Ollie shook his head, laughing. 'Not at all. Sure, I'd be out of business in a week if I had that rule.'

'You're too naïve, Scobie,' said Mole.

'I think that you could really do with Bill Gates' microchip in your head instead of that tiny brain you have, and then you might stop believing that horse shit,' said Scobie.

'Well, I'm tellin' you now, and you can quote me on this, but there's a new world order on the way,' said Mole. 'And this Covid-19 thing could be the way they're goin' to introduce it.'

The three of them raised their glasses and drank. Mole was content to sit and switch off. He was there listening, but at the same time he occupied some other space.

Scobie turned to Robbie. He noticed that the rings around the eyes were not as apparent, and his overall colour was a lot healthier than he'd encountered that first night in Tynan's yard. 'How are ye getting' on?'

'Yeah, all right, I suppose. Got the drawings done for that exhibition in Dublin. It's on next month. But, like, bored most of the time. Spending too much time at home.'

'Anyway, good to see you looking so well.'

'I suppose, yeah, not as many late nights, ye know.'

'Well sure, a few illegal scoops will do us no harm,' grinned Scobie.

Robbie reached for his phone. 'I have a drawing done for you. Must throw it into the house some day.'

He opened a photo on his screen of a charcoal drawing of a giant T-Rex and a superhero-type figure pointing a bazooka at him about to blow him up. Scobie laughed, as it reminded him of all the games they used play when Robbie was a kid.

'It's cool. Real good, Robbie,' said Scobie.

He was moved that this young lad would bother to draw him something, and for a moment the world was a bright place with great hope. He had taken some Klonopin before he came out, and they were working nicely with the drink. He felt open and emotional and not afraid of showing it.

He smiled at Robbie. 'You're a great lad.'

Robbie shrugged and made a 'would ye go 'way from me' face. They drank their pints and ordered more. Scobie felt he was flying now. They bought whiskey chasers with the next few. He felt so good about the young lad. He'd been saved. Yes, that's what Scobie felt. The young man had been saved from himself and the drugs, and now his life could find another, much brighter path. He thought of poor Majella Flynn down in Oz, and decided he would tell Robbie about her, so he could appreciate how badly things could have gone.

'She was from the town here, nine of them in the family, and ye know they had a bad rep, from Castle Park estate and all that. Majella Flynn. You'd know them, Mole.'

Mole confirmed this with a nod of the head.

'She was a nice enough girl, petite and pretty-looking. You know. Tidy. Talked a lot. But nothing prepared me for the shock of laying eyes on her again in Oz. Like, I paid her a visit one night and, ah, things weren't great. I'd split up with the woman, and had a kind of row with Shamie and Therese, and I was out for a night of craic with no strings attached. So I landed over to this kip suburb in Melbourne called Sunshine, or "Scumshine", as the locals know it. I mean, *Fort Apache, The Bronx* wouldn't be in it. Lads in hoodies, smokin' joints on the corner, and there was this older woman shuffling out of a doorway with a shopping trolley full of all kinds of shite. Big sad eyes on her. Anyways, I get to this one-storey house and I sees this lad and a girl out front on the porch. She was skin and bone, and her face was all drawn with sunken eyes, and her looks were gonzo, like. I mean, I didn't recognise her until she called my name. Jaysus Christ, a gust of wind would have blown her away. Anyway, she throws me into a big hug, kisses and saying, "The one and only Scobie Donoghue" and all this craic. So, we started to cane it then, and she's all talk of the various gangs in the neighbour-hood, like the Blood Drill Killers – "But they're pretty harmless," she says. "Just a bunch of lads playing around. Pretending to be hard men. They're grand compared to the people who really run the show in these parts." And then she says to me, "Don't worry, Scobe, it's all cool here. No one fucks with us, like." Ye know, like she's part of all this shit, and then I found out that the boyfriend and this other weird fucker from Kiribati called George were dealing crystal meth, and she was definitely an addict, like. So anyways, it was a real eye-opener. Ye know. What can happen to a person.'

Scobie stopped talking to take a large swallow of his pint. He looked to Robbie. He had only mentioned Majella for his benefit. Robbie nodded back at him.

Mole piped up. 'Do ye remember that Ozzie yoke, *The Sullivans*? Used be on in the afternoons. Jaysus, the Second World War went on for about 20 fuckin' years in it.'

'Before my time, Mole,' grinned Robbie.

'Never watched it,' lied Scobie. Himself and Shamie had often watched it after school.

Scobie got up to go for a piss. Ollie had the back door of the pub open so you could use the facilities inside. Scobie's head was pounding now. He wondered was it the result of the alcohol meeting the Klonopin in his system. He thought of that night in Australia. When he and Majella, the boyfriend and George had driven out into the bush, high as kites. He wished he could forget about what had happened afterwards.

He made himself think about Shamie Jr instead, and the sensitive, nervous little head on him, and then of his father, Shamie Sr, and his sensitive, nervous little head. He had a great yearning to sit with his brother and talk to him. They had planned to phone each other so many times since he got home, but it never seemed to happen. He wondered if they were both avoiding each other because it was too awkward now. They seemed to be set on such different courses through life. Maybe a kind of mutual mistrust had festered in the place where once it was all brothers forever and blood on blood and two sides of the same coin.

Scobie emerged from the jacks and took out his phone. Fuck it, he'd ring him. He'd chance it. Scobie walked across to the far wall of the yard so he could make the call in a bit more peace. He dialled the number, heard the weird foreign ring tone, and then his brother's voice saying, 'Hello, Scobie, is that you?'

'It is of course. Are ye on the site, can ye talk?'

'Naw, day off while they get the place Covid-friendly, ye know, separate exits and entrances, hand sterilisers and all this craic.'

'Well now what you'll do is go into the fridge there, grab a Victoria Bitter, crack it open and we'll have an auld jar together.'

'Jaysus, you're a shockin' man. Go on, might as well. Bit early, but sure there's not much else happening.'

'Good man,' said Scobie. 'How's your lockdown?'

'Oh yeah, not a person on the street. Like a ghost town. It's weird.'

Scobie could hear Therese asking him who it was and him telling her, and she shouted 'Hello Scobie!', and he heard Shamie Jr's voice in another room as Therese called his name to come out and talk to Uncle Scobie.

'I have the beer open,' said Shamie, 'so *sláinte*.'

'*Sláinte mhaith*,' said Scobie.

'So, what about ye?' asked Shamie.

'Ah, the rumour is that we'll be closed down the end of next week,' said Scobie.

'Jaysus, that's a fright,' said Shamie.

Scobie wanted to find a way out of this shorthand small talk shite and into a way of … he didn't know, a way of telling his brother that he missed him. That he'd love to be able to find a way to tell him how lost he feels sometimes, but he couldn't get into that, as Shamie asked, 'How's Ma?'

'She's grand. Missing your man, but she'll survive.'

Scobie heard Shamie Jr charging out of his room, but for once he didn't want to talk to the boy. He just wanted to stay on with his brother.

He became aware of a loud banging on the back door of Taylor's shebeen. He glanced up at Ollie hurrying across to the door. He wished that Ollie would open the door and that some-how, by some miracle, Shamie would be standing there with the cold Victoria Bitter in his hand and he'd step over the threshold into Scobie's dimension and they'd be together again. But when Ollie opened the door, it wasn't Shamie standing there.

Shamie Jr came on the phone with his little high-pitched Aussie accent and just a hint of Offaly in it from listening to his parents.

'How's it goin', Uncle Scobe?'

And before Scobie could answer him, he saw who it was at the back door and crossing the threshold, past Ollie, who looked like he just shat his pants. Delaney. Cool as a cucumber. The whole vibe in the place suddenly went south. People looked panicked. This fucker would take names. There could be fines. Ollie could be sent to Covid jail!

Scobie had to get off the phone. 'Sorry, Shamie, sorry, little man, but I have to go. I'll ring ye later. So sorry.'

Scobie stepped back towards the centre of the yard. Mole, Robbie, everyone looked like they were playing a game of statues, and if they moved a muscle they might die. All except Delaney, in uniform. He moved across towards the bar, took his hat off, rested it on the counter, said, 'Any chance of a drink there, Ollie?'

You could have knocked Ollie and every other living soul in the place over with a drink-sodden beer mat.

Ollie beamed from ear to ear and filled an Old Speckled Hen for Delaney, who sat up at the counter and seemed to be in the right good mood for drink.

'You run the place properly. I'll say nothing, Ollie, for the next while anyway. Let's see how this Covid thing pans out.'

'Absolutely, Guard,' replied Ollie, like a man reprieved from the gallows at the last minute. He plopped the drink down in front of Delaney. 'No charge of course, Guard.'

Delaney took up the glass, took a sip, sighed and said, 'Call me Peter.'

'Grand job, Peter,' said Ollie.

Delaney looked at Ollie and nodded silently. He took another sip. Ollie felt awkward then, futtered around with cleaning glasses, scrambling to make chat.

'So, like hopefully the Covid will help keep the crime rates down, ha – says you,' said Ollie.

Delaney didn't acknowledge this, preferring to glance around the yard. Most of the secret drinking club were now supping up and making for the exits. They tried to pretend that the guard wasn't there for the first few minutes, but then grew nervous and didn't trust the fact that he was being so chilled about the illegal drinking, and even ordering a drink himself.

Robbie leaned into Scobie and Mole and whispered, 'Will we get the fuck out of here?'

Scobie waved him away. 'We're grand. We're grand.'

Mole swallowed down the remains of his glass and slid his buttock down off the stool, wincing as the feet took the full weight of his body. He was clearly heading off, having made the decision that even drinking piss supermarket lager at home in his own kip with his cat Sheba would be more enjoyable than being here in Delaney's presence.

'I'm making like a banana. Good luck,' said Mole as he set off for the back door. Ollie went to let him out.

Scobie leaned up on the counter and turned towards Delaney. 'Good man Peter, how's it hanging?'

'Just fine, Scobie,' said Delaney.

'Fair play, like, not being a bollocks about this place. I mean sure what harm can it do? A few of us having a few pints, like.'

Scobie signalled to Ollie for three more Speckled Hens.

'Do yis want pints with those?' asked Ollie.

'Grand job,' said Scobie, even if the head was a little bit woozy. Must be the auld Klonopin, but sure he'd be grand. He'd press on. Keep the night going.

He put his arm on Robbie's shoulder. 'You know this man, of course. Robbie McNamee.'

Delaney kept drinking and didn't react.

'Robbie, show Peter your art there. Go on, show him.'

Robbie shook his head. Scobie took up his phone from the counter.

'Where are they? Go on and show him,' insisted Scobie.

Robbie gave in, flicked through the phone until he came to the photos of his drawings. Scobie took the phone and stepped across to Delaney.

'See for yourself, Peter. This lad has real talent. He's doing a big exhibition in Dublin and all this craic so—'

Robbie tried to interrupt. 'It's a Youth Council of Ireland thing, but it's a start.'

'So he's leaving his old ways behind him,' beamed Scobie.

Delaney looked through the drawings, said, 'Very good, yeah,' and handed the phone back to Robbie. 'You seem to be behaving yourself anyway,' he added. 'We didn't find you at Number 27 last night when we raided it.'

'How did ye find that out?' asked Robbie.

'We have a new tout around the town.' Delaney glanced at Scobie, who avoided his eyes and took a long drink of his pint.

Ollie slapped down three more pint glasses and the Speckled Hens. Delaney took out his wallet.

'Ah no, Peter. On the house,' said Ollie, waving him away.

Delaney shook his head, saying, 'You have a business to run,' and left a €50 note on the counter.

Ollie hesitated, but picked it up. 'Okay. Fair enough. Appreciate it. You understand the reality of small business, not like them fuckers in government.'

Delaney placed the pints and whiskeys in front of Scobie and Robbie. 'Of course, the real job is to try and stop the supply into the town.'

Robbie shook his head, and was about to say something but then shut his mouth.

'Go on, say it. I'd like to get your opinion,' said Delaney.

'Well, it's just ye are always talking about stopping drugs or seizing x amount worth of drugs at the ports or whatever, and that's your job, but people will always want to take drugs because they feel stuck or left behind, and then kids grow up in houses that are fucked, like, with people who aren't able to bring them up, so I think it's a society thing. Ye can stop the drugs all you like, but if ye don't stop the reason we want to take them then it's fucked. Yeah.'

Robbie was surprised at himself that he had spoken like this in front of a guard. He took a drink of his whiskey. Scobie beamed at him.

'Yes,' said Delaney, 'but isn't it also about some modicum of personal responsibility? Stop looking to others to solve your problems.'

'Yeah, of course there's always that, but it's just a bit easier when your mother and father aren't out of it in the morning and you go to school hungry. Like, that never happened to me, but there's loads of them down at the centre like that. Or worse. Worse types of abuse. I'm not whingeing. I never knew my father, but my ma did her best so ... Fuck it, I'm trying.'

Delaney took a large drink of his whiskey. He suddenly seemed very melancholy. His face darkened. Scobie had never seen him like this. His 'cool as ye like', in-control persona seemed to have been left behind this evening. He noticed how fast Delaney was mowing through the drinks.

Delaney raised his glass. 'Let's get drunk. That's what I need to do tonight. Fuck responsibility.'

Time passed and Scobie and Delaney kept ordering rounds, but Robbie stuck to his own pace. Scobie knocked back another Speckled Hen and it felt like the few remaining brave brain cells who had put up such a good fight were now lying wounded inside somewhere in the dark recesses of his *ceann*. The back yard of Taylor's was now looking slightly out of focus and blurry, and he knew that he had to get a hold of himself. His wiring was faulty. The system was down. He had drunk too much too fast tonight on top of the pills. The horse had bolted. He was fucked. Full-on pissed, mule thick drunk now, his drinkometer had slipped into the red and wasn't coming out any time soon.

'I'll have another heckled spen,' he garbled, but Ollie shook his head firmly with the well-practised publican's demeanour of an old pal who's looking out for ye.

'Now, Scobe,' Ollie said, 'I think it's time for you to call it a night.'

Scobie shook his head, in a 'won't do nothing that anyone tells me' sorta way, and then nudged Robbie. 'Come on, you, and we'll go back to your house or whatever and get another drink. Come on. Bit of craic. Scobie-Wan Kenobi is out. Loud and dangerous. Yessiree bob!'

Delaney was possessed with something else by this point. Any 'drinking buddy' bonhomie had vanished. He finished the end of his drink and took up his hat.

Scobie laughed and banged the counter with his fist. 'Now we're at it. Me, Robbie and the good guard here are goin' to have some craic!'

Delaney turned to Ollie. 'On second thoughts I want this place closed down tonight. I'll be around tomorrow to check that everything has been taken down.'

Ollie looked like a man who had just been told that he was going to be shot at dawn after all. 'Ah no, Peter, come on, I thought we had worked out a little deal, like?'

'It's Guard Delaney, and if there's one more word out of you, I'll report the place.' Delaney turned to Scobie, said, 'Come on you', and went to the back door.

Robbie helped Scobie off the stool and they followed him out the door, leaving a shell-shocked Ollie to look around his beautiful makeshift bar and to contemplate the tragedy of dismantling it.

Outside, trying to walk, Scobie took gulps out of the night air. His head swam even more as he did his best to put one foot in front of the other. Delaney caught one arm, and Robbie the other, helping him along the street.

'Good man, good man, where do ye live now? Have ye got booze?' muttered Scobie into their ears.

They managed to steer Scobie up through the town until they came to the main square, where Delaney's car was in sight.

'I'll drink anything now. I'd drink piss off a scabby leg,' said Scobie.

Delaney and Robbie manoeuvred Scobie until he was leaning against the bonnet of Delaney's car. Scobie launched into a rendition of 'The Boys Are Back in Town', but knew no words bar the chorus.

Delaney opened the passenger door and gestured to Scobie. 'Get in, you dope. I'll bring you home to your mammy.'

Scobie didn't feel like moving from where he was, nice and comfy on the bonnet. He didn't feel like going anywhere.

'Ah, just leave me here, will ye?' he heard himself saying.

Robbie stepped forward and placed his hand on Scobie's shoulder. 'Come on, Scobe, time to move.'

Scobie didn't respond, and Delaney, checking to make sure nobody was around, grabbed hold of Scobie, swung him around and snarled at him right into his face, 'Get in the fucking car!'

'Chill the fuck out, would ye?'

Delaney's face was twisted up. Like now he wanted to inflict some real damage. 'I'd shut the fuck up if I was you, Donoghue.'

Robbie stood rooted to the spot. Part of him wanted to turn and bolt, but more of him wanted to stay and try to snap Scobie out of it. 'Take it easy,' he said. 'He's just locked. I'll get him home.'

He tried to pull Scobie up off the car bonnet, but Delaney shoved him out of the way, grabbed Scobie's arm and roughly hauled him off the car. Scobie rolled down onto the ground with a thud.

'Ah, there was no need for that,' protested Robbie.

Delaney took hold of Robbie, a vice-like grip of his throat. 'You just shut up now, scum. Because you're fucked. There's a load of drugs getting into this town and I think it's you. I think I can make them believe that. I'll make sure you go to Mountjoy. You won't have time for drawing in there.'

Robbie was scared now. His hands shook, all the goodness and confidence so hard won over the past few weeks draining out of him. He looked down at Scobie, who was sprawled out on the ground, wiping his mouth, a pool of vomit swimming around in front of him as it sank from the pavement into a drain.

Delaney advanced on Robbie. 'Go on, I'll give you a chance. Clear the fuck off out of my town. I'll give you until the morning.'

Robbie laughed, a bitter sound. 'That's the way it is, yeah. Sure, more fool fucking me thinking it could ever be any other way.' Robbie turned and took off down the town.

Scobie struggled for breath. He had been seeing a galaxy of stars for the past few seconds. He looked up but couldn't see any sign of Robbie. He heard the sound of Delaney's car pulling out of the square, driving off.

His system flooded with relief and pain. He knew he should get up but he couldn't find the strength so he decided he'd just stay there for a while. The drink and the pills, the pain and the exhaustion had done their job. Scobie Donoghue was out for the count, in the square of his home town, which looked so bare and empty with everything shut down because of a bat in China.

A gentle breeze blew a plastic Lidl bag up the street. The odd car went trundling past the market square, but no one could see the figure slouched in the shadows, in the doorway of what was once a cinema. Scobie's breathing was heavy, his face dead to the world, wedged in at an awkward angle. He'd have a right crick in his neck as well as everything else when he woke up. Something vibrated in his jacket pocket. His phone jingle, the generic electronica sound, was activated. Scobie stirred, but nothing was going to reach in there to cause any sort of consciousness.

The first thing he saw – and heard and smelt – when he opened his eyes to the new day was a long livestock truck and trailer carrying cows to the local meat factory out the road. The ground vibrated underneath him as the truck rolled past the square and on down the town.

Scobie roused himself and rubbed his neck, which indeed was stiff as a board. He felt for his phone and found it in his jacket, then checked the time. Half six in the morning. He felt dreadful. Sick as a small hospital, but then he spied the puke, and it made him feel a bit better, because at least that poison was outside his body now, and not inside. He was cold and bewildered, and felt like some homeless abandoned stray dog in need of a good bath. How in the name of the sweet lovin' divine Jaysus had he ended up passed out in the square all night?

He tried to recall the previous night. A swirl of voices, faces fading in and out of clear focus, but some of the images were beginning to stick. Robbie and Delaney at the back of Taylor's. The drawings on his phone. Delaney's face, genuinely impressed by them. But then what had happened here, in the square, for Robbie to have bolted?

Scobie lifted his head to the world, digging his thumb as best he could into his stiff neck. A breeze made him shiver. He slowly got himself up onto the two feet that he possessed, very gingerly starting to walk down the town. The greatest walk of shame he'd ever walked in his life. He'd lost the run of the drinking and been a fool. He tried ringing Robbie but got no reply.

He walked on and there were very few people around, thank God. He made it to his house, went around the back and took a glance into the kitchen to make sure Angela hadn't woken up earlier than usual. Much to his relief, there was no sign of her as he shoved the sliding door across and entered the kitchen. He walked out into the hall and climbed the stairs as quietly as he could. He slipped into the bathroom and stripped off his clothes. He got in under the hot water and relief and warmth engulfed him.

After towelling down he crept into his room to put on clean clothes and took two more Klonopins. He sat on the bed and lay down for a moment. Let them take effect. He shut his eyes.

He started drifting dangerously into a deep doze but was prevented from going any further by Angela, who suddenly appeared above him.

'You're up early this morning.'

Scobie sat up like a shot.

'Ah yeah, mad for work, Ma, you know me. Out to impress the new foreman. Not as easy-going as Cliff.'

'Well, ye look like shite, Scobe. Where were ye last night anyway?'

Scobie pulled on a shirt and jeans. He noticed a photo album in her hand.

'What's that?' he said, trying to sound as breezy as he could, and to change the subject.

'It's photos of your communion, would ye believe. Found it in the back of a drawer.'

She opened the album and showed him one of the photos. Scobie outside the church with his eight-year-old innocent-as-the-driven-snow big grin and communion rosette, the medal, the hands joined in prayer.

'Jaysus, I look every inch of a lad with a vocation.'

'A vocation for acting the mad eejit,' said Angela.

Scobie leaned in and gave her a kiss on the cheek. Angela winced at the smell of his breath, despite the fact that he was only after brushing his teeth.

'I was going to fry an egg. Do ye want one?'

'Yeah, Ma, that would be great.'

'And you can tell me all about last night.'

Angela left the room to go downstairs. Scobie sat on his bed. His nerves were still hopping. He could still feel the cold ground of the spot in the square where he had spent the night. He remembered the sight of the puke still congealed around the drain. He felt a lurch in his stomach. He may seriously need to relieve the contents at some stage this morning, but for the moment he had to concentrate on eating his eggs and getting to work.

seventeen

Deirdre

Deirdre had made a stew and spuds – Paudge's favourite. He had got picked for the town First XI for the forthcoming match versus Derry Rovers from Edenderry, and the family gathered around the table to eat a celebratory supper. Paudge, of course, had been expected to follow in his father Eamon's footsteps and play GAA, but he had opted instead for soccer. Even so, Eamon couldn't have been more pleased. It was an excuse to get together anyway, even though it was very stiff and awkward at first when Eamon arrived in.

He had rung the doorbell so as to indicate that this wasn't where he lived anymore. Oisín and Paudge answered the door and asked him if he had forgotten his key. All five of them gradually settled into it then. A family meal like no other they had ever had, but Oisín and Paudge began to chat away and laughed and slagged their da. It was as if the pretending was over. The effort of keeping up the charade that their mother and father were happily married was now thankfully a thing of the past, and they could relax.

Deirdre served up the stew onto plates. She passed a smaller portion across to Keelan, who took the plate and smiled at her.

'Thanks Mam.'

She had said those words on more than one occasion over the past few days. Ever since she had managed to confide in her and tell her that she was pregnant, and that the father was Peter Delaney. Deirdre had sat on her daughter's bed, and Keelan had spared her no detail – of how, incrementally, over a few months, she had become so controlled by Delaney. Deirdre held her then, and they cried and laughed, and somehow, they were released from a strain that had suffocated them for so long. All the hurtful words were forgotten, consigned to the past.

Deirdre had been shocked, but didn't interrupt or pass judgement. She tried to keep control of the anger she felt burning up in her belly. Her first instinct was to find Delaney and beat him to death. She had blood-drenched fantasies of the suffering she'd like to put him through. She felt wretched and ashamed that her daughter had sought refuge with someone like him rather than her own flesh and blood who had given her life, who had worried themselves sick when she got colic as an infant. Deirdre remembered the nights she stayed up and sang to her and poured every ounce of love she had into her, and yet, when it came down to it, she had failed her daughter these past few years. She had been completely oblivious to Keelan's ordeal.

Eamon had moved out and was renting a place in Athlone. He had told Deirdre about Paula from the golf club. How they wanted to take things slow, but that he was hoping they might have a future together. Deirdre was genuinely happy for him, but a small shard of resentment lodged in her throat. The years they had spent together, all for nothing now. The patience and under-standing and work she'd put into it. He had changed as a man for the better in many ways, and she would like to think that she had a hand in that. Now, another woman would reap the benefits. Her husband was in love with someone else. This very much confirmed the reality that huge changes had taken place in their lives. There was no going back now.

Keelan had been adamant that she was not keeping the child. She would not bring another one of the likes of Peter Delaney into the world. Deirdre had wanted to make sure that she wasn't just having a termination to spite him. As some sort of revenge because she knew how desperate he was for the child to be born. But Keelan had been absolutely certain. She wanted rid of it. She would never be free of him otherwise. Deirdre told her about her friend Aine in school, who got pregnant when she was 19 by one of her father's friends and she went to England on the boat. All on her own. Told no one, including Deirdre, until she got home. She was never the same girl after that. Like she was haunted by the memory of the child and what they might have grown up to be.

But Keelan had become distressed then. She didn't want this baby growing inside her. 'When I have a baby, I want it to be born in the right circumstances. Not like this. Please, Mam. Ye have to help me.' She had buried her head in her pillow and shook with crying. Deirdre lay down beside her and held her until eventually she calmed down and drifted off to sleep. Deirdre didn't move for a while. She felt her daughter's breathing against her body. She felt a terrible stab in her heart, but would have to accept that a termination was the only option.

Deirdre dished out apple tart and ice cream, which they all devoured except Keelan, who didn't want any.

'On a new diet, is it?' asked Eamon.

'No,' said Deirdre, 'she's cutting out a lot of sugar, that's all. Something we should all be doing.'

Oisín and Paudge didn't look up as they devoured the pie and ice cream. Eamon laughed at them.

Deirdre hadn't said anything to Eamon about the pregnancy. Keelan had made her swear not to tell him. Eamon was vehemently anti-abortion, and he would have made sure to delay or, at worst, even prevent her from undergoing one. He had always held very strong views on this, and campaigned in the referendums. It was his duty to protect people, he had told Deirdre one time, and he believed that everyone had a right to life.

Afterwards, at the door, as Eamon prepared to leave, he looked at his family, and Deirdre could sense how upset he was. She knew, like him, that this was a very unnatural moment. A man leaving a house that he had reared his children in. Stepping away into the rest of his life. Eamon took his key out and placed it on the hall stand.

'Ah, sure, keep it,' said Deirdre.

Eamon shook his head and left it where it was. He hugged

each of his children.

'Thanks for this. Yis are so … brilliant about … ye know … everything. I'm proud of all of ye.'

Oisín and Paudge glanced at their father. 'It's okay, Dad.'

'See ye at the match on Sunday.'

And then he was gone. The door closed. Deirdre went to do the washing up. Life would go on. That was always the amazing thing, thought Deirdre. Life always went on.

Herself and Keelan had gone to the Mullingar hospital the day before. They waited in the queue and Deirdre held her daughter's hand and squeezed and said, for the last time, 'Are ye sure?'

Keelan had nodded, and that was that.

The doctor explained that she would have to get a test, and then receive a cert to prove that the foetus was under 12 weeks old, and then there was a mandatory waiting period of three days before she could actually go through with the procedure.

The next day, the cert arrived and an appointment was booked in the hospital. Deirdre was aware that Delaney was calling and texting Keelan non-stop, so they turned off her phone.

'I'm fuckin' scared of him, Mam.'

'Look it, we'll just sit tight for the next few days, and then once it's done, we'll report the fucker if he doesn't leave you alone.'

Deirdre had made sure Oisín and Paudge were home later that evening, so Keelan wouldn't be on her own, as Deirdre needed to go and help Sister Senan. She could have rung her and cancelled, but truth be told, she needed the space afforded to her inside in the church. The time and peace to gather herself. She told Keelan she'd only be an hour or so.

She pulled up outside the church and greeted Sister Senan, then began to dress the altar with daffodils, and as she did she watched the old nun shuffle around, bent over, but always moving, intent on a task. The church and how it looked was her domain and responsibility, and it gave her a great purpose. Deirdre always thought it kind of extraordinary that an elderly nun like this would never have had sex or had kids or got drunk. Was she ever lonely, or did her faith always manage to fill her life, she wondered. Deirdre had always kind of pitied her, but this evening she envied the old nun's serenity and absolute certainty in her faith and about why she was on this earth.

Deirdre knelt with her then, as she always did when their chores were done, and they spent a few minutes praying.

Deirdre asked God to help and protect her daughter in what she was about to go through. She knew it was a bit mad praying to God for her daughter to have a safe and successful abortion, but she did it anyway. The God she liked to believe in was understanding. She blessed herself and got up from the pews.

'See you next week,' she said to the nun, putting the hood of her coat up, as it was lashing rain outside. As she darted from the front doors of the church to her car she saw there was a Kia Ceed parked up beside her that hadn't been there before. She pressed her key button to open the car door and was about to get inside when a figure got out of the other car and was suddenly up behind her. She turned to see who it was.

Delaney stood in the pouring rain. 'Please,' he said. 'Don't let her do it.'

Deirdre wanted to lash out at him. She could have scratched the fucking eyes out of his head, but she stopped herself. She needed to keep the head. Ignore him completely. She sat into the car.

Delaney reached in and grabbed her arm before she could shut the door. 'Please, I'm begging you. I have a right. It's my child. Please!'

Deirdre tried to wrench her arm free. 'Take your fucking hand off of me or I swear …'

Delaney wouldn't move his hand. 'If I could just see her. Tell her that we have a future together. We could be a family.'

Deirdre gathered every ounce of muscle and strength she had and grasped hold of the door handle and slammed the door hard against Delaney's arm. He let out a cry of pain. Deirdre got the door shut and locked. She started the engine. Delaney banged on the door.

'I won't let you do it. I'll be watching her. *I'll fucking stop her!*'

Deirdre drove away out the church gates. Her whole body shook. Her heart going 90 to the dozen. She didn't relax until she was back home inside her own four walls and had locked all the doors and windows.

She went up to see Keelan in her room and sat on the bed.

Keelan could see the state she was in. 'Are you okay, Mam?'

Deirdre tried to choose her words. She didn't want to panic her. 'I met Delaney down at the church. He said that he wanted to talk to you and all this shit. He's deluded himself into thinking ye can bring up the child together.'

Keelan sank down into the bed. Her face looked tired, and heavy from lack of sleep.

Deirdre reached across to stroke her cheek. 'It'll be okay, but I think we should seriously think about telling your dad. I don't feel safe getting you over to the hospital. He'll be watching the house. We need help, Keelan. What do you think?'

'No, Mam. You can't. We just fucking have to do this ourselves. Please. You know what he'll say. He has that fuckin' big thing about it. He'll try to stop me. Please, Mam, we can't tell him.'

Deirdre took this in and knew she was right. The last thing Keelan needed was Eamon getting in the way of her having the abortion. They would have to do this alone, unless there was someone who could drive them to the hospital. A male who would do them a favour. Immediately the image of Scobie Donoghue handing over the 500 euro to her that Sunday morning flashed into her head. She replayed their embrace once again, their hands all over each other, and thank God Angela had come home when she did. She turned to Keelan.

'Maybe Scobie Donoghue would drive us.'

The decision was made pretty quickly. They both felt they could trust him. Deirdre got on the phone and made the call.

'Hi,' she said, once he had answered. 'Listen, can you call up to the house?'

Scobie hesitated. 'Yeah. What for?'

'Please, it's important. I'll tell ye when I see ye.'

'Okay, I suppose,' said Scobie.

'Thanks, Scobie,' said Deirdre, and she hung up before he had a chance to change his mind.

Deirdre opened the door and Scobie stepped inside.

'Thanks so much for coming,' said Deirdre, ushering him into the sitting room.

Keelan, sitting on the sofa, phone in her *lámh*, looked up at Scobie and nodded. Deirdre sat beside her daughter while Scobie took the armchair.

'Would ye like tea or anything?' asked Deirdre.

Scobie shook his head. He cleared his throat just to break the silence. 'So what's up, like?'

'Okay,' said Deirdre. 'So listen. Meself and Keelan need to talk to you about something. It's very private and … and it can't go outside this room.'

Scobie didn't react. Deirdre could see he was looking increasingly nervous.

'Keelan's pregnant and she's not going to keep it,' stated Deirdre as matter-of-factly as she could.

'Okay. So you've made the decision,' said Scobie, looking to Keelan.

'I have. I've never been more sure of anything,' said Keelan. 'I have to be in Mullingar Regional Hospital the day after tomorrow at ten in the morning.'

Deirdre sat forward. 'I was hoping that you would drive us there.'

'Why? I mean, is your car fucked or something?' asked Scobie.

'No … we'd just like someone else with us,' said Deirdre.

'On account of who the father is,' said Keelan.

'Doesn't the father have a right to, ye know, have a say?'

'No,' Keelan shot back immediately. 'Not this man. No. A terrible mistake. Trust me, Scobie, I cannot have the child.'

'Who is it?' asked Scobie.

'You know who it is. You saw me with him, that morning I was trying to get away from him.'

It took a moment, but when it hit him Scobie sank back into the armchair. 'Fucking hell.'

'He's not right, Scobie,' said Deirdre. 'He's been watching her, so we'd just feel more secure if you could drive us.'

'What about Eamon?' asked Scobie.

Deirdre shook her head. 'We can't tell him. Seriously, Scobie, he's totally against abortion, and we just need to get this thing done with the minimum of fuss. Please, Scobie.'

Scobie was silent for a while. He eyed a photo on the mantelpiece of Keelan and her two brothers when they were young.

Deirdre leaned forward and looked to him. 'She's had a rough time. He was very controlling, Scobie. Like, in every way.'

'Jesus, okay,' Keelan said. 'That's enough, Mam. Please.'

Scobie sat forward and nodded. 'Okay. I'll bring ye.'

'Thanks Scobie,' said Deirdre. She saw him to the door. 'I really appreciate this.'

'Don't worry. We'll get you there.'

Deirdre leaned in and hugged him tightly, and then Scobie turned and headed for the car. She watched him drive off, and afterwards she closed the front door and put the lock on. Turning, she saw Keelan's feet disappearing from the top of the stairs and then heard the sound of her bedroom door closing. Deirdre followed her daughter up and stopped on the landing. 'Goodnight, love,' she said.

There was no answer. Deirdre continued on into her own room, went through her nightly rituals and got underneath the covers. She thought of the day she held the infant Keelan in her arms for the first time. There was a birthmark on her forehead, and Deirdre had kissed it softly. She'd had then a strong impulse to never let her go, and she felt that exact same impulse very strongly now. She closed her eyes and decided to say a rosary, like a mantra that might drop her off to sleep.

'Our Father, who art in Heaven, hallowed be thy name. Thy Kingdom come, thy will be done, on earth as it is in Heaven.'

She wondered whether Sister Senan was doing the same, above in the convent with the other ancient nuns, and she wondered if God had turned his back on the world a long time ago, and was it any use praying at all. But she decided it was. Just in case.

'Give us this day our daily bread, and forgive us our trespasses as we forgive those who trespass against us. And lead us not into temptation, but deliver us from evil. Amen.'

eighteen

Scobie Donoghue settled himself in his father's armchair and switched on the television as his mother called in from the kitchen.

'Is he on yet?'

'No,' said Scobie, who had just taken his last two Klonopin and was in a blissed-out nicely-fuzzy-at-the-edges state of being, so he could put off until later a freak-out about where he was going to get his hands on more of them.

The screen switched to inside government buildings, and the Taoiseach walked down the steps to make his speech to the nation. Scobie had often heard Bob refer to him as 'The biggest Tory since Thatcher', adding, 'I'm not being homophobic in any fuckin' way when I call him a cunt. He can have sex with chickens for all I care.' But Leo couldn't have cared less about what the likes of Bob Bonner thought of him, Scobie reckoned, because as he approached the lectern and microphones, he must have sensed that this might be his moment in Irish history.

Leo paused, looked out at the nation. 'Good evening, I want to speak to you about the next stage in our national response to the coronavirus emergency.'

'Ma, come on, he's started,' Scobie called into the kitchen, and she rushed into the room, parking herself on the sofa, with eyes and ears only for Leo, whom she had greatly warmed to since the Covid crisis began.

Leo went on with his carefully worded speech, attuned to his task, hitting all the notes that the media handlers had put down for him. 'At the beginning of this emergency, I told you that there would be difficult days ahead. We knew that the virus would spread in our country, that tragically, many of our citizens would suffer and that some would die.'

Scobie's head began to fill with the reality of what Keelan was about to do. He felt a sense of pride that he'd been asked. He was needed, and he wouldn't let them down. What did he feel about abortion? Miraculously, he had never had to face the dilemma himself. There had been burst johnnies and subsequent morning-after pills, and a few anxious prayers when there were late periods, but he had never had to get across to England with anyone. The thought of it sickened him, but he knew that in any of those cases he would have been across the Irish Sea like a shot.

Ella had been very adamant about the issue. 'Women are not fuckin' cows, we can't be expected to give birth just 'cause it's nature and somehow our duty is to put up and shut up. We have to be allowed choice. If men could have babies, they would have brought in legal abortion a hundred years ago.' Scobie smiled at the memory of her, when she'd be really het up over something, her eyes burning, and you knew that to argue would be a hopeless cause.

She had been the only woman he had ever felt like possibly having a child with, and even then, something deep down dark inside him had been terrified at the prospect.

Scobie's attention drifted back into the room just in time to hear Leo come to the end of his great address to the nation. 'What happens now is up to each one of us. Show your support to our healthcare staff. Show your support for everyone who is working in essential services or looking after our vulnerable citizens. Show that you care for your families and friends. Stay at home.'

And that was it. The gist of it was that everyone had to stay indoors and not venture outside beyond a two-kilometre limit. The country was in a strict lockdown.

Angela glanced across at him and said, 'I guess it's you and me, kid.'

'I guess so, Ma,' laughed Scobie.

As he always did at that time, Cliff rang, and she went into the kitchen to talk to him. Scobie channel-hopped, his senses not as relaxed as they would normally be under the influence of the Klonopin, because he knew he had to get his hands on some more.

Angela came back in after her call, and he could sense she was feeling sad, as the lockdown meant that she and Cliff might not hold each other again until who knows when.

'Come on, Ma, let's head out for a stroll. That's still allowed, isn't it? A two-kilometre stroll?'

Angela agreed and went into the hall to get her coat. They left the house and started to walk around by the school, the same route that Scobie had taken on his late-night sojourns. They walked mostly in silence, and any talk that did happen was all Angela.

'I'm goin' to miss playing the bridge something shocking. There's some that will really be affected, like the older ones, on their own.'

Scobie could see his mother was becoming upset, and it wasn't over the town's widows. He knew that she was missing the stupid big eejit Cliff. Scobie reached out and took her hand and squeezed it.

'He'll be home soon,' he said.

'I know,' she said, and she smiled in gratitude that her son had sensed how she was feeling.

Later that night, Scobie was sitting in bed looking at stupid videos on his phone. The pills were losing their effect, and he could feel the anxiousness creeping back into his veins. How would he occupy his time? How would he cope with all the free hours to think and nothing to take the sting out of it? Because work was cancelled for the foreseeable, would Scobie's typical routine of a Saturday and Sunday now be repeated every day? Out of the bed at around half nine. Breakfast. Lounge around looking at the

Internet. Help a small bit around the house. Go for a walk on his own to get groceries. Lunch. TV quiz shows with Angela, like *The Chase* and *Tipping Point*. Another walk, this time with Angela. Tea. TV. Internet porn. YouTube. Bed at midnight or so.

He was certain of one absolute fact – that without any pills he simply wouldn't be able to hack it.

The next morning, after a pretty sleepless night, Scobie got on the phone to Doc Byrne, who wasn't seeing anyone because of Covid restrictions. The receptionist said that Doctor Byrne would phone him back some time later that day. Scobie paced the bedroom and tried to watch a show that everyone was watching, about a young lad and a young one riding, but he couldn't concentrate on it. He knew it was good, but he hadn't the head space. Short stupid clips on YouTube were all he could take. And the craving was getting worse. His stomach was feeling sick, so when Angela called him for lunch, he called back down that he wasn't that hungry. 'Fuck fuck fuck fuck, ring you bollocks, Byrne. Ring me,' thought Scobie, who was sweaty now, lying on the bed trying to close his eyes and breathe, the way Ella had shown him, but it was impossible.

The ceiling seemed to swim above him like a great mass of ocean – deep, rough waters, with a hand reaching out above the waves. Were they waving or drowning? It was little Robbie. Like he was as a boy, crying out for help. Scobie turned over on his stomach and clenched his eyes shut. In the darkness the outline of a figure appeared, a hairy, wild, feral animal of great size. Scobie's jaws tightened so much he thought they might snap. The figure had long ears, great shining eyes, like a kangaroo, but with a savage mouth and sharp teeth, and as the figure became fully visible, he saw it had a man's torso and legs. But whatever class of a creation it was, it pulsated with a crazy, wild energy. The creature let out a low growl.

Scobie sat up in the bed, jumped out, stood up, raced downstairs, grabbed his coat and headed on out onto the safe streets of his hometown. Surely to Jaysus there were no monsters out there.

Scobie walked as fast as his legs would carry him up to Doc Byrne's surgery, hoping against hope that he was in there. He rang the buzzer. He waited. The receptionist's voice, with an Eastern European accent, came through to him.

'Sorry, but the doctor is not seeing anyone at present due to the—'

Scobie interrupted, 'Yeah, sure, I know – listen, this is an emergency. I have to see him.'

'I'm afraid that just isn't possible,' said the receptionist.

Scobie knocked on the surgery door. 'Doc, are ye in there? Just need a quick word.'

There was no reply except for the receptionist's voice. 'Please, Doctor Byrne is only taking appointments over the phone at this present time.'

Scobie kept pounding his fist on the door. 'I just need two minutes of your time. It's Scobie Donoghue. Please.'

The door opened, and the receptionist, a small lady with glasses, but with a no-nonsense, don't-fuck-with-me expression on her face, shook her head at him. 'Please,' she said, 'the doctor is busy on the phone all day. He will get to you when he can.'

At that moment, Byrne emerged from a room behind her. 'Everything okay, Katya?'

Scobie shoved his head in the door past Katya. 'Doc, I'm so sorry, but can I just see ye for two minutes? Please. You'd be doing me a huge favour.'

Katya shoved Scobie back out the door. 'Please, you go now or I get the guards.'

'Okay, Katya, thanks, but I'll see him,' sighed the doc.

Katya shrugged, putting her eyes to heaven and stepping aside. 'Okay, but not long, okay, Doctor Byrne? You have many calls.'

Katya went back to her desk. Byrne pointed to the room he had just emerged from. 'Go on in there. Just give me a minute to take a leak,' he said, before heading to the toilet.

Inside the surgery Scobie settled himself, looking to the chart of the human body on the wall, posters for good health practices, and he hoped that this would be a straightforward deal and he'd be up to the medical hall and bingo, he'd be all set up again. Byrne arrived in, sat, reached for his glasses, opened a file and found Scobie's chart. Scobie knew Byrne was into amateur dramatics.

'Thanks so much for this, doc. I hear the last play ye did was great. Me ma went and said you were deadly, like.'

Doc Byrne looked up from the chart for a moment and smiled, but the attempt to butter him up hadn't succeeded. 'Right, what's the problem?'

Scobie smiled, trying to be casual. 'Ah, it's just I've been feeling a bit, ye know, like I told ye the last time, anxious, so I took the Xanax, which were great, and then I stopped taking them 'cause everything was good, but now recently I've begun to, ye know … it's started up again.'

Byrne nodded. 'The same feelings as before?'

'The same,' said Scobie.

'Do you feel worse than you did before?'

'Yes. Well, to be honest, I do feel a lot worse. Like maybe it's the whole Covid thing, ye know, so maybe I need something a bit stronger this time, like there's this stuff Klonopin that someone was telling me about. Do you ever prescribe that?'

Byrne shook his head. 'No, I certainly wouldn't be recommending Klonopin. Not a chance. I would urge you to consider some other way of dealing with this.'

Scobie's whole demeanour dropped. He couldn't help it. 'Oh right, well, I need something, ye know, doc.'

Byrne shook his head again. 'The only thing I'm willing to give you is a small amount of Valium, but I would be urging you to look at things like diet and exercise, which really are key here. I could pass you on to an excellent counsellor.'

'Ah, right. Okay.' Scobie was gutted, and couldn't speak.

Byrne wrote a name and number out on the back of one of his cards. 'John Cronin. He's a really good, straight-up counsellor. I think you'd like him. He's a bit of craic, like.'

Scobie took the card and put it in his pocket like a man who had no intention in the world of ever calling the number.

Byrne wrote out a prescription for Valium. 'I'm telling you, Scobie, that this is the best way to go. It's tougher, but long term giving you pills is not the answer. Have you talked to Angela about it?'

Scobie shook his head.

'It might help if you do,' said Byrne. 'Give me a ring any time.'

Byrne got up and showed Scobie out to the door, patting his shoulder on the way out.

'Thanks, doc,' said Scobie, but he didn't mean it.

He wanted to turn around, pin him to the fucking wall and demand to know where he kept the pills. He imagined a secret room piled high with tablets of every variety, the answer to all his prayers, if only mean little Katya would hand over the keys. Instead, he had to act all polite and apologetic to Katya as he left the surgery to trudge up the town to the medical hall to secure his pathetic prescription for Valium.

Scobie sat in his father's armchair, his foot tapping, the inside of his mouth dry. The TV was very bright in the room, game show lights up and down, and he felt as though he was suffering from that thing – what do ye call it? They had to carry Budgie Burke out of the cinema that time on the school tour because he fainted. What was it? Oh yeah, epilepsy, like he had the Jaysus epilepsy or something, but the lights continued to flash up and down as the contestant stepped up to the mark to take on the Chaser.

Angela watched beside him. 'This fella will be good now.'

The contestant was advised to go for the jackpot and he risked it, so now he could only afford to get two questions wrong or he'd be caught by the Chaser, who's one of the quiz grand-masters on the show. There was a different Chaser on each time, and they had nicknames, like the Dark Destroyer or the Beast or the Governess. Scobie felt anxious now for the contestant, as though he was standing right beside him, as though he had sunk right inside the TV and was standing under the heat of the studio lights, and the contestant looked like Robbie – a healthy, clean-looking Robbie who was all smiles, who winked at Scobie as if to say, no problem, I have the jackpot in the bag.

But suddenly the studio lights went dark, like there'd been some sort of power cut. All Scobie could see was a single light bulb hanging from the ceiling, illuminating the Chaser, who now looked like the half-man/half-kangaroo monster, with his low growl, teeth and long tongue. Scobie looked around for Robbie but he was nowhere to be seen. Then in a flash the studio lights flipped back on again to reveal that the monster, the Chaser, had sprung from its seat to descend on poor, helpless Robbie, who tried to shout out an answer to the question but he was too late, and the kangaroo monster bit his head off with a fierce crunch, and there was blood everywhere. Scobie shot back out of the TV and the studio, back into his father's chair, with his mother's voice next to him.

'Scobe, are ye all right there?'

Scobie came back to this world to find his mother looking at him. 'Ye were dozing or something, shifting around there like a mad yoke.'

'Oh, right,' said Scobie, but he couldn't stay put for a second longer. This was unbearable. He leapt up and out of the room, on up the stairs to his bedside table to rummage for another Valium, but they were like drinking non-alcoholic beer after downing a bottle of Jägermeister. Not worth a hat of shite! He had to be doing something. He had to go somewhere, and so set off on a walk around the town, but as he left the house, an unusual burst of late-afternoon sun came out, and it seemed far too bright for him, so he shielded his eyes and one of the cattle trucks drove by with the noise of the engine cutting into his head. So he put his hands over his ears to block out the sound.

He walked on, as fast as he could, trying to get away from all visions of the half-man/half-kangaroo monster. He could hear its low growl and its breath behind him. He reached a quieter area of the town, on St Kevin's Avenue, and when he turned the corner, he knew that it was all meant to be. He was a stone's throw away from Robbie's grandmother's house, where the lad had stayed when Julie the mother went off to England with the boyfriend. He would call in to her, offer support and help to find her grandson. That's what today was all about. It was clear to him now. It was all about Robbie.

He approached the bungalow at the end of the terrace, searching his internal files for the name, her name – on the tip of his tongue. Kearney? Maura? No. Nora? No. Nuala? That was it, Nuala Kearney, who was married to Noel, who used to train Scobie years ago in the Under-12 football. A big man with even bigger blood pressure, red as a beetroot on the sideline, willing them to win, wanting them to win more than life itself. Scobie had always liked him, and was sorry to hear that he had passed away a few years ago. Scobie went up to the door and rang the bell, as he prepared to offer his belated condolences. He heard footsteps, and then the door opened ever so slightly. A woman in her early seventies, with a smoker's face but lively, intelligent-looking eyes, peered out at him.

'What can I do for you?' she asked politely.

Scobie coughed and cleared his throat. 'Hi. It's Nuala, isn't it?'

Nuala nodded. 'That's me.'

'Great, how are ye, I'm Scobie Donoghue. Your husband Noel used to train me years ago. I just wanted to say how sorry I am to hear that he'd passed away, like I was in Australia when he—'

Nuala cut across him. 'I know where you were.'

'Oh yeah, of course,' said Scobie. 'How's Julie getting on?'

'She's grand,' said Nuala. 'Now if there's nothing else. You know I'm trying to keep my distance from people. I have a bad chest, so …'

Scobie had a wave of nervous energy surging around his body, which made his face twitch, especially around his forehead. Nuala spotted this. There's something off with this lad, she thought. She didn't know what, but he seemed a bit restless in himself. So she went to shut the door, but Scobie put his hand on it, applying a gentle but clear shove to keep the door open.

'Sorry, it's just Robbie, ye know, I was wondering if you'd heard anything?'

Nuala stopped, pausing at the door, glancing down at Scobie's hand. He withdrew the offending paw. Nuala sighed, a hint of sadness appearing in her eyes. 'He hasn't been in touch. Now, if you'll excuse me.' Nuala attempted to close the door for a second time, but again Scobie put the hand out to stop her.

'Listen, Nuala, that's why I'm here, really. You know, I want to try and help find Robbie, because he's a great lad, if he was given half a chance, like.' Scobie hadn't drawn breath, unaware of how fast he was talking.

'Thank you, but there's no need,' said Nuala, pulling the door as hard as she could to try and get rid of this man, who was now beginning to unnerve her just a little bit.

Scobie was forced to whip his hand out of the way as the door slammed. He knocked on the door, with a much greater ferocity then he was aware of, and yelled, 'Please, Nuala, come on, I need to talk to you. I want to help. I need to help.'

He walloped the door with his fist, causing Nuala to shout from inside, 'I appreciate the concern. But please go away.'

'Nuala, I'll go wherever I need to go to find him and bring him back. Nuala. Come on. Nuala!'

But there was no sound from the house now. Scobie did a quick check of the surrounds, but there was only one twitching curtain across the road, so he hightailed it around the back of the house. He was in the throes now of something far more powerful than himself – a manic drive that made him scale the back wall and jump down into Nuala's small yard and approach her kitchen window.

'Nuala,' he called out, 'sorry, do you want to have a chat about Robbie and how I'm going to find him?'

Nuala's face appeared in the kitchen window, pinched and frightened. She was clutching a mobile phone. 'I'll call the guards if you don't get off my property,' she said.

Scobie protested. 'Ah, Nuala, there's no need for that. I'm Scobie Donoghue. You can trust me. You can put your faith in me. I won't let you down. I swear. I swear on my dead father's life!'

Scobie's head was suddenly bombarded with flashes of Eddie, in the truck, watching the westerns in the armchair and something else, something unfamiliar, his father's hand, his nicotine-stained fingers, around his young shoulders, laughing with someone else. Was it a woman's laugh? What type of room did the memory take place in? It wasn't the house at home but some strange place. It mustn't have happened. It's some sort of imagining. It took Scobie out of the moment, stalled his single-minded tunnel-vision need to see Nuala. He saw the mobile up to her ear.

'Go on now like a good man and clear off or I'm going to phone the guards.'

Scobie wished she would realise that he was actually the answer to her prayers. That he was the one to bring Robbie home. He wished she wouldn't look so scared. He changed his mind. The time for talk was done. Time for action. That was what he'd do. Get the fuck away and bring Robbie back to her.

He gave Nuala the thumbs up. 'No need for that,' he said. 'Not a bother. I'm going.' And he turned and lifted the latch on the back door of the yard and let himself out. Nuala sighed in relief when the door closed after him, taking the mobile away from her ear and wondering what was possessing the man. Should she phone Angela, just to let her know what had happened? She had her number somewhere from organising whist drives years ago for the GAA club. Nuala stood pondering, and then thought of Robbie and worried about him and the country and the whole world, because everything seemed a bit unhinged at the minute.

Scobie walked back around home, his head down. He had it all worked out now. He'd drive Deirdre and Keelan to the hospital in the morning and then he'd go and see Eamon. The sergeant would know what to do. He'd report Robbie as a missing person. He'd get Interpol on the job. Scobie went in through the sliding doors and Angela was sitting at the kitchen table, giving him a funny kind of look. Like she was pissed off with him or something. Scobie paid this no mind and was all bright and breezy.

'So, Ange, what's the story? This lockdown craic is grand, isn't it? Nothing to do and all day to do it.'

Angela nodded, but her mouth was tight. She glanced out the window.

'Are you all right?' he asked.

Angela tried to smile. 'Do ye mind me asking ye something there, son?'

'Not at all. Fire ahead,' said Scobie.

'How are ye feeling, in yourself, like?' asked Angela.

'The ol' tummy is a bit off,' said Scobie.

'It's just I got a call,' said Angela, 'from Nuala Kearney.'

'For fuck's sake,' said Scobie.

'She wasn't tellin' tales or anything, she just felt that I should know. I mean, what were ye at?' asked Angela.

'Nothing. I just saw the house, called in on a whim and she wouldn't talk to me. I just wanted to see if I could help in some way with Robbie. He does be on my mind, but she closed the door in my face, like I was some sort of weirdo. Like I was some sort of madman, and I wasn't going to have that, Ma. I wasn't going to be treated like that.'

'Come here, son, it's okay. Ye can talk to me, ye know. What's up with ye?'

Scobie went to the fridge and looked in. 'There's nothing up with me. I'm grand. Just a bit tired and – ah look, I have stuff going on.'

'What kind of stuff?'

Scobie turned and went for the door to the hall. 'Nothing for you to be thinking about, okay? Forget I said anything. Do you want a takeout tonight? Save you cooking. I'll run out to Ping's.'

'No. I have chicken fillets defrosted.'

'Oh, grand.' He saw the worried look on his mother's face. He couldn't bear the sight of it. He moved towards her and held out his arms and enveloped her in a tight hug and kissed her face.

'It's all good, Ma. I'm grand. It's the fuckin' Covid. I heard a lad on the radio. Ye know, apparently, we all feel a fierce amount of stress about it. Under the surface, like. So I went off on one there today, but I'm grand now.'

Angela relaxed a little and put her hand on his head. He kept hold of her. He had to try and keep it together for Ange's sake. Had to protect her above everything else. Not to mention he needed to be steady for Deirdre and Keelan tomorrow. He needed to get through the night with nothing in his system bar poxy Valium. But it was better than nothing. She just didn't understand what he was trying to do. Poor Nuala. She was lonely, and her mind probably played tricks on her. She just didn't understand what kind of a man he was. He shouldn't have scared her like that. But she'd come around some day. She'd realise that he was a good man. Only ever thinking of other people and always ready to put himself out for them.

nineteen

Scobie had a fitful night of sleep, and emerged bleary-eyed from the bedroom at half six after binge-watching some American true crime yoke. He showered and ate porridge alone, as Angela was still in the cot. Then he got a call. It was from Deirdre.

'Hello, Scobie, listen. He's been outside the house all night. Parked across the street. Watching us. So we have to get going to Mullingar hospital as soon as possible. Me and Keelan can get over the back garden wall and come out along the lane. You know it, it comes out at the corner of Ping's Chinese. Pick us up there in half an hour. Okay?'

Scobie didn't answer immediately. Lack of sleep had left him groggy.

Deirdre's voice cut into his ear. 'Scobie, come on. Did you fucking hear what I said? We need to get out of the town without him knowing.'

'Okay, sure. I'll be there in ten. Yeah.'

'Yeah. At the end of the back lane, opposite Ping's.'

'Got it,' said Scobie, but he could feel his guts weren't the Mae West. He'd hoped that the porridge might have helped. The GERD was acting up. The tension was getting to him. He stirred himself to get out of the house before Angela surfaced.

Scobie pulled up across the road from Ping's Chinese on the midland side of the town. He waited. The radio was on. They were playing an old song by The Jam, an English group that Cliff used to bang on about. Then he spotted them emerging out of the end of the lane, like a pair of frightened refugees. They hurried across to him. Keelan got in the back seat. Deirdre sat in beside him.

'Okay, Scobie. Thanks for this,' said Deirdre.

Scobie saw Keelan in the rear-view mirror. She looked real worried, and probably hadn't slept any better than he had himself. She leaned her head up against the window, staring out into space.

'We'll get there in no time,' said Scobie. He reversed and did a U-turn so they could speed off in the right direction for Mullingar. They made it out of the town, passing the building site, closed down, with not a sinner on it. He drove them on in silence out into the countryside, passing the fields and trees and the odd bungalow, and he could feel a kind of collective easing of the nerves inside in the car. They had made it out of the town, away from Delaney, so for now, they could try and relax.

Scobie chanced turning the radio back up. The news was on, the headlines being read out. Seventy-four new cases in Ireland. Four hundred and seventy-five deaths in Italy over the past 24 hours, but coronavirus somehow seemed in that particular moment very irrelevant to the three of them. The classic hits station resumed its tunes from the eighties and nineties, and 'Shiny Happy People' by REM filled the car, and neither Deirdre nor Keelan seemed to object.

As they drove on, Scobie half thought he should try and distract them with talk, but then decided to just let them be in their own worlds, so the only sound in the car was Huey Lewis and the News with 'The Power of Love'. Scobie gripped the steering wheel, checking the rear-view, and saw a country road and two cars behind him. He had a spider sense, like the hairs on the back of his neck were telling him that Delaney wasn't far away. Scobie wiped his tired eyes and heard his sick stomach gurgling. He tapped his finger on the steering wheel along to the next few tracks – Lionel Richie's 'Dancing on the Ceiling', Bruce Springsteen and 'Glory Days' and just as Oasis were revving up to belt out 'Don't Look Back in Anger' they reached the roundabout outside Mullingar. He ignored the first road heading to the town centre and took the road for Mullingar Regional Hospital. He glanced up in the rear-view mirror. Where was Delaney? He must be here somewhere, in one of those cars. A man like him didn't ever let up.

Scobie felt a real compulsion to turn off the road. To drive away and escape into the west. If only he was on a horse. 'Take 'em to Missouri, men!' He saw Eddie hollering at him from across the cab of the truck, and the boy, Scobie, would say, 'A man's got

to do something for a livin' these days.' Eddie, the Major cigarette clamped tight between his teeth, his eyes squinted like Clint,
would reply, 'Dyin' ain't much of a livin', boy.' Scobie wished that
Eddie was here now to help him keep strong and be brave, because
he looked up in the rear-view once more and was sure he saw
Delaney's head in a Kia Ceed behind him. He looked again. The
car was closer now, so he had a better view of the driver. It wasn't
Delaney. Scobie relaxed, but his nerves remained on high alert. He
pulled into the car park of the hospital and found a space.

Scobie turned off the engine. 'Well, *sin é.*'

Keelan nodded, but seemed very ill at ease, a look of great
apprehension on her face. Deirdre gathered her bag and opened
the car door.

'Hope it all goes okay,' said Scobie.

Deirdre got out of the car. Keelan followed her. Scobie watched
them like a hawk as they made their way across the car park.
Deirdre would be forced to leave her daughter at the hospital doors,
as she wasn't permitted inside because of Covid. Scobie pushed
the seat back, turned off the radio and tried to settle himself. He
was overtired and fidgety, and he reached for another Valium.

He looked at the hospital building and had a vision of the day
in Melbourne when they pulled up in the mad emergency, Ella in
such pain with desperate cramping, and it was only five months
gone, and the fear in her eyes as he tried to bolster her up with
empty words and gestures. Rushing inside and being confronted
with the hive of hospital activity, trying to be seen and heard
among all the mayhem, but they ended up being treated incredibly
well in the place. The doctors and nurses had been amazing, but

the one thing they couldn't manage was to save the baby.

Scobie came back into the here and now as Deirdre and Keelan reached the front entrance and stopped, still deep in conversation. Deirdre held her hand tightly. Keelan still looked worried. Scobie knew how tough it must be to have to let your daughter go on through on her own, into the world of disinfectant and white coats and the invasive nature of what was about to happen to her. Scobie shut his eyes but his stomach churned, his head swam. He took a breath, wishing he had the proper pills. His nerves tingled. His whole body was on high alert with nerve-twisting tension, clenching his fists. It was like the night in the outback in Oz. The same fear. The same feeling of trepidation. Like the poor creatures hiding behind the gum trees knew that something bad was about to happen. The heat, the sound of the cicadas, the tequila, the weed high. Majella's infectious energy as she asked him, 'Do ye know how many kangaroos have to be culled each year?' Scobie had no clue. 'Three million,' she'd told him. 'Like, they'd overrun the country otherwise.' And she'd laughed.

Scobie suddenly felt very sick again, like down to his toes. He opened his eyes. He knew what he was going to see before he saw it. He could feel it, deep down where all his instinct and secret wisdom was buried. Inside in that cave they had it drawn on the walls. The hospital car park in Mullingar, a Kia Ceed pulling in and a man getting out. Hell-bent on entering the building and stopping what he would see as murder of his flesh and blood.

Scobie scrambled from the car as Delaney moved past, marching through the car park. He felt the pain in his guts as he stormed past Delaney and stood in front of him. Delaney looked straight through Scobie, as if he didn't exist, like he was just an empty space. In Delaney's line of vision there was nothing except the hospital and the girl who was about to go inside it to terminate his child.

Scobie spread his arms. 'Listen, leave her in peace, just back off now.'

Delaney continued to ignore Scobie's presence, just kept ploughing on through the car park. Scobie smelt the fresh drink on Delaney's breath as he grabbed his collar to try and force him back.

'Please just turn around,' said Scobie.

Delaney stopped in his tracks. 'This has nothing to do with you.' He tried to push Scobie aside, but Scobie held firm. They grappled, and fell up against one of the parked cars. Some of the patients out smoking spotted the scuffle.

'It's over, Peter. Just let it go.'

'No. Get off me or I'll fucking kill you!' roared Delaney. He pushed Scobie away and kept going. Scobie looked to see Deirdre giving Keelan a final hug before she disappeared inside. He gathered himself then charged after Delaney and grabbed his jacket collar again, trying to reef him back. Delaney swung around viciously with his arm and caught Scobie on the forehead, knocking him sideways to the ground. As Delaney stormed on, Scobie wiped the blood from his face, got to his feet, jumped for Delaney and managed this time to pull him down.

The two men wrestled with each other, and although Delaney was gym-strong and in much better shape than him, something primal took over inside in Scobie and he managed to pin Delaney to the tarmac. He wanted to crush him, but not physically. He'd never manage that, so he opened his mouth, and a guttural sound formed words in the back of his throat – 'She doesn't want your child! After what you've done? Are you fucking insane? She'll be relieved to be rid of it.'

This hit Delaney in the guts. He was stunned for a second, speechless. All eyes in the hospital car park were trained on them. Scobie looked over at Deirdre, who had turned away from the front doors and had seen them for the first time. A look of fear struck her face, and for a moment, she was paralysed. What should she do? She spotted a security guard in the foyer of the hospital and dashed inside to alert him to what was going on.

Delaney let out a roar into the heavens, and used the energy from this to push Scobie off of him. He hauled himself up to his feet, stumbled across to where he'd left his car. He collapsed in behind the wheel. Shut the door and started the engine.

Scobie stormed across, a man possessed, in the madness of the moment, to put himself in jeopardy, because Delaney had to be stopped. The man could not be allowed to get away. Scobie stood in front of the car. Delaney revved the engine. Scobie banged the bonnet of the car and shouted, 'Come back, ye coward, face up to it! You're fucked!'

Delaney roared back, 'Out of the way! I swear to God, get out my fucking way or I'll run you down!'

Scobie felt a rush of fear all over his body, but his nerve endings were numbed somewhat by the pills. Somebody shouted something behind him. He turned to see the security guard charging out from the hospital, with Deirdre alongside him. Time seemed to stand still. Scobie's whole sensory perception seemed to narrow its focus. It was just him and Delaney in the universe. The car revved and its thousand kilograms of metal moved off, straight for Scobie, whose whole body tensed, ready to leap to safety, but instead he threw himself onto the bonnet and grabbed hold of the side mirror as the car accelerated through the car park.

Delaney's view was blocked by Scobie's body, and he swerved to avoid the side of a parked car and veered off, heading slam bang towards a low wall. Scobie flung himself off the bonnet and landed on the ground with a dead thud, shouting out in pain. Delaney managed to brake hard, and the car slowed before it hit the wall, lessening the severity of the impact, which caused his head to jolt forward, and he caught the side of his forehead against the steering wheel, and blood and tears rolled down his face.

As Scobie lay on the ground his eyes flickered open and pain shot down his back and leg. Delaney sat in his stationary car, his head in his hands, looking like a man who wanted to curl his whole body up into a ball, like all he craved was to be buried in the bowels of the earth. He knew that he had lost all control, and for a man like him, this meant that he had lost everything.

twenty

Scobie settled himself into his father's armchair with a steaming mug of tea, and Angela placed a slice of her famous lemon cake in front of him. The way his mother had treated him over the past eight days – with fries cooked every morning for when he eventually surfaced from the bed at noon, and instructions that he wasn't to lift a finger to do anything around the house – made him feel like the vainglorious hero of the hour. He basked in her attention, as the cakes and desserts and tarts she'd produced in abundance made his belly stretch against every shirt he possessed.

Eamon Freeman had called around with a bottle of 12-year-old malt whiskey. Scobie presumed that Deirdre must have put him up to it, as Eamon was not his biggest fan, and it probably annoyed him no end to have to acknowledge Scobie's part in the whole affair. But Eamon had sat in the kitchen and drunk tea with him, and had spoken very candidly. 'I feel very bad about the whole thing. I was the one who introduced him into our home, who trusted him. I was completely taken in by him. I don't mind admitting to you that I even considered handing in my resignation after the other morning. What kind of sergeant am I to have misjudged a man's character so badly?'

Scobie had poured him more tea and indicated the bottle of malt. 'Do you want a drop?'

'Ah, no thanks. I have a drive ahead of me. I'm not staying in the town at the moment. I'm sure you've heard that myself and Deirdre are no longer together.'

'I'd heard that, yeah.'

Eamon took a sip of tea.

'And what about Delaney?' asked Scobie.

'He's been suspended pending an investigation. He could face charges of police brutality and coercive control, and we'll be in touch with you and other people to give evidence. There've been other complaints, including from his ex-partner, for harassment and controlling behaviour. Anyway, I won't rest until he does some time.'

'And is there any sign of Robbie McNamee?'

'No. He was seen leaving the town on the bus. We know that. His grandmother has been in touch with us. So we're looking into it.' Eamon stopped then and looked into his tea, and he shook his head slowly. 'I was very upset about the termination. I don't care what anyone says. I think it's a tragedy that it was voted in. No civilised society should allow it. I know women have rights, but to end a life before it's even begun? I lie awake some nights and imagine holding the child in my arms, or taking him to his first football match. I wish I'd been given the chance to persuade her to keep it. You know … Poor little thing.' Eamon took a moment before looking Scobie squarely in the eye. 'You were around to tackle Delaney, and I thank you for that, but you had no right driving Keelan to get that abortion. No right.'

Scobie shrugged. 'Sorry, Eamon, but it was her choice, like.'

Eamon got up then, and Scobie saw him to the front door and watched him drive away. He'd heard that he was seeing the widow from the golf club. Scobie genuinely wished him well for the future. Love was a very hard thing to find, and it was even harder to keep hold of. A feeling of sadness came over him then as he went inside to be bombarded by Angela with questions about Eamon's visit.

Deirdre and Keelan had also called around with a hamper of stuff, and Scobie was glad to see that the girl was doing well after her ordeal. No regrets. She had plans for the future, with an idea to apply for a Canadian visa. She said she felt like she had been released from something. Her head was clearer, so she could see some kind of way forward. Above all, they both felt incredibly grateful to Scobie, and they weren't shy about spreading the word around about how Scobie had helped to expose Delaney.

Scobie would walk through the aisles of Lidl now and was nodded to by complete strangers or older townsfolk he hadn't seen in years. Of course, a few denizens of the parish weren't too impressed with him having caused a crash in a public car park while aiding and abetting an abortion, not to mention fighting with a member of An Garda Síochána. But the likes of Hog Hughes were fierce impressed, and Hog had burst into the chorus of Tina Turner's 'We Don't Need Another Hero'.

'*Maith an fear*,' Hog had said. 'Good man. I heard what ye did there.'

Mole Mulvin insisted on buying him a six-pack of cut-price German beer. 'Well rid of that fucker,' wheezed Mole. 'Scobie-Wan Kenobi, you're some man for one man.'

And, best of all, Kimberly Nolan stopped to chat to him. She was a 'posh bogger' solicitor's daughter, now living in Dublin but home for lockdown with her parents. A 100 per cent horn-on-brass monkey's ride of a thing who'd stopped him on the street, and this was the best bit, while he was having a stroll with Bob and Niallers. The two lads' eyes were out on stalks as Scobie let on to be real cool, the height of modesty. 'Like, anyone woulda done what I did' kinda thing, which made Kimberly even more impressed. Oh, yeah! Scobie Donoghue felt as tall as the town hall clock. He had his balls back, and no doubt.

Scobie finished his lemon cake. He felt weirdly empty, as if he had really enjoyed something and looked forward to it, but now it was gone. He had an empty plate. He could make more tea. He could do anything – he was Scobie Donoghue, man of the hour – but somehow, he felt a kind of hollow feeling inside. It was back to ordinary life, which meant his brain could settle and muse on what he was at.

A terrible sadness welled up in him over the next few weeks, sending him into a downward spiral, sinking in quicksand, and now even the Valium had run out. He continued to have sleepless nights, sweaty and too warm, or he'd be woken by bad coughing, so he was absolutely certain that he had the Covid. That was it. The night terrors struck him. He'd end up in ICU, gasping for air, and they'd just have run out of ventilating machines, so he'd be left to die in agony. But when he woke in the morning the cough was always gone and his breathing was fine.

The long days stretched out ahead of him with nothing to do and no way of getting the medication he needed. A huge anxiety chased through his system. He could sense the kangaroo monster lurking somewhere nearby. Making noises. A harbinger of dread. He couldn't be here, he decided. He had to move. He stood up, flung on his jacket and scampered out of the house, past his mother, who looked up from her flower bed.

'Where are you off to?'

Scobie kept going, and waved back at her. Where *was* he going? The usual. The mouse run. He walked the well-worn path past the school to Dinny's Hole, but suddenly felt tired and short of breath. He needed to take the weight off his feet. His energy was dropping right down because he hadn't eaten properly. He lay down under the yew tree with his head resting against the bottom of the trunk, and when he closed his eyes he was sure he could hear the low growl of the kangaroo monster. It had been following him. It wouldn't leave him alone. Why should it, after what he'd done?

In his mind's eye he saw the clear Australian night sky above him. He was in the back of the pick-up truck, sprawled out and heading into the outback. For a while he had been able to banish that night to the back of his mind, but now it hurtled forward and took over. Bumping around in the back of the truck, over potholes, taking corners, tearing away down the road, down the rabbit hole of a warm, humid Aussie night. He swigged at a bottle of tequila, feeling warm and fuzzy, grinning as his eyelids began to close. He would fall away for a moment. Ella appeared to hover over him with a child in her arms. The child cried and Scobie took it from Ella and held it close and he spoke to it, saying 'I will keep you safe and sound', and then the child was gone and all Scobie could see was the bottle of tequila in his arms.

The truck moved faster and more smoothly now, as though it had reached a proper motorway. He heard the engines of other vehicles. The movement created a welcome cooling breeze in the back of the truck. Scobie noticed the light attached to the roof of the truck's cab. A kind of searchlight. He wondered what the fuck it was used for. He heard Majella let out a laugh from inside the cab, the loud drunken voices of her boyfriend, Declan, and the big man, George, yammering away.

He had been introduced to both men earlier that evening, when he'd found his way to the house of his one-time girl-friend from back home and been shocked that she'd ended up in Scumshine. Majella had nodded towards a gangly looking lad who wore a sun hat that said 'Up the Rebels', as if he was on the way to Semple Stadium for a Munster final. 'This is Declan.'

'Pleased to meet ye, Declan,' Scobie had said, reaching out to receive a weak fist bump. 'What part of Cork are you from, boy?'

'Baltimore,' muttered Declan, wearing a fixed smile, eyes

focused somewhere in the middle distance. He'd offered a joint to Scobie, who'd taken a deep drag. Just what the doctor ordered.

Majella had been full of energy and jittery excitement. As if she might stand up and scream at any given moment. 'Isn't this the most fucking amazing thing that has ever happened in, like, forever? Like, would we have ever pictured when we were messing at the back of Screwy Huey's maths class that one day we'd be sitting on the other side of the world getting high and drinking beer?!'

Scobie had felt his head blasting off as the joint hit him. It had been proper gear, whatever it was. 'It's crazy shite all the same. Life. Ye know. We have no clue really, Majella darlin'.'

Majella had thrown up her arms then. 'I spread me wings, Scobie! I absolutely love Oz and the pals I've made here. I am free here to really be myself. Nobody knows my business or judges me, and I don't give a fuck anymore about nothing.'

Scobie had noticed the deep throatiness to her voice, sounding older than she was. There was an unhealthy rattle when she coughed, which she did at regular intervals. She had rested her face on Scobie's cheek then, and left it there. He had felt her hot breath. His head swam. Minutes passed in suspended animation. Scobie realised that he was very stoned. As if he had stepped out of time. Reality was now behind a fog. He had passed into a netherworld. There were shapes in front of him. Voices. Laughter. He registered them on some level, but his whole system had momentarily been completely paralysed by the strength of the cannabis.

Scobie had opened his eyes then to see that a big bloke had arrived. He had a beard, and he wasn't white, but native-looking, the type of lad who could be any age. He held out his hand for Scobie to shake.

'Hi, the name's George. Pleased to meet ye!'

Scobie took his hand and George squeezed hard. Scobie was glad when he released it. 'How's it hangin', George?'

'Bloody good, man.'

'Where are you from, boss?'

'I'm from Kiribati originally, and I'm sorry to tell you that I have no Irish blood in me at all, and more's the pity. I fuckin' wish I had. I have a bit of English in me, on my father's side. Some English magistrate bastard had sex with one of my ancestors. She was a maid in the colonial mansion. Probably raped her. That's a lot of trauma handed down the line, man. Don't let my name fool you. Slaying the dragon and all that shit. I hate the fuckin' Brits! Fuckin' evil empire. Invaded all but 22 countries of the world.' George stopped then and closed his eyes in deep concentration. 'Right. Here goes. Andorra, Belarus, Bolivia, Burundi, Central African Republic, Chad, Congo, Guatemala, Ivory Coast, Kyrgyzstan, Liechtenstein, Luxembourg, Mali, Marshall Islands, Monaco, Mongolia, Paraguay, São Tomé and Príncipe, Sweden, Tajikistan, Uzbekistan and, last but not least, Vatican City. The only ones to escape the bastards!'

Declan waved at George to distract him, holding out a pipe, and George took it and inhaled with three or four short, sharp intakes of breath. Scobie took up the pipe and repeated the action. Whatever the hell was inside in it, this batch had really got to him.

George's mouth was still moving. His eyes like giant saucers of translucent greens and browns. 'Could get up to 34 degrees tonight, maybe we could all go for a little drive to cool down.'

Glasses were thumped down on the table. Majella and Declan chugged back tequila slammers. Scobie grabbed his, put his hand over the glass and slammed it on the table. The liquid fizzed as he gulped it down. '*Whoooooooaaaahhhh! Now we're at it!*' he shouted. Just the right injection to get up, up, up again.

They did another round of slammers and then George bawled out, '*Roll up! Roll up for the mystery tour!*' at the top of his voice, jumping into the cab of his pick-up truck. '*Come on and hop in. We're goin' for a ride!*'

Majella and Declan both yelled 'Shotgun!' at the same time, and then they clambered into the cab with George. Majella called back out to Scobie, 'Sorry, Scobe, you're in the back.'

And so there he was, splayed out, hurtling along, downing tequila and looking up into the vast night sky and wondering if there was a lad like him millions of light years away looking up at his sky and wondering if there was a lad like him, a million light years away ... and then the vibration underneath him came to a halt. The truck's engine had cut out.

Majella hopped out of the cab and walked around to the back of the truck and climbed in beside Scobie. She grabbed the bottle off of him and took a swig. 'All right, Scobe,' she said, 'this is gonna be some craic!'

Scobie could barely make her out in the pitch darkness. They were out in the fucking sticks, and then a bit further out than that. He heard the noises of the bush. A full chorus. The cicadas and all sorts of birds, or God knows what Aussie creatures. The searchlight on the roof of the cab suddenly powered into life and a strong spotlight cut through the darkness. Majella stood and grabbed the lamp and pulled it around. She aimed it until the light illuminated a group of gum trees and shrubs.

'Where the fuck are we?' asked Scobie.

Majella was focused on the job in hand, manoeuvring the beam of light around the trees, lighting up the slender, bluish-green leaves of the eucalyptus, and its buds like pointed caps.

Scobie saw a set of luminous eyes shining out from behind the smooth, creamy barks of the skinny tree trunks.

Majella lowered her voice. 'Do ye know how many kangaroos have to be culled each year?'

Scobie shook his head. He had no clue.

'Three million,' Majella informed him.

Scobie could now see a group of the creatures. They stood stock still. They sensed it. Danger was in the air.

Majella leaned in close to Scobie and took a swig of the tequila. 'Like, they'd overrun the country otherwise.' She passed him back the bottle. 'It's exciting, Scobe, it's fucking brilliant, like. Wait till ye see. A real rush.'

Majella transmitted an energy that Scobie picked up on. It was infectious.

The driver's door slammed shut. George let out a roar into the night. The roos scattered and disappeared into the trees. George climbed up into the back with Scobie and Majella, holding an automatic rifle in his hands. He grinned at Scobie. His eyes seemed different now, as if his pupils had changed to jet black.

'Get ready, Irishman.'

George banged the top of the cab. The truck took off, Declan at the wheel. It sped on in towards the gum trees then swerved around them, just narrowly avoiding a crash. There were three or four very close shaves. Scobie let out a scream, then burst out laughing. This was a fuckin' rush!

George pushed Scobie towards the searchlight. 'Take over the light, Scobe!'

Majella let go, and Scobie did as he was told and took over.

They drove on out into a flat tract of land, and George roared in his ear, *'Keep the fuckin' light on the roos!'*

Scobie took the strain, using all his strength to keep the lamp steady and pointed in the right direction. The roos hopped and jumped at an amazing speed up ahead. George yelled and shouted and took aim: *'Faster, Declan, foot to the fuckin' floor, mate!'*

The truck revved up and accelerated. They came within range of one of the roos. George fired. The noise of the gun gave Scobie a fright. Majella grabbed hold of his shoulder and squeezed. She was completely caught up in the moment. In the thrill of the hunt. George pulled the trigger again, and this time he hit one of them. The creature fell over and rolled around, dust flying, and Scobie saw blood. He was momentarily distracted, but George kicked him in the arse. *'To the right-hand side!'*

Scobie swung the lamp around as the truck took a turn in the direction of about 10 or 12 terrified creatures, hopping and bounding for their lives. A volley of shots were fired. One, two, three animals fell and hit the dirt. George and Majella cried out, as alive and alert as they would ever be.

George turned to Scobie and held out the rifle to him. 'Take it, Irishman, have a go!'

Scobie felt dizzy now, started to feel a knot in his stomach. Like the old anxiety thing. He could feel it creeping down his arms, and he had dry mouth and the panicky feeling of dread was bubbling up. The rough features of George's head filled his line of vision. The lips curled into a weird kind of smile. George licked his lips. Scobie flinched and moved his head away to avoid the awful, shit-smelling breath, rancid with drink, cigarettes and raw onion. He felt like throwing up.

'Come on, Irish, take the fuckin' rifle!' shouted George.

Majella gave him a slap on the back. *'Scobie, come on, will ye!'*

Scobie felt a primal urge to take the rifle that was being offered to him. Maybe he could be that man with a gun, taking life that had to be taken. Like a real John Wayne! One of the Wild Bunch! Clint Eastwood, as the man with no fucking name! Da would have loved it. He wouldn't miss. He would draw blood. He had an overpowering instinct to cause pain and death and bring home the meat!

Scobie took the rifle in both his hands from George who shouted, *'Up the 'RA!'* and grabbed the searchlight. Scobie put his finger on the trigger.

George kept shouting, *'Don't forget to breathe, relax, aim, squeeze the trigger and keep it fuckin' squeezed!'*

Scobie picked out a kangaroo, which was jumping away from the rest. He took aim. He fired off a round. In that moment, he was so focused and alert and alive that he could have cried out with relief and happiness. He continued to fire. The automatic rifle emptied. He felt the recoil but he held firm. He kept firing. At last, he hit it. The kangaroo fell. The truck braked to a stop.

George jumped down off the back, his boots landing on the dusty earth. 'Time to go and collect some meat!'

Majella let out a scream of exhilaration. She turned to Scobie and kissed him on the lips and hopped down off the truck. Declan suddenly appeared beside her, holding a large, very sharp-looking knife. He grinned up at Scobie then kissed Majella. They made their way over towards one of the corpses. George wheeled around and pointed at Scobie. '*The fuckin' Paddy did well. Killer Irishman!*'

Scobie stepped down onto the earth. It felt good to be on solid ground again. George signalled him over. Scobie moved across the sandy, dry soil, dotted with scrub, carrying the rifle in his arms. If only Eddie could see him now. He followed behind George and they approached the area where Scobie had brought his animal down. They heard something in the shadow of a gum tree. A low whimpering. They saw the corpse. The roo lay stone dead. Scobie could see guts and blood and intestines hanging out of the animal, and then he saw the head of a joey. In the pouch. Very much alive. Making small, frightened noises in its throat, grieving for its dead mother.

George looked across to Scobie. 'Kill it.'

Scobie felt as if he had just been landed a massive kick in the stomach. He felt very sick, dizzy, the adrenaline rush subsiding. He felt like puking. He had landed back into the real world with a bang.

The little creature bleated with distress in its dead mother's pouch. George roared at him, '*Kill it!*'

Scobie was frozen to the spot. He was in a state of shock, numb. George grabbed the rifle off him.

Scobie turned around. He couldn't bear to witness it. He heard the shot. The bleating stopped. Scobie turned and walked away into the trees, then bent over and vomited all the night's intake onto the ground. He crumbled down onto his knees and lay his head on the earth, crying tears for Ella and the baby they never had, and for Shamie and Ma and Da and the town at home and his life in Oz and who he was and why he drank so much and his body emptied out. He heard the others roaring and shouting and he looked around to see Declan cutting the head off one of the roos.

Scobie lay back down against a tree. He could smell the eucalyptus. He used to use it at home years ago to clear his sinuses. He'd lean over a basin of hot water with the oil in it, with a towel over his head. Now, he felt an itch all over his legs. He realised that he was being eaten alive by the mozzies. Scobie closed his eyes. He tried to breathe the way Ella had taught him: in through the nose, out through the mouth. But he could still hear the whimpering distress of the joey. It sounded so much like a small infant. Scobie felt that he might throw up again, but there was nothing left to get rid of.

He suddenly sensed George's hot breath near his face. The breath came quicker and nearer to him. He opened his eyes to see George's head looming so close that Scobie could count the pores around his nose. Scobie flinched and moved his head away, but George slowly placed his hand around Scobie's neck. He applied pressure. His fingers tightly wound around the throat. Scobie was too sick and drained to move. He was caught in a rapt, horrible fascination. His whole nervous system was now on high alert.

Then he heard Majella calling his name, '*Scobie, where are ye?!*'

George turned around and shouted back, '*Scobie's okay. He's here with me. We'll be back in a minute.*'

George released his hand from Scobie's neck and moved it up onto Scobie's cheek. He wiped the sweat and tears away with his thumb. He was so tender in this moment that Scobie felt a strange comfort. George took his hand away from Scobie's face. He shook his head and sighed, taking a step back from Scobie. He said, 'Crying like a fucking baby. That's put me right off.' George turned on his heels and marched back towards the others.

Scobie could see them throwing bits of kangaroo carcass up into the back of the truck. He dreamed of getting up and walking into the bush, like the Aborigines used to do. Disappearing into the land and being free of it all. He would walk back to the county of Uíbh Fhailí. Where he was born and raised. He needed to get back there.

And now, from his position under the yew tree, he could see the town, stretching out below him, the square and main street and the various pubs and the schools and Dinny's Hole, the field where he lay. Yes, he needed to get back home to Mam. So he got to his feet and walked as fast as he could. He wasn't stopping for anyone or anything, because he needed to get back home to Angela and make sure she was okay. What if the monster had crashed through the walls, mouth open, teeth bared, the giant kangaroo out for vengeance, and poor Ma was murdered and eaten? He twitched with the fear of what he might discover in the house, blood on the walls ...

On the main street, a voice called his name. He turned to see Deirdre and Keelan coming out of Centra, all smiles and waves and, 'Howsitgoin', Scobe,' but he couldn't stop, not even to bask in the glow of their adoration. 'Have to get home,' he said to them, walking on. One foot in front of another, turning right at Babby Brennan's corner and up to Father Paul Cleary Avenue, to the homestead, and at last, turning the key in the front door and shouting out to the hall, 'Howya, Ma, I'm back.'

There was no blood on the walls. Everything was normal, his mother's voice coming from the kitchen: 'Hi, Scobe, where did you take off to?'

'Ah, just needed a breath of air,' said Scobie, so glad to be back inside the four walls of the home. The place where he had taken his first steps and said his first words, where safety and security were encased into the bricks and mortar.

twenty-one
Angela

Angela was at the cooker frying a few chops when Scobie walked into the kitchen. He came up behind her, enveloping his arms around her and giving her a mighty squeeze. 'I love ye, Ma,' he said to her.

Angela laughed and pushed him away. 'Jaysus, have you been on the sauce?'

'No, not a drop, just telling you how I feel 'cause it's, like, a mad fucking crazy world and there's a disease going around that's killing people so none of us know what might happen so, like, we have to fucking value what we have and be safe, like, you know, like, not be going out of this house, only to shop, which I'll do from now on. I don't want you undertaking any unnecessary risks, do ye hear me?'

Angela nodded her head, turning the chops. Was he okay? He seemed very agitated and the spake of him. I mean when had he ever talked like that? 'Are ye feeling okay in yourself, son?' she chanced asking him.

'Good, yeah, just, I want to make sure you're safe and well.' Scobie smiled, heading for the door. 'Just going for a quick shower.'

'Grand,' said Angela. She went on tending to the chops, deciding that, not for the first time, he must be feeling it all a bit today. The fact that the whole world was being turned upside down by Covid was bound to affect everyone at different times. She stared out the kitchen window at the clouds moving across the sky, wishing Cliff was with her. She didn't know what to do without him. The phone call from Nuala, Robbie's grandmother, was still preying on her mind. Her voice had had a nervous quality to it, as if she had been shaken by the encounter with Scobie. She wasn't going to report it or anything, she had said, but she felt that Angela should know.

Angela went to the pot to mash the potatoes. She turned on the radio to incessant chatter about the nursing homes and the number of deaths, the voices like knives in her brain. She switched the radio off. She'd been sensing for a while that her son was not the man he used to be. She tried to trace a line back through the last few weeks, to try and work out when she really started to notice the little differences in his behaviour. What would make him go around and hassle a woman in her seventies? I mean, what the fuck was he at, and how could she possibly try and broach it with him again?

She heard him descending the stairs. He came into the kitchen. She turned and smiled and started to plate up the food.

Scobie went to lay the table, reaching for the good placemats and glasses that only ever made an appearance on Christmas Day or Easter or the odd special birthday.

'No need for that, son, sure it's only a few chops.'

'No, no, Ma, nothing's too good for you.' He proceeded to set out the good plates and cutlery onto the table. Angela was about to protest again, but let him at it. She placed the chops onto the plates and brought over the bowl of mash and the carrots and parsnips.

Scobie rubbed his hands together in anticipation. 'Lovely,' he said, but as he dug in, she could see that he was only feigning enjoyment of the food. He was lowering it into his mouth, but there was no relishing of it.

She ate steadily as he slowed down, picking at the meat, like he had no real appetite.

'It wouldn't be like ye not to devour the plate and all,' said Angela, doing her best to smile.

She cut up her meat, chewed and swallowed and prepared to speak, but didn't quite know how to say what she wanted to say. The kitchen clock ticked. The fridge hummed. She was very aware of the silence between them.

She opened her mouth. 'So, how's it goin'? Are you missing work?'

'Nah. Well, I don't miss having to get up in the Jaysus mornings, but like, yeah, a bit, like. The days stretch out a bit when you're not at anything.'

'It's just you seem a bit, not yourself or something.'

Scobie speared a bit of chop with his fork and stuck it into his mouth. 'I'm grand.'

Angela could hear how shaky his voice was now, like it might break. She tried to keep herself in check. She had never seen her son like this. 'Come here, son, it's okay. Ye can talk to me, ye know. What's up with ye?'

Scobie couldn't meet her eye. Head bowed. 'Dunno. All too much … it's just all too much,' he muttered to himself.

'I know how ye feel. Stages in life get on top of ye. Like, I got fierce low with the menopause that time. It was tough.'

Scobie looked up at her. 'Ye never said anything.'

'Ah, sure, what was I goin' to say to a pair of young bucks? Ye would have run out of the house.'

Scobie laughed. 'Yeah, Shamie would have been mortified.'

'I got great help from a doctor in Athlone. I still go to her,' Angela said.

Scobie perked up now. 'Do ye? Would she take me on?'

'Are ye not happy with Byrne?' asked Angela.

'Yeah. Just … he won't take me seriously enough. I need a very specific kind of medication. Like, I was taking Xanax, and then this other stuff, Klonopin, and it was really helping but I ran out and he won't put me back on it.'

'Well, he's probably only looking out for ye. It's not so great to be taking them things, Scobie.'

He picked at the half-eaten chop. 'Well, yeah, whatever, but I wonder, could you ask your doctor for some? She'd give it to you.'

'Ah, no, Scobie. Come here now and talk to me. What's wrong with ye?'

'I … I'm just a bit … tired, and there's no let-up. I want to be in the full of me health, to be able to mind you properly.'

'Don't worry about me. I'll be okay,' Angela said, trying her very best to reassure him.

'But I do worry, ye know. I mean, what the fuck, like. There's no solid ground. Thin ice. What if we fall through? It's hard to breathe, Ma, sometimes. Have to keep the head above the water, and there's so much to do. I have to try and find Robbie, but I don't want to leave you … not safe, like.'

'Okay,' Angela said, 'but just listen to me now. What is it you *do* want, love?'

Scobie tapped his foot and rapped his finger against his cup. He closed his eyes and clenched his fists and pounded the table.

Angela didn't flinch. 'Go on, son, talk to me.'

Scobie spoke. 'I just wish it was the way it was long ago, when it was you, me, Shamie and Eddie, and a few Sundays, anyway, we drove out the country and had picnics and it was sunny and – remember them days?'

'I do, Scobe,' said Angela sadly. 'Come here to me, son.' She reached across the table to try and touch his face.

Scobie moved and avoided her touch. 'Please, Ma. Just ask her. Please. It would be such a help. Just say that you need them.'

'I don't think that's a good idea, but let's talk to her tomorrow. She's a good listener. She might have other options to explore bar pills. Half the feckin' country is hooked on all them things. That's what we'll do. I'll make an appointment now and hopefully she'll be able to phone us tomorrow. Obviously, it would be better to go and see her in person, but that's not possible.'

Angela watched on tenterhooks, to see what his reaction would be.

Scobie remained perfectly still. Then he moved his hands above his plate and lowered them to grab hold of the mashed spud, and started to squeeze it between his fingers.

'Son, please. What are ye doin'?' Angela had a sick ache in her stomach now. It was as if he were somebody else, had been taken over by some alien force. Angela steeled herself. She placed her hand on his hands to try and get him to stop. 'Please now, Scobie, you're not a child.'

Scobie went dead still. He lifted his hands from the plate and then he exploded. 'No, I'm not a child! Not a fucking child, I'm a grown fucking *man*! Please help me – I just need you to *help* me! Just get me the pills! *Fuckkkk!*' Scobie took up the plate and threw it against the wall. It smashed into pieces, globs of spud sticking to the wallpaper. And then his face broke, tears rolling down his cheeks.

Angela didn't react. She was not putting up with this. Her instinct was to go to him and throw her arms around him and give him as much comfort and solace as she could, without any thought for herself. But something hardened in her heart. She had to maintain a distance now. There was something seriously wrong, and it wasn't a case of trying to kiss it better. She got up and went to the door.

'Clean that up, mister. I'm going out.'

Angela closed the door behind her, slipped on her coat and headed out the front door, leaving him alone. She got into her car in the front yard and placed her hands on the steering wheel, key in the ignition – but where was she going? She eyed her phone and thought about calling her doctor, Doctor Sangi, a Pakistani woman, who had a lovely, calming sort of voice and a great manner. You felt completely at ease with her.

She thought of Scobie as an eight-year-old boy in his Holy Communion photo. How totally caught up he'd been in the whole occasion in the church, getting the few bob, getting the photos done, but then his mood had seemed to dissipate during the meal in the hotel in Moate. Shamie did his best to gee him up, but little Scobie just wasn't himself. She thought of how Eddie was at the time. She remembered how moody he'd been that day in particular, all smiles and jokes outside the church, and then a kind of withdrawal during the meal. Had Scobie picked up on this? He reminded her so much of Eddie. The way they presented themselves to people who didn't really know them, in a way that wasn't anything to do with who they really were.

Her marriage to Eddie had run the gamut of ups and downs, of deep love and connection and troughs of distance and emotional loneliness. She felt the responsibility of keeping everything in the house happy for the boys, so there would be nothing to upset them. Looking back, she felt that she'd overcompensated. Eddie had stuff going on in his heart, partly because of a tough upbringing, which she was never quite able to understand. He would withdraw from them, and she encouraged it, so her two young lads could be blissfully oblivious to his moods.

Angela thought about how much had been buried with Eddie. Her stomach did a turn when she imagined ever going back into all of that again. She had done her level best for so many years to keep the box tightly shut on those memories and difficult times, but she supposed now that she had only ever been fooling herself. She pictured the envelope in the bottom drawer of her dressing table, under a jewellery box, where it hadn't moved since the day after Eddie's funeral. A letter that he'd given to her in the hospital, a couple of weeks before he passed away. She thought about the contents of that letter. She thought about a dream she had had about Scobie recently. He was lying in a gutter with blood and puke spilling out of him and his double appeared and just stopped and stared. He did nothing to help. Angela had fashioned a theory about this. That there were two sides in Scobie, and they were in a constant battle. One half craved security and love and home and the other half wanted wildness and drink and carry-on, which always ended up making him feel depressed and alone. She knew in her heart that Scobie had been cut from the same cloth as Eddie.

Angela waved at a neighbour who was walking his dog up the road. She knew she had to move or do something. She couldn't sit in the car forever. She couldn't have her son suffering like he was. She needed to get him straightened out in some way before she could have a proper talk with him. If that took pills, then so be it. She needed him to be calm and not mad as a box of frogs the way he was now.

Angela picked up her mobile, punched in a call, waited while it rang, and a voice picked up. 'Hello. Doctor Sangi's surgery, can I help you?'

'Hi, Angela Jones here, I'm a patient of the doctor and I need to speak to her very urgently.'

'I'm sorry, but she's got calls booked for the day, so we'll have to try and fit you in later in the week,' came the well-worn response.

'No, please, just say that Angela Jones needs to speak to her now.'

'I'm terribly sorry but—' the woman began.

'Sorry, I didn't get your name?' asked Angela.

'Eh, my name is Denise.'

'Okay, good woman, now listen to me here, Denise, I am suicidal. Absolutely on the fucking edge, and if I don't get to speak to Doctor Sangi, I am liable to do something stupid. Like, I mean it now. I am sitting in a car and I am in no fit state to drive it bar off a fucking bridge because I have been pushed to the very edge here, so get me the doctor after she's finished whatever call she's on now, or I will come around and reef ye all out of it. I'm serious, Denise. Don't make me have to come over there!'

'Eh, okay. Jesus … please, hold on. She shouldn't be too long,' came the flustered response. Angela knew that the very last thing Denise wanted was some crazy bitch arriving on her doorstep.

'Thanks, Denise. I appreciate that,' said Angela, taking a breath, laughing at herself and wondering where the fuck that all came out of, and it was confirmed for her in that moment that a mother's love knew no bounds.

Ten minutes later she pulled out of the yard on her way to the medical hall to pick up a prescription for Xanax. Doctor Sangi had been very reluctant at first, and insisted that she couldn't offer Xanax or any similar medication unless she had an in-person consultation, which was impossible because of Covid. Angela was like a dog with a bone. She just needed them for a short time while her husband was away. She was finding Covid very frightening, and she wasn't sleeping. In the end the doctor had acquiesced, but with very stern warnings and caveats as she sent a prescription for a limited amount to the chemist. Angela picked them up, not being able to hide her feeling of acute self-consciousness in front of Matty Morgan, who served her, even though he was his usual very chatty and pleasant self and gave no sign of disapproval.

She went back to her son, who she found curled up in a ball on the couch in front of *The Chase*, and his face broke into an expression of sheer relief when she produced the packet of Xanax. 'I'm so sorry, Mam. I just need some rest, ye know. Thanks so much.' She watched as he tore the packet open to get the pills inside him as fast as he could. He lay back down on the couch then for a few more hours, not wanting anything to eat, and he went up to bed after the nine o'clock news and weather.

Angela was left to take her nightly phone call from England, but she didn't say anything to Cliff about it. Not yet. He was stressed to the nines over the mother and her finances, which had to be sorted out so they could afford to get her into a nursing home, as it was clear that she couldn't remain at home, not without Cliff there to mind her. All a pain in the Nat King Cole, by the sound of it.

'I miss ye, Ange,' he had said to her.

'I miss you too, Cliff, but it's okay, we have each other, ye know, so let there be no panic. We'll be back together in no time.'

'I'm fucking sick of it. Sometimes I look at her and I just wish she'd kicked the bucket years ago.'

'No such luck,' said Angela, trying to keep it light.

'Not a word of thanks when you fetch the tea up to her or …
Look it, I'm tired and stressed out this evening, Ange. I'm sorry.'

A sense of the devil came over Angela then. She whispered
into the phone, 'I know what we need. I've had a shit day as well.
All I want to do now is to get into the bed with you and eat ye!'
She didn't believe she'd just said that.

'Oh, fuck me, Angela, I'm getting excited here,' said Cliff.

'Good. Now listen to me. I'm gonna tell ye what to do.' And,
for the first time in her life, Angela made an attempt at phone sex,
doing her best to describe all the stuff that they had ever done
and the stuff that she knew Cliff especially liked. Gradually, Cliff
was able to join in and describe what he wanted to do to her. They
kept it up, and much to their mutual delight, were able to finish
around about the same time.

The next day, Angela stirred home-made leek and potato soup
in a pot. It was nearly there. She smirked at the boldness of her
phone antics with Cliff, and wondered what had got into her. She
had felt something new lately, a compulsion to act on her instinct
rather than holding back or feeling that she mustn't or that she
should be thinking of other people first. She didn't quite understand this new impulse in her. It kind of scared her, but made her
feel that she was really living life.

She glanced at the kitchen clock. Half twelve. Time to go up
and see if he was awake. She took the tray with the bowl of soup
up the stairs then stopped outside her son's room, preparing to
face him. She knocked on his bedroom door, which she found
odd, as she had never done that before, even when the two boys
were younger and could have been up to all sorts. She had never

felt the need to knock, until now. She pushed the door open and stuck her head into the room, not touched since both sons had departed for Oz over a decade ago. The head stirred in the bed, then the rest of the body belonging to it turned and the arms stretched out and the eyes opened.

Angela stepped into the room, indicating the tray in her hands. 'Could ye eat something?' she said. 'It's only a drop of soup.'

Scobie sat up in the bed. Groggy-looking, hair like an exploded mattress. Angela put the tray down into his lap.

'Thanks, Ma,' said Scobie. 'I'll give it a go anyway.'

Scobie took up the spoon, dipped it into the bowl, lifted the spoon to his lips, blew on the soup and then tasted it. This reminded Angela of a thousand school lunch hours, himself and Shamie racing home on their bikes to get the dinner, absolutely starvin', they'd have 'ate shite off a scabby leg'.

Angela glanced around the walls again. 'Jaysus, we must do something with this room. Like a fresh lick of paint or something.'

Scobie nodded as he slowly took in another spoonful of the soup.

Angela indicated the poster of Jeanette, the perfect girl. 'I mean poor aul' Jeanette has been up there a long time.'

Scobie managed a smile. 'She has, fair play to her.'

'I mean, we could get rid of Shamie's bed, get you a double, ye know, for the bit of comfort,' suggested Angela.

'I suppose,' said Scobie, but he didn't seem too enthusiastic.

'How are ye feeling anyhow?' said Angela.

Scobie shook his head slowly. 'I dunno. Better anyways. Me head is sore, but at least I got a bit of kip. Thanks again, Ma, for, ye know, for them lads,' Scobie said, indicating the packet of Xanax on his bedside table.

'Yeah, but Scobe, come on, they'll have to stop. You know that, like. If ye need to go and talk to someone—'

'I know,' Scobie said sharply.

Angela sat down on the end of his bed and surveyed the ceiling. 'I have a bit of paint downstairs left over from when Cliff did the lounge that time. It's a kind of oatmeal white. What do ye think?'

'I have no idea what oatmeal white looks like, Ma,' said Scobie.

'Ah, it's kind of a darker white. Sure, ye know it, and it on the Jaysus walls of the lounge and the hours you've spent in there watching telly.'

Scobie put down his spoon for a moment and managed a smile, but felt full or slightly sick again after getting through only around half the soup in the bowl.

'Just another few sups,' encouraged Angela.

Scobie attempted another spoonful, but he knew that that was it, for now anyway.

'You know your father had to go on them things one time,' said Angela. 'Not them exact pills, but something like them. He used get very down in himself.'

'No memory of that,' said Scobie.

'Ah, ye were only boys. Like five or six. Sometimes he'd light up this house, ye know, with the craic and chat of him, and then other times …' Angela looked away from her son, back across to Jeanette on the wall, and she again pictured the envelope in the bottom drawer of her dressing table, under the jewellery box.

Eddie's last chance at some sort of confessional. A last chance to set the record straight, which he had found much easier to write down than to speak. The most gut-wrenching thing that Angela had ever had to read in her life. She imagined how Eddie must have sat up in the hospital room, with a pen in his hand, painstakingly etching out his words. They had spent many hours in that room towards the end, a bedside vigil, snatched conversations when he was conscious enough to be able to half-understand what they were trying to say to each other.

Scobie closed his eyes for a moment.

Angela turned towards the door. 'I'll be back in a minute,' she said, and leaving him alone she went into her own room.

She opened her dressing table drawer and reached underneath her jewellery box and took up the envelope. She thought of the spidery, at times illegible writing of the letter within. She sat on the bed for a moment. Was she going to do this? She remembered the last few lines. *Show this to the lads someday if you want. If you feel it wouldn't be too much for them to know the truth. You'll know what's best to do. You always did.*

Angela never intended to show them this letter. She didn't want to besmirch Eddie's memory for them – or was it that she didn't want her sons to think bad of her? To see her as the helpless little woman who put up with things. Who took him back when she had every right to kick him out. If she was being entirely honest with herself, it was the fear of losing their respect in some way.

She stood up off the bed and headed back out of the room and across the landing and pushed open the door to Scobie's room, because she was certain now. She was going to share it with her younger son, because he was so like his father. A man who was a kind of stranger to himself, always on the run, a man in danger of going under. Stuff gets passed on, she knew that, through the generations, a restlessness of the soul, a hurt caused by other hurts that were inflicted and, somehow, she knew that Eddie's words might speak to Scobie from beyond the grave and help him in some way.

Angela's heart pounded in her chest and her palms were sweaty as she stepped up to the bed. Scobie's eyes were half open. Angela took a moment and then sat on the bed. 'I want to show ye something.'

She offered the envelope to Scobie. He took it off her, seeing her name scribbled on the side of it.

'It's a letter your dad wrote to me when he was in the hospital, just weeks before he left us. I think ye should read it.'

Scobie reached inside the envelope and took out the letter, consisting of three pages, written on both front and back. Angela could see that he recognised his father's small, scrawny handwriting, as if it was a class of insect that had walked over the sheets of paper with inky legs. Himself and Shamie used to slag him over the state of his writing, and his father would slag back, 'Fuck ye, I had to leave school after the Inter, ye got two more years and ye did very little with it.' This was true. Angela knew that her sons had not exactly sat the Leaving Cert exam with any great distinction. They got through with a few passes and honours each. Shamie was not an academic kind of lad, doing best at the mechanical drawing, whereas Scobie wasn't bad at English and that craic, if he had bothered his hole. But he had been too busy being head of entertainment at the back of the classes, or the front of them – it didn't really matter where he was sitting, he was always the instigator of disruption, and many's the time Angela had been called to the school because some young teacher had been sent home a nervous wreck, questioning their very future in the profession. His son's lack of focus and wilful acting the eejit had irked Eddie, especially as he himself had been of a bright disposition and would have liked to have had the opportunity to stay on at school, but that had not been possible at the time. His father and mother needed him on the farm. Eddie had no say in the matter.

Scobie squinted to get a better view of the scrawl, and Angela could see that he felt something in his blood, a response to holding this paper that his father had once held. She could see the wave of emotion come over him.

'Just read it and I'll talk to ye after, okay?' said Angela.

She leaned in, placed a tender kiss on his forehead, then grabbed up the tray and went for the door. She took a last glimpse back at her son, the first page of the letter in his hand, his eyes in a serious state of concentration, and she knew he'd begun to read and she hoped to Jesus that she had done the right thing in showing him.

twenty-two

Scobie realised after half a page that it was going to take a while for him to get through the letter due to the handwriting, but also, he'd already had to stop several times to try and absorb what he had just read. He heard his father's voice in his head, his turn of phrase, as if he'd landed into the room in some kind of way. A primordial presence. A ghost on a day trip back to the house that he'd first moved into in the spring of 1977, when it teemed with rain as he'd carried his new wife across the threshold, his heart bursting with happiness and hope as they kissed in the kitchen and drank their first pot of tea and ate Marietta biscuits with butter, like a pair of excited children. The ghost sat at the end of Scobie's bed, and Scobie kept on reading, aware of the apparition, but for now, there were only the words and sentences on the light-blue Basildon Bond paper, and this is what they said:

Dearest Angela,

The other day, when you came in for the visit, there was so much that I wanted to say to you, but I ended up saying nothing bar the usual, and it's hard to keep the chat up when we know that one of us is going to croak. So I got this mad notion then to start a letter to you and so this is it. I hope you'll be able to make out my writing.

I've been thinking a lot about not being around any-more. Like, it's mad to picture the house at home and my armchair empty and the fact that you'll be sleeping on your own in that bed. Life is so mad. Hard to understand half the things that happen to us. I think about the funeral and who'll turn up and the fact that I'll never see a grand-child, although you could be waiting a long time for that at the rate our two are going. I'll miss driving the truck, watching hurling and football and your apple tart with a cup of tea and smoking a fag and the two lads pulling up outside in the car after work and the craic we'd have around the table. Slagging and chatting and talking shite, but most of all, above any of that, even them two lads, I'll miss you, Angela. I'll miss you. There's no other way to put it. I don't want to have to leave you.

There's plenty to look back on, the if-onlies. I should have gone into the business with Foggy Flynn that time, we could've made a real go of it, but I was too cautious. Stuck with Tynan's. I could have made a better life for all of us, and I regret that now. I keep thinking about a match I played in 1978 against Bracknagh. I pulled on a ball, kind of half-knowing that I'd miss the connection and land the hurl into the face of this bollocks who was marking me, and I was sent to the line, and I often think about what got into me in that moment, because I was playing well and the county selectors were there to watch me. Who knows. It was like part of me wanted to fuck it up. Was I afraid of making the highest level? I don't know.

Other things fly into my head. There's a lot of time for that, lying in the bed. Like, I woke in the middle of last night and was full sure I was back home in the old farm-house talking to my father, and he was being real friendly and we were having a great chat so it must have been a dream. I regret that, Angela. That I never told either of them what I thought of them. That I just stopped talking to them and left them alone and barely went to their funerals. Terrible really. But they weren't right. Took me a good few years to realise that.

There is one time I always remember. I was around ten or so and we were doing fencing up on one of the back fields. Da was teaching me how to do it, and of course he had no patience, but anyway, he left me to it and I did my best but didn't hammer in a post properly, and during the night it keeled over and some of the cattle got out onto the road. He woke me and brought me outside and told me there'd be no breakfast, as I had to go and find the three missing cows and herd them back up into the field and fix the post. Rain, hail, sleet, snow, everything but shite fell out of the sky, and I was at it all day. Eventually, I got the three cattle back in and had the fence mended and got back to the house but they had the door locked. They sat inside in the warmth of the fire with full bellies, and I knocked on the door and shouted into them but there was no answer. I had to sleep in the barn. In the hay, freezing and starving, but at least he hadn't hit me. You could put up with anything if it meant he didn't come near you like that.

I managed to doze for a few hours and woke to find himself standing over me. He hoped that I'd learned a lesson, but I talked back. I'd never done that before. I told him to fuck off, and he went at me then, as you can imagine. He really went at me, and my mother stood inside in the house and never came out. She must have heard me, trying to get him to stop, but she never did anything. Do you remember me telling you this before? The thing I want you to know now is that I think I ended up hating her more than him, for not helping me. I was only a child. I needed help from her. She let me down, Angela. Do you get me? And it's only hit me this last while, in the hospital like, that something in me hardened after that time. Like, I split meself into two or something. That's the only way I can try and describe it. I had the hard, fuck-you bit of me that I put on for the world, but there was another, softer lad underneath, a lad who never got to come out that often. When I met you, Angela, he came out. He wasn't afraid to come out when I was with you. I couldn't believe that life could be so good that time when we were having the craic in the pubs and discos and all that, but my favourite thing was when we were alone, just chatting, and the day we moved into the house was the best day. Fixing it up and making plans and spending one weekend in the bed. Remember that! I do. I'll never forget it. I think that was how the first lad came about!

It's getting harder to write this letter now. It's trying to find a way of being honest with you. I remember the two lads being born, of course, and I remember very clearly me and a few pals went to McKeon's for a few pints and I swore to Benny McGrath that I was going to be a good da, and not take after me own. I said it and I meant it, but I couldn't seem to be able to hack it. I left the bulk of it up to you. I started to stay on the road for longer, volunteering for the overnight jobs, so I could get sleep away from the kids. I was frightened of something. Of the huge job of being a da, I dunno.

I hate to admit it but I think that I resented you because you were so understanding and parent enough for them. I was not being a good da, and you were letting me away with it. I dunno. The soft lad disappeared then cos he was ashamed. It seemed that way anyhow, looking back, like. The hard man took over and wanted his sons to take after him. The eldest lad wasn't able, so I concentrated on Scobie, chip off the old block, ye know. I was going to make a little man out of him and, for a while, we were great pals going around in the truck, but I lost me temper one day and it was never the same after that. He'd been messing with the truck and trying to drive it while I was inside in the office and I got a real fright and let on to be okay in front of the other lads but then I lashed out at him on the way home. I regret doing that. I remember the day because Eileen was there. I'd been in talking to her in the office.

Look it, I know we agreed never to talk about her that time you took me back, the day that I agreed to give her up, but I'm writing this letter to try and work these things out a bit. Before I go. I think it's important. For years I was glad to leave it alone but I'm not anymore, Angela. As I said, when a man knows that he's going to die it really has an effect. Anyways, I have to tell you that I never loved Eileen, not in the way I loved you. I felt so odd in meself at that time, and we'd grown so separate. You dedicated yourself to the two lads. I didn't feel I deserved any of ye. I was a selfish bastard like my old man, so I behaved accordingly, telling Eileen a heap of lies about you, how you were cold and uncaring and all this, like I was really describing me ma to her, not you, but it made her forget any qualms she was having and she was willing to continue on with me and wait until the lads were a bit older. God forgive me, but that's what I said to her. I'd leave my family and set up with her. Of course, I had never the slightest real intention to do that, but that's what I'd been saying to her that day in the office when Scobie nearly drove the truck through the bloody window. I felt like such a fraud and took it out on him. It was funny, though, I'll always remember the way he looked at her, like he knew something. Like he sensed there was something going on. I don't know. I regret so much of it all. She didn't deserve the lies I told to keep her reeled in. I'll carry that with me now until I go. How was I capable of that? Being so cruel? And I hurt her, like really hurt her, and she did nothing wrong really, except fall for a married man.

I was never sure how you found out about us. You didn't want to tell me. You had no interest in talking about it. You just asked me to finish it. You made me promise. You told me that you could forgive me and it was the most amazing thing anyone ever did for me. To trust me that much. You have no idea what that meant to me. You told me that I was needed and loved and that I was a great da. You told me to try and have trust in myself. It was a short chat we had there in the kitchen at home, but I'll never forget it. You didn't waste words or mince them. I knew in that moment that everything else was a hang-up, a left-over from the fucking barn and my father and mother's unhappiness and a misery that I was destined to have for the rest of my life, until you came along with your strength and love. I have been blessed and I hope I have managed to give you some happiness since all that happened. You deserve so much.

When I'm gone, I don't want you to be on your own forever. I can't bear to think about another man, but I would hate it more for you to be miserable and lonely. I will love you and cherish you all the rest of my days, and hopefully we might see each other again, up above, if we're to believe in all that stuff. Either way I will carry you in my heart for eternity.

Your husband, Eddie

PS. Show this to the lads someday if you want. If you feel it wouldn't be too much for them to know the truth. You'll know what's best to do. You always did.

Scobie laid the letter down on his lap and looked up slowly to see that the apparition at the end of his bed was still there. Head slightly bowed, as if his father was listening to something, or in deep thought. His face settled in a gentle smile, as if he was at great ease, but the sight of him still caused Scobie's nerves to jangle. The blood seemed to thicken in his arteries as the now-familiar wave of tension spread around his body, so he reached for a Xanax and swallowed it with a glass of water.

He closed his eyes and felt himself drifting out to the edge of somewhere, beyond himself, away from the confines of the room with the apparition of his father, as if he'd floated right out through the window and up into the sky beyond, ending up in the grounds of St Mary's church, drifting in through the front doors to find a packed church and a line of children queueing up for their first taste of Holy Communion. He could smell the church smell. He could feel the nervousness as he knelt at the altar in a row of children as the priest approached with the chalice. Scobie Donoghue was all done up in the First Communion suit and rosette and medal, feeling all self-conscious but kind of grown-up, and he put out his hands to receive the host into his palm. He could hear his thoughts, the goings-on of that little eight-year-old head. He started to tune in to them, as if he was that boy again …

Jaysus, don't drop it now – sorry for cursing, Lord – okay, pick it up now and say the 'Amen'. That's it, all done. Thanks, Father. Off ye go there to the rest of them. I like the taste of the Communion. It's a pity they don't give ye a bigger bit. Anyways, stand now, bless meself and get back to the seat. Look at Mucky Mahon's hair. His ma musta put too much Brylcreem in it, state of him – 'How are ye, Mucky?' Now back to the seat. Da, Ma and Shamie smiling at me, it feels good, I have to say. Like, I feel kinda shy with them all looking at me but grown-up, too. I wonder how much money I'll make. A lad last year made over two hundred quid, but he came from a huge family, whereas I have hardly anyone, only one uncle, I mean, it's pathetic. Sad dose. I'll be lucky to make twenty.

Come on, now, the rest of ye, peg the communion out a bit faster there, Father, let's get the show on the road, as Da does say. I'm gonna drink as much Coke as I can and eat sweets and chocolates until I burst. Like the young one in Willy Wonka, *I want to eat until I blow up like a big balloon. Raymond Kelly says that* Willy Wonka *is for babies, and that his da lets him watch* Rambo, *so I* said to him that my da lets me and Shamie watch Clint Eastwood films, but Raymond doesn't know who Clint is, the fucking eejit, all he knows is Rambo.

Anyways, Father McAvoy is sending us off now to love and serve the Lord, which we will. Promise, Father. We will do our best. Like, it's good to be a bit holy on a day like this. No harm in saying your prayers properly and thinking about God in Heaven and how he's looking down and guiding us and all that craic. Go on there, Mucky, get a move on there, that's it, into the aisle, single file, that's the job. Look at the state of the girls. Thank Jaysus us lads don't have to carry those little white bags and stupid umbrellas, and look at Aoife Hynes there, thinks she's on the telly or something, with her hair and smiling all the time, and her ma looks like a one off the telly, too, but I don't like Aoife, she's sly. Not that I'd be bothered having girls as friends, but in the High Babies we played together in the yard, kinda chasin' each other, and some of the girls like Aoife would try and kiss ye and all this. We don't do that anymore. Why is that?

Outside, Ma has the Polaroid camera out. Okay, let's just get this over with. The quicker we stand and pose for the camera, the quicker we get out of here and to the hotel. Okay, grand. Me on me own. Snap. Me and me family. Snap. What! Mucky wants me for a photo with him. The adults are looking at us now, laughing, pointing, saying how cute we are, little men all dressed up. Mucky once told us he'd take a shite on the street if we gave him 50 pence, that he'd take his pants down and go for it. I wasn't bothered, but Raymond gave him 30 pence as it was all he had, so Mucky took down the pants and knickers and shat in the street, down the town, *like. Laughing. And I remember no adult saw it, or if they did, they let on that they didn't. But Mucky is taking no shite now, not today. He's all posing and delighted with himself, and Father McBride is coming over to us and he's dead sound and a bit of craic, and he doesn't talk to you like you're a fuckin' baby. Quick, good man, Father, get into the photo and then we're done. Good man. Ah, that's right, Father, I've never looked so clean and smart in my whole life. Me ma laughs and me da laughs too, although he doesn't always go to Mass. I wonder about that, actually. Does he ever go to Mass when he's away at weekends driving the truck? Don't know. Anyway, he's not very holy. I hear him giving out about the priests sometimes, and even the Pope, which is kinda dodgy, like. Ye can't be giving out about the Pope.*

Anyways, it's time to go. Come on. Race ye to the car, Shamie! I get there first as usual. Shamie is fierce slow. He takes ages to do anything, from eating to walkin', runnin' or even talkin'. Like, I sometimes think that I'm the older one, even though he's nearly two years older than me. 'Let's take 'em to Missouri, men,' I say to Da, but I know Da doesn't really go in for all the cowboy craic unless it's just the two of us in the truck. Hope he takes me out again soon. Love sitting up in the cab. Real high up. You can see over all the hedges, into the fields. It's brilliant.

There's Raymond and his family heading off, with a load of brothers and sisters and cousins and aunts and uncles. I'd say he's made well over a hundred quid, and he'll be sure to brown me over it, but the thing is, his family isn't going to the hotel. He told me that they're just going back to have a meal at home. Boring. We're going to this hotel to eat a savage big dinner. I can't wait!

Out in the car I feel the breeze on me hand – love it! Window rolled down, me arm stuck out. Ma doesn't like it. Says she's afraid me arm will get whipped off some way. Da shakes his head. He always lets me do it. Especially today, as it's my First Holy Communion! My day. I see the hotel car park. Won't be long now. Shamie and me go around the revolving doors of the hotel a few times until Da tells us to cop on. We laugh and head into the lobby and look it, there's the big restaurant. Families sitting around at all the tables. But, like, my family is the best. Look at the dessert trolley, Black Forest gateau and trifles and baked Alaska. Howsitgoin' there, Mister Waiter, grand job, here's the table. Can I, Da? Brilliant. Okay. I'll sit in this chair. So I can see the whole room, ye know, so I'll be able to tell ye when our food is comin'. I don't know what to order, Lord Jaysus, look at the menu. Chips, anyway. Maybe fish and chips and mushy peas, or roast chicken or chicken with whatchamacallit kinda breadcrumbs around it and ah – yeah, Da, what's that? How much did Mucky and Raymond get? I don't know. They didn't say, but I bet it was loads.

What? Ah, thanks. White envelope, open it up, look inside, A tenner, and not just one. No way José, there's five lovely new tenners in the envelope. Ah, thanks so much, amazing. 'Ah, that's too much,' says Ma, and Da ignores her. I love the feel of the money in me hands. This is going to be the best day ever. I'm so happy. Hello Mister Waiter, steak for Da, fish for Ma, chicken for Shamie and burger for me and soups to start. Thank you kindly and hurry up now, don't be too long. Ye can peg the bottles of Coke for me and Shamie over this minute.

Shamie asks me to do an impression of Mister Scally, my teacher, and I do him real well. 'Any boy who doesn't bring something into the nature table will not be eligible to play soccer in the hall.' He has a real accent, from some other part of Ireland, and he talks through his nose, so he's easy to do, and Ma laughs despite herself. Da is looking at his watch. Don't worry, Da, the food won't take too long. He grins and lights up a smoke. Can I have one, Da? Ma, don't look like that, I'm only messin', although I would love to try one. I thought about sneaking one out of the packet when I was in the cab of the truck the last time but I chickened out in the end. One day I'll give them a go. For definite.

I see our waiter coming through the kitchen doors with a tray and four soups. Here we go. I knew it. It's for us. Sure enough, he comes over to our table. Four soups. Cream of tomato. And lovely fresh rolls and butter in the little packets. Deadly. Dig in. Slurp at the soup. Me and Shamie. A thing we do to annoy Ma. Okay, we'll stop and drink the soup and stop acting the maggots. Da is a fast eater. Ma always says for him to slow down but he never does. His soup is nearly gone. Then he gets up. He has to use the loo. Grand job. I could do with the loo meself. I'll come with ye, Da. Just scoop back the last few spoonsful of soup and away we go.

Walking with Da, into the lobby, we're on the way to a gunfight, me, hands down, like I'm getting ready to draw. I look to Da. 'Hey now, that ain't no way to talk to my mule.' Come on, Da, do Clint with me, Fistful of Dollars. No. Not on for it. He's not doing Clint today, no—

'Come here, son. I just need to make a phone call. You go on into the jacks.'

Okay, grand. Into the jacks I go. Out with the lad, and really, I have very little piss. I kinda just wanted to be with Da. There ye go, little sprinkle, shake him and there we go. Wash the paws, love the soap, it's all runny in a tube thing. Love the hot air out of the yoke for drying your hands. Head back out. There's Da, he's on the phone in one of the booths in the lobby. Watch him now, he's talking a lot. Real serious-looking. He can be great craic sometimes, doin' Clint and all that, and then other days he does be in the chair with the telly on, and you know to kind of leave him alone. Adults can be funny sometimes. All chatty one day and then another day not a word for the cat, as Ma does say. His brother, Uncle Ned, could be the same. He's gone to America and sends the odd postcard, but Da says he'll probably never come home. They aren't brothers the way me and Shamie are brothers. I never knew Da's ma and da, and Ma told me not to be asking about them. How long more will he be? I want to walk back into the restaurant with him. Come on, Da. Get off the phone. Stop talkin'. I'll go up to him, will I, and point my pistol in at him and say something. Just for the craic. I'll say something from Clint, like 'We got ourselves the Josey Wales, now you put those hands where I can see them.' The Outlaw Josey Wales is Da's favourite Clint film. I prefer Fistful. Walking towards him now, hand out like a gun, get up next to him, his back to me, hear him talking.

'I can't just leave them. Not today.' Who is he talking to? 'Of course I love you.' Who does he love? Who does he love, if he doesn't love us? No, must have misheard. What was I doing, oh yeah. The line from Josey. Just do the line.

I stick out the hand, finger pointed like a pistol and prod his back. He swings around and I say, 'Hey, Josey Wales, let's put those hands where we can see them!'

Da shakes his head and gives me a little push. Like a shove, enough for me to fall back a bit. Why? He says something else into the phone before he puts it down.

'Sorry. Sorry, son.'

'Okay, Da,' I say. 'I was only trying to play Clint with ye.'

'I know, Scobie. I know. That was Paul Tynan, ye know, just had to talk work stuff so I couldn't be messing. Understand? Ye can't be messing when your boss is on the phone.'

He must have to tell his boss he loves him. But that doesn't make sense.

Da laughs, all Clint now as we walk back into the restaurant doing the lines from Fistful. 'My mistake, four coffins.' Everything's deadly again. Back at the table. All happy as Larry. Food has arrived. Shamie tries to tell a joke, which he's no good at. Ma says he's funny. Maybe she has to say that. Anyway, it's a joke he heard at school, Paddy Irishman, Paddy Englishman and Paddy Scotsman, and I've heard it before. Da is laughing. My Ma is laughing and so am I, but not really. I'm putting it on. Why am I doing that? Everything's great. Me burger is absolutely lovely and me and Shamie are burping after all the Coke. But I keep thinking of me da on the phone. Who does he love? Who does he love if he doesn't love us?

Me tummy is still bursting from the meal, lying in bed, thinking through the day. Hear voices down below. They're talking about something. The front door closes. Who's gone out? Shoot outta the bed quick. Get to the window. Have a look out. It's Da, walking down the road. Where's he going at this hour? Maybe he has to meet his boss, Mister Tynan. Maybe that was what the phone call was *about. 'Of course I love you.' Who does he love? Have to make sure he loves me. Have to be good for Da. Have to be like him. Ye know. Not like Shamie. I'll drive a truck like him and smoke cigarettes like him. I know he does love me. But maybe I do things to annoy him. Sneaking up on him today. Like, I shouldn't have done that. I have to watch that sorta thing. Only play the Clint when he wants to do it. I'm gonna get good at the hurling as well. Da will like that. I'm gonna try extra hard this summer at the hurling. He'll love me for that.*

Scobie floated back inside the room again, returning into his 40-year-old body, glad to be back, because wherever he had been had been almost too much to bear. A place between sleep and dreams and reality and memory, gently nudged along by the Xanax, and now, in the depths of his consciousness, Scobie really understood that thing that Ella had told him in Australia, when they had visited Hanging Rock. The ancient belief that when you sleep people come and steal your body. It made so much sense to him now because it felt so much like he was being returned to his physical self. He then realised that his father's apparition was still present in the room, at the end of the bed.

Eddie looked over at Scobie and gestured to him with one of his big, calloused, hard-working hands, the nicotine stains on the fingers looking so familiar, but Scobie wanted to settle back into himself, back into the here and now. His father wouldn't let him. He was insisting, and before he knew it, Scobie was off again, but this time, his father was with him, guiding him, and they were no longer inside in the bedroom. They were up in the cab of the truck with the smoke from a Major cigarette wafting across to 10-going-on-11-year-old Scobie. The two men on the open road with the radio playing out the hits of that summer of 1991, and the roads and fields and bogs flying by them. Scobie could feel the breeze on his elbow leaning on the window. He saw the front of Tynan's yard approaching, and they drove on through the open gates, to the 'How's the men' greeting of the lads inside, who Scobie knew real well, as he'd often help onload the timber onto the back of the truck in the morning time. A big job that could be tough on the muscles, but which Scobie loved. Working with the men who'd slag him for trying to lift too much.

They parked up the truck and Scobie was starving and wanted to get home, but his father needed to just pop into the office for a minute. Scobie waited, fidgeted with the inside of the glove compartment, always hoping against hope that his da would have left a spare stick of chewing gum in at the back of it. The thoughts sped through his head, and again 40-year-old Scobie was privy to them, wherever he was now, on the edge of here, some liminal place of the mind. He could hear little Scobie's head turning over, as the minutes ticked by and there was no sign of Eddie.

Won't be too long, he says, and he gone ten minutes now, I see by the Jaysus clock on the dash here, like what is he doing? Come on, Da, I'm starvin' to get home, although Ma's only doing a salad tonight on account of the good weather. I dread hard-boiled eggs. Shamie loves them, puts loads of salad cream on them, but I hate them. Come on, Da. Where is he? Most of the other workers have left now. Not a sinner around the place. I do often wonder what it would be like to drive the truck. Ye know, just to get behind the steering wheel and start up the engine. I see the keys on Da's big chunky brass key ring in the ignition and everything. Ah, would ye stop? Come here, I've had enough of this now. I'm gonna go in and see what the fuck he's doing. Come on, Da, we need to get home for the tea – that's what I'll say.

Out of the truck, walk across and enter the office and there's no one around. Like the receptionist Monica is gone, sure, but there's Paul Tynan's office door and it's a bit open. When is a door not a door? When it's ajar. Remember that stupid joke that Shamie kept saying to everyone when he was younger. Thought it was real funny. God help him. Come on, sure, walk up to it anyway. Should I knock? No. Just push it open. No. I should knock, listen now. Voices. A woman's voice, it's Eileen, she works here. The secretary. Eileen. Why is she still here? What is she saying? Can't really hear. Go closer and take a peek in. I wonder will she be wearing her red lipstick? I like looking at Eileen. There she is, standing beside the desk. Mister Tynan isn't in his office. It's just her and another man. It's Da. Eddie Donoghue. What's he doing? Should I say something? No. What's Da doing? His hand is kinda touching her face, real gentle. He never touches Ma's face like that. She leans into him and places a kiss on his cheek. He moves his mouth over to her lips. They kiss. Like people do in the films. Like you're supposed to kiss. Get away. Aaaaahhhhh! Get the fuck out of there. Speedy Gonzalez, fucking Road Runner, out the door of the office, back outside. He must love her. That's it. Not us. Ma or me or Shamie. He must love her. That's it. We must have done something wrong. What did we do? Scramble back up into the cab of the truck and wait and let on to have seen nothing. It's something I've done. I mustn't be a good-enough son. I want to hit something now. Fuck! Fuck! Hit the fuckin' dash. I see that key in the ignition. I'll show him what kind of son he has. A mad notion now! Go on, Scobie, ye boya! I'll show him what kind of man his son is! I know what foot goes on what pedal. I've seen him do it loads of times. That's it, slide across over in front of the steering wheel. Grab the hand brake with both hands and release it. Jaysus, it's hard to move. There we go! True Grit. *Fill your hands, you son of a bitch! Turn the key in the ignition. Rev her up! Stretch down now to put the feet on both pedals. Release the clutch with one foot. Push the accelerator with the other. She's revving, boys! She's moving! Wait till Da sees this. He'll love me then. He'll think that I'm the best son in Ireland! Rev it up, boys! There he is. Da coming out of the office, he must have heard the engine.*

Hi, Da. Look at me! He shouts something at me but I don't hear him because I'm driving full throttle towards the office door and I can't stop. He lets out a roar. I crash straight into him, mow him down and bang into the office wall. The front of the truck smashes on impact and the glass flies out of the front window. Da stone dead, but at least he knew before he died what kind of a man I was. Scobie Donoghue, who never told anyone about what he saw. He never told his mother or brother about Da and Eileen in the office in Tynan's. You have a son, Da, who was able to stand up and be a man. A son you can be proud of! A son you can love. I know you do! I know you do, Da!

Scobie fell through the seat of the truck, plunged, fell further through space and time and darkness and light and a cacophony of voices and sounds, until he landed back down on solid earth. There was no further to fall. There was nothing underneath him anymore.

'Scobie. Son. Scobie. Are you okay?'

He opened his eyes. His mother's face was in front of him. Her hand on his shoulder. 'Sorry, but I just came up to see how ye were.'

Scobie sat up, wiped his eyes, checked for his father's apparition in the room, but there was no sign. He was home, for real, in his bedroom with his mother, Angela, who sat on the edge of the bed and wiped his forehead. 'You have a fierce sweat on ye.'

Scobie felt as if he'd been away for days and only just landed back into the here and now. He took hold of his mother's hand, mostly out of a need to show her affection, but also to double check that she was actual flesh and bone, and then he put his arm around her and squeezed her tight and he said into her ear, 'Sit down, Ma. I had the most – I dunno. It musta been a dream. I need to tell you all about it.'

twenty-three

It was the tail end of the summer, a bright late-August morning, as Scobie parked up the car at the canal bridge at Rahan. He sat on the bank to take in the stillness of the water, the gentle sounds of the brushing of the reeds, the birdsong, going through a mindfulness routine 'kinda meditation thing' that the counsellor, John Cronin, had told him about. Then Scobie drove back to town and dropped into the shop to grab the paper for Angela and Cliff, delivering it in time for them to read over the breakfast.

Cliff had arrived home from his mother's in late July, as Ethel had made a full recovery and, with home help and a special nurse, she would remain in her own house until the day they carried her out in a box. Cliff could broach no argument with this, once he had satisfied himself with the carers, a fine-built matriarch from Hull with Jamaican roots and a younger woman called Rachel from Derry, both equipped with the right amount of patience, sardonic humour and take-no-shit attitude to be able to manage Ethel.

Scobie was delighted for his mother that Cliff was back, although he had to cede territory to the couple and let them spend time alone together. Scobie began to sense, though, that Angela and Cliff were making a little strange with each other for the first week or so, as if they had been dying to see each other so much that a nervousness about meeting expectations had affected both of them. Neither wanted to overburden the other with their separate worries, him about leaving Ethel behind and Angela about Scobie's welfare and mental state. So they walked on eggshells, one trying to be more helpful to the other, falling over themselves to make the dinner or offering back rubs and cups of tea. Both desperately trying to please, to not upset, to make life as easy as possible for the other.

But then on the eighth day back, Scobie was lying on his bed when he heard raised voices coming from their bedroom. Cliff couldn't find a favourite T-shirt. As far as Scobie could make out, it was one with 'The Jam live at Hammersmith Apollo, '79' on it, one of the best gigs Cliff was ever at. Scobie could hear rummaging around in their wardrobe. Drawers being opened and closed, and his mother's voice.

'Sure, ye never wore it.'

'Yes, because it's a collector's item. I haven't worn it for 20 years! Come on, Ange, it must be here somewhere. Scobie would never have taken it or anything, would he?'

'No. He wasn't near it.'

'You didn't try and wash it, did ye?' said Cliff, now sounding really worried. 'Angela, come on, tell me the truth.'

Angela's voice was annoyed now. 'Ah, look, I didn't know it was so fucking precious to ye or whatever.'

Scobie sat up in the bed so he could hear better.

Cliff was getting thick now. 'I told you the story about that T-shirt one of the first days I moved in here. How me and my mate Denny hitched to London for the gig, had to walk around the city for the night after, but we didn't care because we were so excited after seeing The Jam.'

'Sure, it was ages ago since you moved in, I can't remember every feckin' concert you ever told me about,' said Angela.

'That T-shirt means something to me,' said Cliff, 'so I'm going to find it if I have to go through every nook and cranny of the house!'

'I threw it out, Cliff,' said Angela. 'I fecked it out while you were away. I reckoned it was too old and discoloured even for the charity shop, so it went in a bag of clothes for the dump.'

'I don't believe it. I wonder do you ever fucking listen to anything I ever say to you?'

'Well, I'm sorry, your fucking highness, if I don't hang on your every word, but you fucked off to England to that mother of yours and left me high and dry here!' shouted Angela.

'I know I did, and I'm sorry,' shouted Cliff.

'No, I'm sorry,' shouted Angela, and then there was silence.

Scobie strained his ears to listen, but then it slowly dawned on him what was happening. The bedroom door was slammed shut, and then he heard the bedsprings. Heavy breathing and whispered voices and groans and moans. Scobie dived off his own bed and ran downstairs, into the lounge, where he put on the television and turned up the volume.

The next day Cliff knocked on Scobie's door. He came in and stood nervously at the end of the bed. 'I know it's been tough for ye,' he said, 'but you're doing the right thing. Seeing this counsellor chap and all that.'

Scobie really didn't want Cliff trying to do his substitute daddy act, even if it was very well intentioned.

'Thanks, Cliff.'

'So you know you can always talk to me about anything?'

Scobie smiled.

Cliff, having made his offer, retreated to the door.

'Cliff,' said Scobie.

Cliff turned back to him. 'Yeah, Scobe, what is it?'

'Cliff, where do babies come from?' said Scobie, grinning.

Cliff shook his head and smiled. 'Feck off, you.' And then he closed the door, leaving Scobie on his own.

In those days Scobie sometimes didn't feel like getting up. He covered his head with the duvet, dreaming of oblivion, the other existence, the furry-edged safety net, which he craved half of the mornings. The kangaroo demon, or monster, or whatever you'd call him, still made an appearance in his dreams, and he would wake in sweat-soaked sheets as his body weaned itself off the drugs. He still used the Valium to help things along, and the first few weeks had been hell, but he had promised his mother to kick the Xanax and see the counsellor, as recommended by Doc Byrne. This firm promise had been made to her the morning he'd read his father's letter.

They had sat and talked for hours that morning. In that moment, Scobie felt like he was starting over again in some way. The experience that morning, so vivid and startling, had profoundly altered him. Trying to describe it to his Ma had been difficult, so he just called it a mad dream – easier for her that way. But he knew it had been something else. Something deeper within. Sometimes he preferred to just blame the pills and dismiss the whole episode or put it down to the fact that he had indeed completely lost his fucking mind, and sometimes, in quiet moments, out in the bog, or sitting on the canal bank, he really did believe that, yes, absolutely, the Aborigines are right, when you sleep people do come and steal your body.

In those early summer months Scobie had to drag himself into the car every Tuesday to drive to Athlone to sit with an old *GQ* magazine in a small waiting room and face the truly awful prospect of having a lad ask you questions about yourself and your life.

John Cronin was a thin, wiry man from Walkinstown, with wisps of hair still left on his head. He was in his early sixties, a seen-it-all alcoholic who had turned the corner when he was in his mid-forties, after setting fire to a chip pan and nearly burning down a house with his son upstairs in it. John had a big grin, a bold intelligence and a soft timbre to his voice, which gently prodded Scobie with questions about why he was there, sitting in front of him. Scobie gave the answer he thought was expected of him. 'To get my life back on track again. To get off the pills.'

John nodded and asked him to talk about where he was from. His family background. His job. Scobie gave the bare essentials. John upped the ante then, and asked him about his drinking, and when he'd felt it had got out of control. Scobie shrugged and talked about Australia and the drinking with the Irish lads down there and feeling a bit lost and lonely and the strip club, and he mentioned Ella, but then wished that he hadn't. John asked him about the relationship and how had it ended. Scobie clammed up. He said that it was a mutual decision. Both started to lead different lives. He knew John sensed that there was more to be got out of this, but Scobie wasn't going to open up about it. No way José. He began to resent being in the room, and he eyed the window and wondered how far it was to the ground. He could run and take a jump through it – anything to get out of the situation. His body felt itchy and sweaty. He just couldn't abide having to sit there under the microscope, and for the rest of those early sessions he was evasive and irritated.

He was also burdened by thoughts of Robbie, was worried about him, and he desperately wanted to apologise to Nuala Kearney. He even got Angela to phone her, hoping to be able to speak to her, but Nuala had no wish to speak to him. She told Angela that Robbie was in England, and that that was all she knew. He'd phoned her one night to tell her not to worry. That he was doing okay. Scobie was relieved to hear that Robbie was still surviving somewhere, but he tried not to think of his sunken eyes, his scrawny body eking out an existence in the streets of some cold, bleak English city.

Scobie knew that his leaving the town had something to do with Delaney. Something had happened in the square that night.

He wished he could let Robbie know that Delaney was off the force and facing a trial. Scobie himself would be due to give evidence whenever it came about. But Scobie needed to keep focusing on his own shite. He had to keep going to the counsellor once a week, every Tuesday, to talk about himself, even though he hated it and felt that really it was doing very little for him.

But then, on his sixth weekly visit, Scobie arrived over to the office in a real pissed-off sort of mood. So much so that when he sat down in the seat in front of John, he was kind of glad that he was there to listen to him. 'Niallers and Bob, who I used work with on the sites, came over to see me this morning,' he started.

Scobie went on to recount the visit to John. He had spotted the two heads at the glass sliding doors and had completely forgotten that they were going to call up. He had seen very little of them for months, not since the buildings had closed. Niallers opened his mouth into his big toothy grin and was waved in. Both himself and Bob were sporting the most overgrown Covid hair, like two hedges on top of their heads.

Scobie greeted them with a 'Jaysus, look who it is, Dumb and Dumber. I suppose ye'll be wanting tea', and he got up to boil the kettle.

'Ah, well, that'd be mighty,' said Niallers, all shy and fidgety.

'Sit down, lads, I'll get the fuckin' garden shears,' said Scobie.

'My mot keeps threatening to cut it, but I won't let her,' said Bob.

'And Aine doesn't give a shite what I look like. She never did. She was attracted to my personality,' claimed Niallers.

'Well, she hardly had a choice there,' said Bob, who reached into a Centra bag, taking out a packet of Jaffa Cakes, a Curly

Wurly and a Crunchie bar for each of them.

'How's your two young lads, Niallers?' asked Scobie.

'They're very lively, like, ah, ye'd be semi-strangled with them.'

'Not surprised, the way you run around after them. Honest to God,' said Bob, 'when we were kids, like, our folks used send us out in the morning and lock the back door. Now ye seem to lock the door to keep the kids in, or spend all your time arranging fuckin' play dates and all this shite. Honest to God, I hear parents trying to reason with their kids when they're bawling cryin'. My ma used say, "Birds fly, children cry." She had no truck with any of that.'

'You don't have a clue,' said Niallers. 'It's different when they're your own.'

'How are you getting on anyway, Scobes?' asked Bob.

'I'm doing okay, lads, still not sleeping that great, ye know.'

The lads nodded, but there was a bit of a lull then. Scobie busied himself with the tea. Bob opened the Jaffa Cakes, and they took two each.

Bob said, 'I read this specialist in viruses lad, and he was saying that there's another two years in this thing.'

'No way. Sure, when the vaccines come it'll be all over,' said Niallers.

'Variants. That's what this expert is talking about. Mutant strains that vaccines will be less effective against,' insisted Bob. 'Anyway, I'm not sure whether I'd get a vaccine to be honest. I don't trust those drug companies, money-grabbin' bastards.'

'Ah, you trust no one,' said Niallers.

Bob distributed the Curly Wurlys. There followed lots of chewing.

'We might be back to work soon enough,' said Niallers.

'Yeah, well, I dunno whether I'm going back, lads,' said Scobie. 'Not for a while anyway, just until I feel up to it, ye know.'

'Ah, sure ye have the PUP anyway,' said Bob.

Niallers fidgeted with the Curly Wurly wrapper, like he was preoccupied, glancing up at Scobie every now and again, like he wanted to say something. Finally he said, 'Sorry, Scobe, but, like, we were wondering exactly what happened ye. Did ye have a—?'

Bob kicked Niallers in the foot. 'Shut up, you, none of our business.'

'You were the one that said you reckoned that Scobie had had some kind of breakdown,' said Niallers.

'I fuckin' did not,' said Bob.

Scobie laughed, making a face, with his tongue hanging out. 'Yeah, went stone batshit crazy.'

'I didn't mean that,' protested Bob.

'Lookit, I had a bit of anxiety and got too fond of the pills. That's it in a nutshell.'

'Good man,' said Niallers.

Scobie paused, but then decided to tell them. 'Like, I'm going to see a counsellor lad, a Dub, just to talk things out, like.'

Bob winced visibly at the thought of it. 'What? Lying on a couch and spouting on about yourself to a stranger?'

'Yeah,' said Scobie, 'except there's no couch. I just sit in a chair.'

'Like your man outta the Jaysus *Sopranos*. Does it help ye?' asked Niallers.

'It seems to. I dunno. Sometimes. I dunno.'

Bob shook his head. 'Well, what has the world come to when Scobie Donoghue is being made go to a shrink. American shite. Sure, that would melt the head off ye.'

'Jaysus, thanks Bob. Just what a fella would need to be hearin',' said Scobie.

'Sure, everyone's goin' to therapists nowadays, Bob,' said Niallers.

'Ara fuckin' come walkin' with me and Niallers. A bit of air in the lungs, never mind all your shite talkin' to strangers. Sure you'd end up more fucked-up after the likes of that.'

'No, you're all right,' said Scobie, but he was pissed off with Bob.

Scobie sat in John's office, and as he continued to tell him about the morning, he could feel his irritation rising. 'I mean, for the rest of the time, Niallers did his best to talk shite and try and keep the craic goin', but to be honest with ye, I couldn't wait until they left. It was like they were fierce uncomfortable with the notion that one of their own, ye know, good old Scobie Donoghue, from the town, like, if something could go wrong upstairs with him, well then it could happen to them, ye know?'

'And how did it make you feel?' asked John.

'Fuckin' annoyed. Just annoyed with them.'

'What specifically annoyed you?'

'The way they looked at me. Like, I saw something in their eyes. Then I realised what it was. They felt pity for me. I mean, the pair of them.'

'So, how do you feel now?'

'Fuckin' angry with them. Stupid fuckers. Pitying me. Scobie Donoghue – I used to be king of this fuckin' town. I mean, to have the pair of them looking at me like that. *For fuck's sake!*' Scobie stood and kicked the chair away, then shouted, '*Fuckin' cunts!*' Almost immediately, he was mortified and went to pick up the chair. 'Jaysus, I'm so sorry. I didn't mean to. So sorry.'

'It's all right, Scobie. It's all right to be angry, you know.'

Scobie replaced the chair. He sat and hung his head.

'What's going on there with you?' asked John after a minute or so had ticked by.

'Dunno. Feel bad. Ashamed or something.'

'About what?'

'Kicking the chair.'

'Is it really about that?'

Scobie didn't move or speak. He seemed near to tears. He took a breath, couldn't look up. 'Ashamed at their pity.' Scobie put his hands over his face then. To hide the tears.

John let him alone then. Scobie cried. He couldn't stop. 'Jaysus, this is fuckin' embarrassing.' Then Scobie laughed. He felt that something had been released. From then on, he didn't find the sessions as toe-curlingly awkward. He felt freer in himself to talk.

The sun shone through the kitchen window as the radio news for Saturday 21 August came on the radio and Scobie, Angela and Cliff finished off a fry and listened intently. The county of Offaly had been locked down along with Kildare and Laois for the past two weeks on account of the high number of Covid cases, and the restrictions were due to be lifted today. Cliff raised his arms and shouted 'Freedom!' as the newsreader confirmed this, but then went on to say that Kildare would have to remain in lockdown for another week.

'The poor old Lilywhites,' said Angela.

'Ah, feck them,' laughed Scobie.

Cliff, gesturing towards Angela, said, 'Right there, Ange, fancy a run out somewhere?'

'Where would we go?' asked Angela.

'I don't know, Ange, somewhere over the county limits.'

'For why?' said Angela.

'Because we can, for the craic, come on,' said Cliff.

'Okay then,' said Angela. Then she looked to Scobie. 'Will you be all right on your own?'

'Yes, Mammy,' sighed Scobie. 'Sure, don't I have the call with Shamie?'

'Oh, yeah, maybe I should stay and say a quick hello.'

Cliff took Angela by the hand. 'Come ahead. Leave the lads to it.'

'Okay. I suppose. See ye, Scobe,' said Angela as they barrelled out through the sliding doors.

Scobie took himself upstairs and sat on his new double bed to wait for his brother to call. Shamie didn't like Zoom or Skype, only if the young fella was coming on with him, so he insisted they talk on the phone. 'We don't need to be lookin' at each other.' The brothers hadn't spoken on their own in ages, not since the night in Ollie's shebeen, which had been interrupted by Delaney's appearance. An unnatural state of affairs, and one neither could have possibly imagined when they used to live in each other's ears, working, driving, drinking and lying in their beds, having long bullshit conversations into the night. Maybe it had been a necessary part of their development that a knife had been taken to separate the conjoined twins that they used to be. They needed to become their own men. But now, Scobie was so looking forward to hearing his voice, his kind, sensitive, bit-of-a-goon older brother who he loved with all his heart.

Scobie surveyed the new paint job on the walls and the empty space where Jeanette used to flaunt her ample breasts to them every morning when they woke up. He hadn't replaced Jeannette or Shamie's poster of the red Corvette with anything as yet. His phone rang and he answered it.

'Hiya, bro,' said Shamie on the other end.

'How's it goin', horse?' said Scobie.

'Great. Awesome, as they never get tired of saying here. What's the weather like?' asked Shamie.

'Okay, ye know yourself, four seasons in one day. But anyway, fuck the weather, how are you and Therese, how's the boy?'

'All good, ye know, yeah, Shamie Jr is flying it in school, like. He's some boy to spell, gets first place every week. Mad. I could barely spell me own name.'

'Well sure he's such a great little reader.'

'Yeah, but the dreaded video games are creeping in. There's been some fierce battles with his mother.'

'Is she working in the same place?'

'She is, yeah, she likes it in there. Good little firm, and the boss is decent, so. But, like, she's working from home at the moment. We're in another emergency lockdown here now. Anyway, they both send their love.'

306

'Well, tell them I said hello and sure we'll do a Zoom real soon, then I can show you the state of the new bedroom. You wouldn't recognise it, double bed and everything.'

'Go way, where will I go if Therese kicks me out and I land home?'

'Too late, even Jeannette has been retired.'

'Ah no, poor ol' Jeannette,' Shamie laughed.

'Honest to God, the walls are a kind of white paint. Oatmeal white, according to Ma.'

'Anyways, so how's the Covid numbers with ye?' asked Shamie.

'Ah, they seem to be manageable enough, like, after the lockdown, so we'll see, whenever these vaccines come in. Terrible pain in the hole. But sure …'

'We'll keep at it.'

'We will.'

One, two, three seconds of silence passed, but it seemed longer, and Scobie couldn't stand any more of it. 'Listen I wanted to say to you that, ye know, we haven't been talking much, and I wanted to apologise about the way I was that time in Oz, near the end, like I was—'

'Ah, no, look it, you were goin' through a tough time.'

'Has Ma told ye anything?' asked Scobie.

'She tells me the odd thing. I know ye got a bit fond of the pills and that.'

'Yeah. But I'm doing better now, seeing a counsellor.'

'I'd love to be a fly on the wall for that. Scobie Donoghue in treatment.'

'I know. Fucking desperate,' Scobie said.

'Well, no problem to you to be talkin' about yourself anyway.'

'Feck off. The first session, I'll never forget it. So mortified, like. I wanted to get up and walk out and go straight into a pub. But he got me talking over the weeks about what had happened to me since breaking up with Ella, and I was getting more and more upset and feeling more and more of an eejit for getting upset. Then do ye know what he asked me, Shamie? He asked me did I like myself. Real simple question. I laughed and said that Scobie Donoghue loved himself, but he asked me again, real serious, and I couldn't answer him. I wasn't sure. I wasn't sure. I got upset then. Couldn't help it. And it's not the only time I've, ye know, cried and everything.'

'Fair play. Cos you don't get upset too easy. I know that. Not even when we buried Da. I was thinking about it lately. You were mighty that day. I'll never forget the morning of it. I lost it above in our room, trying to tie me fuckin' tie properly, and you talked me through it. "Let it out to fuck," you said to me, and you held me, and I fucking bawled and felt a hundred times better.'

'I remember that, yeah,' said Scobie.

'Ye were always there for a lot of people when they needed ye. You should give yourself a bit of credit.'

'Yeah, but I think I was only distracting meself half the time. Too scared of me shite to bother with things inside me, ye know?'

'Like what, Scobe?'

'Like why I run from myself, or don't fully trust meself. All this craic. It's hard to talk about it. And then some days I wake up and want nothing more than just to head straight for a bottle and a smoke, and John said that's all right, too, I'm not a fucking monk. But he thinks I've made progress, or at least I don't think about the future and dread it as much anymore, because ...' Scobie hesitated then, because he couldn't fully go into what had happened to him in the counselling sessions without talking about their father's letter. The spidery handwriting on the blue Basildon Bond paper came into Scobie's head, and what his mother had said to him about it. How she had only shared the letter with Scobie for a reason, so that a drowning man might learn from what his father had gone through before him. She didn't think Shamie needed to know. He was happy and making a great life for himself. Leave him alone, she'd said. So he would.

'Anyways, I've missed ye, Shamie.'

'And I've missed you too, ye stupid bollocks.'

'Not as big a bollocks as you.'

'I *am* a bollocks, for not trying to get talking to ye sooner.'

'Ah, well, you have a life there, Shamie.'

'No. I coulda easily picked up the phone. I suppose I just didn't know what to say.'

'You don't have to say a thing.'

'Okay, well that's easy,' said Shamie.

There was another few seconds' pause, but this time Scobie was comfortable in it. The bros were at it again. The Donoghue boys were back!

'Oh, yeah. Me and Therese were just wondering,' said Shamie, 'if ye'd been in contact with Ella at all?'

Scobie paused and cleared his throat, trying to sound all casual. 'I have, yeah. I just e-mailed her a few weeks ago, so she's doing good. She's seeing this teacher lad. It's only in the early stages, but who knows.'

'Sorry to hear that.'

'Ah, no, I mean I have no hold on her.'

'Do ye still love her?'

'Jaysus, you're worse than the fuckin' counsellor.'

'Do ye?' asked Shamie again.

'Will ye stop, it's history now. I'm just glad to be on civil terms with her again.'

'You should Zoom her, talk to her face to face,' Shamie suggested.

'Ah no, I mean I'd love to see her but … might be too much, ye know, like she has a boyfriend and—'

'And nothing, she's the one for you, Scobie. I always thought that, so go on now and promise me you'll Zoom her.'

'I don't know.'

'Promise me.'

'Jaysus, okay, fuck's sake, leave it alone now,' Scobie grumbled.

Another pause followed, then Shamie said, 'Anyway, Scobe, it was great talking to ye.'

'Absolutely, Shamie, and I just want to say that … that I fuckin' love ye.'

'Wow, that Jaysus therapy must be working. That's the first time you've ever said that to me sober.'

'Feck off. I mean it.'

'I know ye do. See ye, bro.'

'See ye, Shamie.'

Scobie put the phone down and stared at the blank white walls, seeing Ella's face, thinking about how great it would be to talk to her. He imagined the craic they used to have, the back and forth. But would she want to actually talk to him? She'd written a friendly enough response on the email, but she had probably moved on. With this new boyfriend. All he could see now was himself waking up on their veranda, still sick and bewildered from drink, and Ella stepping over him, a look of complete disgust and disdain all over her face. No. He'd leave it. He was afraid of it. He knew that. Afraid to hear the possibility that she might be in love and blissfully happy with a fabulous new man who wouldn't be afraid of loving her. Who wouldn't be afraid to have a child with her.

twenty-four

Scobie didn't get a great sleep that night. He kept drifting in and out, but with that old sense of unease, like the kangaroo monster was just around the corner. He tried to focus on all the meditation stuff he'd been doing with John. He did his slow belly breathing, and the simple eye exercise to settle his vagus nerve. That was a nervous system inside you that counterbalanced the fight-or-flight impulse, or so John was forever going on about. How to use it to calm yourself down and all this craic.

Scobie sat, bleary-eyed, at breakfast the next morning, half-eating his muesli, when Cliff arrived in from the hall with a handful of letters and one larger hardback envelope. Angela went through them and it was all bills except the envelope, which was for

Scobie. He opened it up, and couldn't believe his eyes. He unfolded the thick sheet of paper inside to reveal a beautiful sketched drawing, in Robbie's trademark graphic comic-book style, of a man holding hands with a blonde woman and a crazy-looking giant baby standing over them. There was an inscription on the back: 'Hope you're doing okay. Just moved back into Mam's over here in England. In better form. All cool. Best, Robbie.'

Scobie showed the drawing to Cliff and Angela.

'That's brilliant,' said Angela. 'We'll stick it up on the fridge.'

Scobie took the car out for a drive and parked up as he usually did, at Rahan Bridge. He sat by the water, listening to the small sounds and the odd car trundling past over the bridge. He felt a great relief that Robbie was okay. He decided he would text him. Just to say he got the drawing. *Hi Robbie. Got the drawing. It's brilliant, as usual. A bit of a departure though. Not a T-Rex in sight! Hope you're good. How long have you been in your mam's? Scobie.*

He waited then, closed his eyes for a few minutes. The phone bleeped. He looked at it. *Hi Scobe. Two weeks or so. Was kinda homeless before that up in Manchester and then Leeds, until I got meself arrested for drunk and disorderly. Anyways, the cops traced me ma and she came up and got me. She's much better in herself and the boyfriend's been kicked out. She has a grand flat. So, anyway, I'll be home to see Gran at some stage, so might see ye then. I hear Delaney is in trouble. Fair fucks to ye. I heard ye took him on. Anyway, thanks for everything. You're a real good man and you'd make a real good dad. That's you in the picture with the woman from Australia you showed me. And that's a baby that ye might have.* He'd added a smiley-face emoji.

Scobie stared at the text. He smiled. He felt a great warmth inside in his belly. He wanted to shout out. He was thrilled that the young lad was okay. He got back in the car and drove back home. Pulling up into the yard, he chased into the house, into the kitchen, and he stared at the drawing now stuck to the fridge. He looked at Ella and himself and the outlandishly large baby. He knew what he must do. He went upstairs to his room and shut the door. He took up his phone and sent an email that read simply, *Hi Ella, just wondered did ye want to do a Zoom chat some time. It would be great to have a proper catch-up.*

It winged its way to Oz, and Scobie wondered what he'd do now. There was nothing he could do except get comfortable on the bed and wait for a response. But he didn't have to stew for long. One came back almost immediately. *Sure. I'll be up for another hour or so, unless you want to do it tomorrow.*

Scobie didn't think about it. He replied, *I'll set a meeting up. Talk in the next short while.* He couldn't put it off. He was as ready as he'd ever be.

Scobie hopped off the bed, opened the wardrobe and checked himself in the mirror inside. His hair was sticking up, and hadn't seen scissors in months, and although he had lost a bit of weight recently around the face, his skin looked blotchy and red, so he raced to the bathroom, splashed water on it, then reached for moisturiser, rubbing it onto his forehead and cheeks and under the eyes. He dampened down his hair and combed it to try and tame it in some way. He grabbed Cliff's electric beard-trimmer yoke and tidied up the facial hair. Now what would he wear? A blue shirt that Ella always liked. But would that be too obvious?

Like she'd know he was trying to look his best for her? Ah fuck it, he put on the shirt and settled down on the bed. He eyed the time. He was nervous, but was genuinely looking forward to seeing Ella and catching up, even if it meant he had to hear all about this wonderful new shit-hot man in her life.

He picked up the phone and set up the Zoom meeting, then sent Ella the link. He opened the meeting and waited for her to join. A few minutes passed by, Scobie staring at the screen, until suddenly Ella's face was in front of him. She looked every bit as good as he ever remembered her. She had great colour, of course, the golden Aussie tan, the brown eyes, but her hair was different, cut shorter. It looked fierce well, and she smiled at him before she spoke. That was the best bit.

'How's it goin', Scobie, nice to see you, to see you, nice,' she said, using Bruce Forsyth's famous catchphrase.

'Yeah, great to see you too,' Scobie spluttered.

'Yeah, sorry,' laughed Ella, 'but I've been watching that channel we used to watch sometimes, with all the crap old Brit game shows. It's the only thing I can concentrate on at night. Gets me off to sleep.'

'Ye can't beat a bit of the *Generation Game* – or of *Bully,*' laughed Scobie.

'Stay out of the black and in the red, you get nothing in this game for two in a bed,' said Ella, and she grinned. 'I can keep this up for hours.'

'So how's tricks down there?'

'Ah, fucked. Schools are off, so I'm sitting at home trying to study for a master's in child psychology.'

'But ye keep getting distracted by *Bullseye.*'

'You said it, mate.'

'Anyway, how's it goin', the study and all that?'

'I'll get there. I mean, this fuckin' pandemic has given me paid leave, to be honest, so I have no excuse.'

'Cool. Well, that's great you're busy, like.'

'Gives the day some kind of shape. And yourself? You wrote that construction is still closed down.'

'It is, yeah, but there's talk of it coming back soon, so we'll see.' He paused a beat, then said, 'It's mad to be talkin' to ye.'

'Yeah, I know. How are you?'

Scobie looked at her, trying to figure out where to start, or whether he'd say nothing and spare her the details.

'What about that girl you were seeing?' asked Ella.

'We broke up. She was getting too fond of the Scobemeister General so, ye know, I had to back off.'

'Ah, right, the poor girl had it bad, did she?'

'Ah, yeah, ye know. How's things goin' with your new lad?'

'Okay. He's a good guy but, ye know, I'm not sure. I mean, you don't wanna hear about this ...'

'I do,' insisted Scobie. 'Honest to God, go on.'

'Okay, well, he's a bit ... he has it all worked out, his life, like he has it organised just the way he likes it. Into different boxes. He has a 10-year-old son who I've never met and his buddies he likes to hang out with, and then there's his work and then time with me. He likes to compartmentalise, which is his thing, but I don't know. I do like him, he's smart, and we're interested in a lot of the same kinda stuff ... Anyway, we'll see.'

Scobie smiled, appreciating her honesty, realising he now owed her the same courtesy.

'Yeah, well, can I admit something to ye?'

'I suppose you can,' said Ella. 'Let me guess – you've become a Jehovah's Witness?'

'Eh no, although I wouldn't rule it out,' laughed Scobie. 'It might bring me more luck. To be honest, I haven't been near a girl since I came home. I only made someone up, didn't want you to think I'd lost me mojo.'

'I bet ye haven't,' said Ella. 'It's hard to get laid during a world-wide pandemic, Scobie.'

'I suppose. I've been lying low anyways.'

Ella took a moment. 'Have you lost weight around the face?'

'Yeah' Scobie nodded. 'It's so great to talk to ye, I really want to … tell you something. But I don't want to make a bollocks of it.'

'Go on. Talk to me,' urged Ella. 'Listen, we went through a lot of shit together, but I still care about ye, ye know.'

'Me too, Ella. Ye see, things got difficult, to say the least. I kinda lost it a while ago. The walls seemed to be closing in, and then something happened to me. It was batshit crazy, but maybe you're the only one who might understand or not laugh at me or call me a mad bastard.' Scobie paused to gather himself and gauge a response from her.

'Go on, then, I'm always game for a bit of crazy, ye mad bastard,' she said, and then she laughed.

Scobie let out a burst of nervous laughter. 'Okay. I got addicted to Xanax and these other very strong mood stabilisers, and I was losing the head. I mean, it was scary, Ella. I was drifting so far away from the real world, like I hadn't a clue what the fuck was going on anymore. I was getting involved in all sorts of drama-rama around the town. To feel something ... I dunno, to feel that I had some sort of purpose or ... I'm not explaining this very well. I don't really understand what happened but ...' Scobie felt an emotion building up in his throat, but he swallowed it down. Not yet. He needed to keep talking. Go away and let me speak, thought Scobie, let me get the words out.

'I get it, Scobe, yeah, take it easy, mate,' said Ella.

'Right. Well, I was in a very bad way, and my mother decided to show me a letter that my father had written to her on his deathbed. I read it, and fuck me but his words floored me. He admitted to depression and anxiety, and then an affair when we were younger lads – the details aren't important. He did what he did, and somehow my mother took him back for our sakes, but something happened to me, Ella. It was like I had the most vivid, clearest dream, like I was a child again, right back there. I can't explain it, but I heard meself as an eight-year-old lad, and then as a 10-year-old. It was like they needed to be heard or something, like these young lads were told to shut up years ago, they were locked up and told to stay quiet forever, and something broke in me, and shit that I've been carrying around with me for years just ... I swear to Jaysus, it just burst out of me. I've been seeing this counsellor-therapist lad who's trying to help me look at the whole thing. I dreamt of killing me da and the counsellor kept at me about what that might mean and I got fierce thick, like, real angry, and he said that this was good. I had all this anger, all bottled up, because I'd never forgiven him. Because I'd finally had enough of trying to be like him, never being able to settle with anyone and all that. And I was thinking of us, ye know, in that regard. So I'm sorry. So sorry about everything that happened.'

He could feel a sensation sweeping up over him, a feeling so raw that it threatened to squeeze his throat and choke him. He took a few breaths.

'That's it, Scobe, you're okay,' said Ella. 'There was two of us in it, you know. I took a lot of stuff out on you.'

'Pure mule, what do ye think?' said Scobie.

'Pure mule all right, but pretty fucking amazing that you've – I mean, Scobie Donoghue talking to a therapist!' said Ella.

'Everyone thinks that's the maddest thing,' laughed Scobie.

'You feel things, Scobie Donoghue. You feel things so much, I always knew that.'

They looked away from each other then. To try and absorb what had been said. Scobie gathered himself to speak again. 'I'll never forget those waking dreams, though. It felt so real, ye know. The whole experience reminded me of what you told me one time, when we visited Hanging Rock, remember? About the belief that when we sleep, people come and steal our bodies. That's what it was like. I was lifted from this world into some other place, and I had some sort of better understanding of things. And I don't regret anything. I mean, I am who I am, and fuck it, but I'm seeing a bit more light these days. Ye know, not every day. Some days are – like the anxiety sets in, and I have to do this cognitive practice to try and … Jaysus, did ye ever think ye'd see the day?'

'No way, Scobie Donoghue. Cognitive practice, are you fucking joking me? The only cognitive practice you ever did was trying to work out the price of booze in the offie.' Ella leaned forward towards her screen. 'I think about you, too. I remember that trip to Hanging Rock very clearly. Some things you just can't really explain. There are so many mysteries to our existence. Life is stranger than shit, Scobie Donoghue.'

They kept their eyes on each other now. Like they had entered their own special space, unoccupied by any other living soul, full of their good times and good feelings, like before they drifted apart.

Ella broke the spell. 'So, Ian, that's the guy I'm seeing, he's got some Irish blood in him. From way back. Convict stuff, but he's anxious to visit Ireland, so who knows, whenever we're allowed to, I might take him to meet you in Offaly.'

Scobie laughed, but his heart sunk like a stone. 'That would be some craic.'

'Well, ye know, have to see what happens.'

'Ah yeah. With the Covid and all that.'

'No, with Ian. I mean, as I say, I'm just not quite sure where it's headed at the minute.'

Scobie's heart lifted again. His mind raced. What to do? Let it go. Another time. Another call. We're back on track, so don't want to fuck it up. Make it a gradual thing. Take it easy. No. What if he misses the boat? What if this Ian lad suddenly gets his act together and pulls it out of the bag and buys the ring and takes her out to Hanging Rock and gets down on one knee? No. He had to say something. Because he was sure now. He was certain. He needed to say something. To not let the moment pass.

Ella spoke before he could. 'I see you still have the blue shirt.'

'Oh, yeah, just threw it on today,' said Scobie.

'I always liked that on you,' Ella smiled.

'Did ye? Oh right, well, it barely fits me anymore.'

There was another pause. Scobie willed himself to say what he wanted to say to this woman that he loved, but something was holding him back. A paralysing grip of fear that closed his throat and cut off his voice box.

Ella shifted in her seat. She rubbed her hand through her hair. 'Scobie. It's so fucking cool you've managed to, you know, be so honest and open. No bullshit. You seem to have really gone through something very profound and come out the other side. I've been a bit haunted myself. Caught in the grip of something. Every morning when I wake up it's there. I'm scared in the world. I keep being brought back to the hospital and the moment they told me that the baby was dead, and I swore to myself that I could never risk going through such a moment in my life ever again. But then what is life? Hiding out. Being afraid and living safely or to try and live like … to try and live like there's no tomorrow.'

Scobie heard the floorboards creak on the corridor outside his room, and he knew it was Angela going into her bedroom for something. His head filled with moments he would never forget, the kangaroo lying dead with the joey inside her pouch, the fur splattered with the mother's blood but the little tummy still breathing. The yard of Tynan's and Eddie getting back into the truck beside him with Eileen looking on. He saw his mother handing him Eddie's letter and Shamie's tears the day of the funeral. Ella kissing him under the stars and telling him she thought she was pregnant and how now he yearned for her and another chance.

Scobie Donoghue yearned to be a da. Like as if all the bad and the beautiful, the craic and the heartbreak, the drink and the drugs and the pure fuckin' mule times he'd had were all just a lead-up to this moment. He looked up at the screen. It felt like they'd been silent for ages, but actually it had just been a little over a minute. And he found that all his fear and anxiety was gone and he was able to speak then and tell this woman, over ten thousand miles away, exactly how he felt about her and why they needed to be together. He opened his lips, the words escaping.

'Hey, Ella.'

'Yeah, Scobie?' she said softly.

'I need to tell you something.'

acknowledgements

I would like to thank all those who made *Pure Mule* the TV show happen. The producers, David Collins and Ed Guiney. The directors, Declan Recks and Charlie McCarthy, and script editor Lauren MacKenzie. To the fantastic crew and cast, which included Garret Lombard who brought Scobie to life.

I would also like to thank Melbourne resident Olivia Sinclair Thompson for advice on the geography of the city.

Thanks as well to Deirdre Nolan (formerly of Gill Books) and all those at Gill who offered me the chance to do this book: Seán Hayes, Rachel Thompson, Teresa Daly, Claire O'Flynn and Fiona Murphy. A huge thanks to editor Alison Walsh, whose expert hand guided me through the process with great clarity and encouragement.

Finally, I'd like to thank Mari Kennedy, for her amazing support and love.